Praise for Lili St. Ge...   ...rter trilogy

'Good lord, this series ... this book ... these characters ... they are seriously playing all sorts of havoc with my emotions, my feelings, my nerves and my anxiety levels'
THE HOPELESS ROMANTICS BOOK BLOG

'Possibly the best series I've ever read. Powerful, emotional, entertaining, confronting yet clever storyline with plots, twists and shocks – I could not put these books down'
NAT COOLS FROM OZ, iBOOKS

'Had me on a tight grip for the entire ride ... I was completely immersed' THE READING ESCAPADE

'Finally, a book that grabbed and kept my attention from start to finish!' BOOK VIGILANTE REVIEWS

'Awesome job Lili ... I am ready to hop on the back of a bike and join the club!' THE LITERARYGOSSIP BOOK BLOG

'Sensational, shocking, compelling and totally addictive ... the best when it comes to dark, brooding and bloody romance'
KELLY, PERUSING PRINCESSES

Lili takes you for a walk on the dark and dirty side of life. She makes you question how far you'd be willing to go to save those you loved and what lengths you'd go to to survive. What happens when the lines of right and wrong blur and when the lines of hate and love are crossed ...' OBSESSED BY BOOKS

'Fast-paced. Thrilling. Violent. Dark. Raw. Ruthless'
WICKED READS

'Cartel is just the beginning to what promises to be an erotic, twisted journey' THE ROMANCE REVIEWS

Lili St. Germain is a publishing phenomenon. The first of her seven serialised dark romance novellas, *Seven Sons*, came out in early 2014, with the following books in the series released in quick succession and selling over a million copies worldwide. The bestselling Gypsy Brothers series focuses on a morally bankrupt biker gang and the girl who seeks her vengeance upon them. *Empire* is the gripping conclusion to the Cartel series, a prequel trilogy of full-length novels that explores the beginnings of the club.

Lili quit corporate life to focus on writing and is relishing every minute of it. Her other loves include her gorgeous husband and beautiful daughter, good coffee and Tarantino movies.

Find out more about the author at lilisaintgermain.com

Other books by Lili St. Germain

THE CARTEL TRILOGY
Cartel
Kingpin
Empire

THE GYPSY BROTHERS SERIES
Seven Sons
Six Brothers
Five Miles
Four Score
Three Years
Two Roads
One Love
Zero Hour

EMPIRE

LILI ST. GERMAIN

HarperCollins*Publishers*

HarperCollins*Publishers*
First published in Australia in 2017
by HarperCollins*Publishers* Australia Pty Limited
ABN 36 009 913 517
harpercollins.com.au

Copyright © Lili Saint Germain 2017

The right of Lili Saint Germain to be identified as the author of this work
has been asserted by her in accordance with the *Copyright Amendment
(Moral Rights) Act 2000.*

HarperCollins*Publishers*
Level 13, 201 Elizabeth Street, Sydney NSW 2000, Australia
Unit D1, 63 Apollo Drive, Rosedale, Auckland 0632, New Zealand
A 53, Sector 57, Noida, UP, India
1 London Bridge Street, London, SE1 9GF, United Kingdom
2 Bloor Street East, 20th floor, Toronto, Ontario M4W 1A8, Canada
195 Broadway, New York, NY 10007, USA

National Library of Australia Cataloguing-in-Publication data:

Saint Germain, Lili, author.
  Empire / Lili St Germain.
  ISBN: 978 1 4607 5006 3 (paperback)
  ISBN: 978 1 4607 0430 1 (ebook)
  Series: Saint Germain, Lili. Cartel trilogy ; 3.
  Subjects: Man–woman relationships – Fiction.
  Drug dealers – Colombia – Fiction.
  Fathers and daughters – Fiction.
  Colombia – Fiction.
813.6

Cover design by HarperCollins Design Studio
Front cover image by shutterstock.com
Back cover image by Sybille Sterk / Arcangel
Author photo by Rachel Roscoe
Typesetting in Sabon LT Std by Kirby Jones
Printed and bound in Australia by Griffin Press
The papers used by HarperCollins in the manufacture of this book are a natural,
recyclable product made from wood grown in sustainable plantation forests. The fibre
source and manufacturing processes meet recognised international environmental
standards, and carry certification.

I loved you at your darkest.

Romans 5:8

MARIANA

People aren't born monsters.

They're made that way.

After all, how do you fight the darkness when you're thrust into it?

Same goes for vengeful beasts. They aren't born. They're created, fuelled by one singular moment in time when the universe wrongs them and their existence shatters.

I'd been with Dornan Ross for almost a decade. Slept in his bed, sewn up his wounds, tasted his blood, seen inside his soul.

I was the mistress of a monstrous man. Dornan Ross, vice-president of one of the most feared biker gangs in the United States.

Son of the most powerful drug kingpin along the West Coast.

A man whose entire being was predicated on violence, blood and death.

But even I wasn't prepared for what he did.

He killed our child. He put his boot into my stomach and *kicked our baby to death.*

He killed the love I had for him.

And he took away the only family his son had ever known. Left his mother in a bathtub full of blood and a hotshot still hanging from her arm, for a sixteen-year-old boy to find.

I'd been foolish enough to question the brutality he'd delivered to his son's mother, and lost my own child as punishment.

I should have known it would always come down to this, from the very moment I laid eyes on him in that motel.

I should have known his salvation was too good to be true.

Because it's all gone now, the dark secret love I had for him bleeding away in the darkness that came afterwards.

Now, there's only hate.

Now, I just want to escape.

Even if it means I have to kill him to be free.

***

I loved Dornan Ross once. I loved him so much that he became a part of me. I loved him despite his darkness, despite the impossibility of us ever being able to have a real life together.

I fucking *worshipped* the man. But false Gods always betray your devotion eventually. They peel off their mask, and you stare at a stranger. They are the shark and you are the prey, and you wonder how you ever thought you could trust them not to devour you on sight.

2

CHAPTER ONE

MARIANA

You might've walked past us and wondered why a woman like me – twenty-eight years old, no tattoos, modestly dressed – was with *him*.

The president of the most lethal biker club in California, the Gypsy Brothers MC – John Portland. Covered in tattoos, smoking, the crest of his brotherhood inked on the flesh above his heart. That tattoo was hidden from public view as we stood side by side on the Santa Monica Pier and watched his daughter and my kind-of-not-really stepson ride the Ferris wheel, two teenagers clearly experiencing the first stages of love. Fifteen and sixteen. When I was their age I'd already given birth to my only child and had him taken from me. I'd already been tainted by life.

My not-stepson had found his mother dead, murdered by his father – my lover – a few months earlier, and it was safe to say he'd been tainted by life, too.

John's daughter had been too, to a lesser extent. Junkie mother. A father who presided over criminals and murderers.

3

Despite her beginnings, she still had traces of the naivety that summer love and an overprotective daddy provided. She still slept soundly at night, from what I could gather.

Sadly, it wouldn't always be that way, but on that pier, in the sunshine, none of us had any way of knowing the horror that lay ahead, its gaping maw ready to scoop us up when we least expected.

'We'll have to watch out for him,' I teased, tilting my head towards Dornan's youngest son, Jason, as he rode the Ferris wheel with John's daughter, Juliette.

Beside me, leaning against the railing that flanked the pier, the man I was secretly in love with shook his head. 'Don't even,' he murmured, rubbing his stubbled chin with his palm.

I started to laugh, until I saw John wasn't laughing. Or smiling at all. I gestured to the two teenagers as they rode in a carriage high atop the Santa Monica coastline. 'They're kids. You can't seriously be worried about him.'

John's eyes cut through me, making me wonder if I should be worried.

'John,' I tried again, 'he's a kid. He's sixteen years old.'

John's knuckles turned white as he gripped the railing feverishly. 'He's not a kid. He's Dornan's kid.'

I rolled my eyes. 'He didn't even know Dornan until a few months ago.'

'Yeah, but he's still Dornan's blood. Still Emilio's blood.'

I shrugged. 'She's not that much younger than I was when Emilio came for my family.' And left with me as a consolation prize.

John appeared pained. 'Jesus Christ, Ana,' he said, his words like bullets, forceful and cold, metallic. This was our

4

eternal impasse, our universal hesitation. We were in love. We wanted to run away, to flee Los Angeles and the eventual death it promised us.

But he wouldn't leave with Dornan's son, Jason.

I wouldn't leave without him.

And so we were stuck.

'Will you miss him?' John asked me.

My heart squeezed painfully. 'I'm not leaving Jason, John.'

He shook his head, his eyes glued to his daughter as she laughed and pointed out things to her crush. 'Not Jason. Dornan.'

Oh.

Dornan Ross, the man who'd been my lover for almost ten years, since the day he collected me from a dirty motel in San Diego and claimed me as his own. From the instant he'd stopped his drug kingpin father from selling me as a sex slave to cover my father's impossible debt.

John Portland had been Dornan's best friend for longer than I'd known either of them – twenty years or more, I'd guess. I knew they'd met as teenagers, formed a fast friendship, a friendship that soon became a brotherhood of bikers called the Gypsy Brothers, a club that John had presided over since its inception.

I smoothed down my tank top, painfully aware that we were out in the open, an afternoon ice-cream date with his daughter and the stray I'd taken in. Dornan's son Jason, the one he'd been unaware of for sixteen years, emerged from the fairground ride with Juliette, stepping back onto the pier, two teenagers in love, even if they didn't know it yet. It was a rare day for any of us to be out, but the weather was so beautiful,

John had collected us all in his beat-up car and brought us out into the sunshine for some fudge sundaes and a chance to dip our toes in the cold water.

It wasn't a typical outing, to say the least. On a day like today, I'd normally be working for my boss, Emilio, cooking his books and making sure his hefty cartel profits were funnelled into all the right places. Or, if I got a day off – rare for a Saturday – I'd inevitably be on my back, or my knees, or my stomach, with Dornan. But today was Emilio's birthday, and he insisted on a great big family celebration – one that none of us were invited to. I was surprised Dornan hadn't insisted on taking Jason to the family event, but I think he worried about how unstable Jason might be in a large gathering of the people who'd inadvertently caused his mother to die.

Yes, I was sleeping with two men. I was in love with one of them, and I was terrified of the other. When I first arrived in California ten years ago I'd loved Dornan, but now I loathed him. I was ready to leave him, or kill him, or both. Anything to get away.

But the world kept spinning, and the cartel kept trading, and I kept my feet on the ground, too scared to make a run for freedom lest a bullet find its way between my shoulder blades.

'Can we go feel the water?' Juliette asked her father.

'Sure,' John shrugged, his face lighting up for his daughter like she was the sun. And she was, to him. That made me fall for him even more than I already had, to see the love he had for his daughter. Without thinking, I reached out and placed my hand on Jason's shoulder. He was only sixteen, but already well taller than me, and the picture of his father – all olive skin and deep brown eyes, a product of their Italian heritage.

Jase flinched when I touched him; I pulled my hand away and smiled instead. I didn't want to apologise and bring attention to how jumpy he was, so I left it. Juliette grabbed his hand – the contrast between them night and day, what with her bamboo green eyes and straw blonde hair – and pulled him towards the beach. He didn't flinch when she touched him, and that's how I knew it was already love in bloom.

I realised I'd been daydreaming and turned my attention back to John. He was just as stunning as the day I'd met him, but age had weathered him in a way that only made him more attractive to me. He was barely forty, but the lines around his eyes told a story of far more trauma than a man his age should have seen.

I loved his hands. Rough palms from the mechanical work he did, but smooth on top. Rough fingers that spread me open and worshipped me, not missing an inch of my flesh; smooth on top, for those times when he'd brush a knuckle along my cheek or put my hand on his as I travelled on the back of his motorcycle.

Dornan's hands didn't have an ounce of smoothness; they were rough and big and good for holding over my mouth while he fucked me until I screamed. I won't pretend that I didn't like it. I lived for his brutal touch. I was addicted to it.

But the addiction had become too dangerous. It was a nasty habit that was going to kill me one day, a day that would come very soon if I didn't figure my life out and get out of Los Angeles.

I was entirely certain that if I didn't make a bold move soon – run, or hand myself over to the police, or just plain kill my dark lover while he slept beside me – I'd be the one who'd end up dead, dumped on the side of the road in a ditch somewhere, or maybe cut into little pieces and fed to the sharks. Because Dornan Ross had changed. He'd grown cruel. He used to use violence in the most delicious of ways – a hand over my face to stifle the noise that accompanied the mind-blowing orgasm he was giving me with his other hand; a subtle choke that made me see stars as my heart sped up in anticipation; a finger forced into my mouth so I could suck on it, tease him, pretend it was his cock I had my lips wrapped around. A violence that would have me smashed up against the nearest wall, fingers that bruised me with their passion as he wrenched my thighs apart and entered me so hard that I ached for days afterward.

That violent love was the thing that made us. When we met I was only nineteen years old and his father's property, thanks to a deal I'd brokered to repay a debt my own father had racked up, and to keep my family from being slaughtered. One set of parents. One sister. One brother. I had given my servitude for their lives.

Emilio had killed them eventually, anyway. Loose ends and all that.

That violent love reached its peak when I saw the blood on my lover's hands and the body of the woman he'd killed for daring to flee from him. Her face had been so badly beaten she was unrecognisable.

I still saw her when I closed my eyes at night. *Stephanie.* He'd killed her for concealing a pregnancy and leaving him seventeen years earlier, and he had punished her by beating her until she was almost dead, and then giving her a hotshot of heroin to finish off the job.

That this was the man I'd fallen fiercely in love with as a young woman was impossible to me. This was a man who'd risked everything for me, a lowly Colombian slave on her way to auction. He'd defied his father, and in doing so, had taken my heart and my loyalty. He'd done it out of some goodness that existed inside of him, something that couldn't bear to see me come to harm.

'He's struggling,' I said, nodding my head towards Jason. 'He has nightmares. He barely talks. He barely eats, and teenage boys are supposed to eat everything in sight. I'm worried about him.'

John side-eyed me. 'And your son? Luis? How's he doing?'

I immediately baulked at his line of questioning. He was inferring that I cared more about a boy who wasn't my son than the boy who was waiting for me in Colombia, my beautiful son, Luis. He was thirteen. I hadn't laid eyes on him since the day he was taken from me by my father – the day he was born.

'He's safe,' I said, my throat itching. 'He's with family. And that's where we should be going. All four of us.'

John pulled a face. 'You really want to take Dornan's son after you saw what he did to the woman who kept him secret his entire life?'

I didn't want to think about that. About how Dornan had become the monster he'd been trying to save me from all those years ago.

About how a lover could become your captor.

I didn't want to think about how a lover, in a rage over your incessant questions and your disbelief that they could murder somebody in cold blood, could beat you until the baby inside you, the one that was still a secret, died.

9

Didn't want to remember how a lover, in a post-murder-fuelled high, could pin you down and rape you, while still covered in the blood of the woman he murdered hours beforehand.

Didn't want to reconcile all the ways a lover could become the person you hated the most in the world.

Especially because, if you were like me, black-hearted and completely corrupted, you already had *another* lover.

John Portland. Of course he had to be Dornan's best friend, just to dial shit right up to eleven on the crazy scale.

It was complicated.

It was wrong.

I didn't care.

I was in love with a man who was not my lover, and soon we would leave this place.

Together. I'd convince him that Jason needed to come with us. That he needed protecting from Dornan, the man who would surely mould him into a beast if given half a chance.

We were leaving.

And we were *never* coming back.

***

'Hey,' John said, snapping a finger in front of my face. God, he was fucking beautiful, with his dirty blond hair, tanned skin and those brilliant blue eyes that looked just like the ocean we were standing before. With his tight black T-shirt and dark denim jeans, he looked casual. Add the steel-toed boots and the biker tattoos that covered his arms and neck, and he looked lethal. *Casually lethal.* That was my John.

'Will you miss Dornan?' John repeated. His question wasn't born from jealousy, or insecurity. He seemed genuinely ... curious.

'I miss him already,' I said, shrugging. It was so bright, and I could already feel my skin start to prickle under the Californian sun. I'd spent so long indoors over the years as the cartel's captive that my skin didn't know what to do when I was allowed out into direct sun. 'I miss the person he used to be. Don't you?'

John nodded, running his tongue along his teeth, seemingly deep in thought himself.

'Will you miss Caroline?' I asked softly, my stomach squeezing painfully at the mention of John's crazy wife.

Yes, I was fucking not one, but two *married* men, one by choice, the other through necessity. I was not a good person. I was just trying to survive, stay one step ahead, and I was so fucking tired of it all.

John shook his head. 'Caroline was already an addict when I met her. I never got to know her well enough away from the drugs to be able to miss her.' He paused for a moment, the lines around his eyes creasing as he frowned. 'My wife and I are basically strangers who share a child.'

I thought back to the countless times I'd seen John's wife stumbling down the hallways of the Gypsy Brothers clubhouse, high as a kite, sometimes with a thin trail of blood still fresh on her arm from where she'd injected the heroin. I'd seen her in all kinds of trouble – a couple of overdoses, plenty of times when she'd plain forget that she was naked from the waist down as she wandered around.

I'd seen the shame in John's eyes every time she did something to embarrass herself. I knew the shame wasn't for him, it was for their daughter, Juliette.

I hated Caroline bitterly, not because I was in love with her husband, but because she had everything I'd ever wanted and yet she spent her life cruising about in a drug-addled haze, because she couldn't cope with the fact that she was somebody's mother, or wife. She'd been a nurse, once, and I'm pretty sure she'd started on pain pills before she graduated to smack.

When we left and made a run for it we were taking John's daughter, but we were categorically *not* taking his wife. A part of me selfishly hoped Dornan would kill her once we left. She deserved it more than Stephanie had.

I swallowed thickly, a sense of impending doom settling upon me like a plague of ants crawling over every inch of my skin. I glanced at John, and we both knew what I was thinking.

'We can't take him,' John said firmly. 'They will hunt us to the ends of the earth if we take their blood.'

We both watched Jason, down on the sand, as he spoke to Juliette beside him. They were sitting now, him hugging his knees and her cross-legged, her eyes only for him. Something squeezed painfully in my chest as I watched Jase and Juliette, knowing the destruction that lay ahead. Because even if we pulled this off, even if we managed to get away and make a run from the Gypsy Brothers, we'd be running forever. For the rest of our lives, we would be looking over our shoulders and sleeping in shifts to make sure we didn't all wake up dead, courtesy of Dornan and his family.

I chewed on the inside of my cheek, tasting blood. 'We have to take him,' I countered. 'Or I will never forgive myself. Or you.'

'You're going to be the death of me, woman,' John sighed, pulling a packet of cigarettes from his pocket and offering one to me. I took it, because I needed something to do with my hands, and since we were in public I couldn't be using those hands to unbutton his jeans and squeeze his cock.

Even though that was what I'd really, really prefer to be doing. If we didn't have these kids with us, I wouldn't have been able to stop myself from dragging John into a back alley, dropping to my knees, and sucking his cock until he came down my throat. John might have been the tender lover, the man who took his time, but it seemed we didn't have an abundance of time as of late. It was hard to be gentle when you didn't know if somebody was waiting around the corner to blow your brains out at any given moment. It was impossible to slow down and enjoy each other when we were both trapped in a constant vortex of crushing reality – that we might die very horrifically, very soon. And, despite the impending doom that floated around us like a choking fog, we both still found it impossible to keep our hands off each other. Which was kind of hard, in a crowd of tourists and locals alike, all getting their fix on a sunny day while we tried not to give in to carnal desire and go screw in the backseat of John's car.

Lucky we had these kids with us then, because if anyone we knew ever saw me do that with John, we'd both end up with our heads sawn off and hung over a freeway overpass as punishment.

I happened to like my head very much. John's, too. So we never let ourselves be tempted anywhere remotely public.

'Those jeans look good on you,' I said, glancing at him. Something to break the malaise, because otherwise we'd talk in circles and never come to a decision one way or the other.

'Your skirt, too,' he replied, looking straight ahead as he lit his cigarette. 'It'd look better off, though. You wearing underwear?'

I felt my nipples stiffen to hard peaks as I took the lighter from his outstretched fingers and held the flame to my own cigarette, wishing he was doing it for me. Along with my tank top, I was wearing a loose black skirt that sat just above my knees. 'Not today,' I murmured.

John shook his head, turning away so he could readjust his jeans as subtly as possible. 'Goddamn it,' he swore, holding his smoke between his teeth as he used two hands to fumble with the waistband of his jeans.

'I'm so wet right now,' I said casually, just loud enough for John to hear. 'If I sit down in your car, I'm going to mess your seat up.'

'Fuck you. I'm going to get coffee,' he muttered. 'Make sure that little shit doesn't touch my daughter.' He walked away without looking back at me. I snickered, wondering how obvious my nipples were underneath my black tank top.

I didn't mess John's car seat up, but we did ditch the kids pretty soon after that. Dropped them back at my apartment and made sure they were securely inside before we drove to a deserted football field and fucked until we were raw and panting.

We were getting careless.

Looking back, it was a miracle nobody found out about us sooner. But I couldn't focus on that then, naked and spread open along the backseat of John's car as he pounded me into the leather. Both of us slick with sweat, my head slamming against the car door with every thrust, his hands pressing my knees so wide it felt like I'd break in two. We fucked like two people about to be murdered, two death row prisoners tied together, devouring each other, one last meal while we waited for the executioner to come and blow a bullet through each of us.

We fucked like we were starved, like dirty, raw copulation was the only thing that could feed us, the only act that could make us whole again.

We loved each other so much, it was a wonder we didn't just burst into flames from the strength of our desperation right then and there.

We'd burn eventually.

I think we both understood that.

We just didn't know when the Reaper was coming to collect our corrupted souls.

CHAPTER TWO

MARIANA

I was cutting into a red bell pepper a few days later when my phone buzzed. I still remember the moment like it was yesterday – the way the sun was perched high on the horizon, ready to swallow up the shadow of my apartment building that overlooked Santa Monica Beach; the Ferris wheel on the pier, a giant silhouette against the bright blue sky. I can taste the pepper in my mouth, sharp and cold from the refrigerator; I can hear the waves as they crash onto the shore beneath my apartment. I can still remember opening the window, a cool breeze hitting my face as I marvelled at how the sky and John's eyes could be exactly the same colour.

Peace was always fleeting in my world.

My twenty-ninth birthday and I was still here. Still with Dornan. Still with John. Trapped between three men: one that I loved, one that I used to love, and one that I despised with every fibre of my being.

And number three, lucky last, was calling me. *Emilio*

flashed up on my cellphone, and I was so startled I almost chopped my fingers clean off.

Emilio never called me. I wasn't even sure he had my number until that moment. Why would he call me? Maybe Dornan was dead. The thought briefly occurred to me, and then it was gone, a wisp of smoke on a summer breeze. *Maybe Dornan is dead.*

I set my knife down and hit the green answer button, bring the phone to my ear.

'Happy birthday, Mariana,' Emilio drawled. I heard loud noise, traffic in the background. I remembered Dornan telling me his father had travelled to Bogota for a meeting with his brother, Julian. Perhaps that explained the noise.

They were still searching for Christopher Murphy, shady DEA agent and Emilio's right-hand man. They'd never find him, though – this I knew for certain.

They didn't know, though. They were still searching for answers to his disappearance. *If only Emilio knew what I'd done*, I thought to myself, a sick feeling in the pit of my stomach as I remembered how Murphy's blood had tasted, how my ears had buzzed for a week after I'd shot him in the face at point-blank range.

'Did you kill my family?' I whispered. Realisation spiked in his eyes, and his entire body tensed. A wave of nausea rolled through me.

He didn't respond, but the answer was clear as day in his eyes; in the way he looked away for a split second before meeting my gaze again, in the stunned expression on his face, in the heavy exhale that came from his chest. His mouth around the gun was revolting, the metallic knock of tooth on polished steel enough to make me cringe.

I saw the questions in his eyes. How? How did I know? How had I found out what he'd done?

'You really think I didn't check on my family in nine years?' I whispered. 'How stupid are you? How stupid do you think I am?'

And then, before I lost my nerve, I pulled the heavy trigger back. I'd just killed a man as he hate-fucked me, and I was pretty sure I was going to be murdered brutally for it.

I was the murderess who had finally put Christopher Murphy in the ground – or, more accurately, in a crematorium – and Emilio could *never* know.

'Thank you,' I said, pressing my fingers against my eyelids. Emilio Ross wasn't the kind of man to wish me a happy birthday. He was the kind of man who thought I took up too much air just by breathing in the same room as him.

'I got you something,' he added, and I stiffened. Swallowing thickly, I tried not to panic. *It's probably nothing.*

But it was never nothing with Emilio.

'You didn't have to do that,' I breathed, clutching the phone harder.

'I did,' he replied, his tone betraying nothing. 'I got you something ... appropriate.'

My stomach twisted violently. *Appropriate?*

'Go to the front door,' Emilio instructed.

I bristled, looking towards the entryway of my apartment.

'Are you going to shoot me?' I asked. *Shit.* I hadn't meant to say that. The words had come out of their own volition.

Emilio snorted. 'And cut short your valuable working life with me? I think not,' he said, and he sounded amused. 'Go. Now.'

With knees made of rubber, I shuffled towards the front door of my apartment. It was no longer a secret that I was free to the outside world; Emilio knew. He'd never said a word about it. And in my head, I'd figured it was because, after almost ten years, he'd finally started to trust me. Or because I had Guillermo, a Gypsy Brother and key cartel shitkicker, as my permanent roomie. My round-the-clock bodyguard.

Maybe I was wrong, though. Maybe Emilio didn't trust me at all.

Maybe he'd found out my secrets. There were *so many* secrets. Killing Murphy. Killing Murphy's girlfriend and DEA partner, and screwing John all over this goddamn apartment whenever Dornan and Guillermo were elsewhere. *My son.* Yeah, I had plenty of secrets for Emilio to unearth.

I keyed in the code to disarm the front door and let it open a crack. I peered around the corner, spotting a slick black SUV downstairs.

So Emilio wasn't in Colombia then.

'Open it all the way,' he commanded, and I did.

On the front stoop, there was a large plain cardboard box, big enough to fit a carry-on suitcase, or maybe a new computer. Maybe that was it, I thought numbly, trying to shake the crawling feeling that pervaded every inch of my skin. Yeah, I decided. I'd told Emilio about my work computer getting slower and how it'd be a good idea to replace it soon. *He was giving me a computer.*

It sounded so unrealistic, but I clung to the benign possibility that it was something normal at my doorstep, because I couldn't begin to fathom what it would be if it were not.

19

'Going somewhere?' Guillermo asked, from his spot on the couch. Sprawled out in front of an old episode of *SVU*, he was eating a slice of Papa John's pizza and swilling Budweiser. I tucked the phone between my ear and shoulder, squatting in front of the package.

No, I turned and mouthed at him as I picked up the box – it was heavy – and carried it to the dining table. It was rarely used for dining, and most often used for fucking, with its convenient height and width.

The box was sealed with thick duct tape. I placed it in the middle of the table and took a few steps to the kitchen to grab a pair of scissors.

'Is it open yet?' Emilio asked, and I remembered that he couldn't see what I was doing in the safety of my own apartment.

'I'm cutting through the tape,' I answered, trying not to sound too impatient.

'Good, *cholita*,' he replied. 'You enjoy. Happy birthday.'

He ended the call. I took the phone away from my ear, staring at the screen for a moment before placing the phone on the table beside the mystery box.

I didn't want to open the package – something screamed at me to just get rid of it – but I knew Emilio was outside waiting on me, and my curiosity won over my suspicion.

Like a bandaid, I ripped the box open as quickly as I could. The cardboard packaging fell away to reveal an innocuous-looking pink suitcase, one of those hard-shell ones with four wheels that glides like a dream when you're pushing it through a crowded airport. Not that I'd remember. I hadn't been on a plane since Murphy had brought me to

America almost a decade ago and released me into Dornan's clutches.

Dornan. I wondered, briefly, if he'd remember what day it was. Probably not, unless John reminded him.

John had already called to wish me a happy birthday, because he was a stand-up fucking guy with things like that. He had the capacity to think about people outside of himself. It was one of the reasons I'd fallen in love with him.

Yeah. Crazy, isn't it? Being in love with two men at the same time, knowing one is poison and one is safety but not being able to do a damn thing about either of them.

The suitcase. It sat on my table, prompting a thousand questions. Was Emilio sending me away somewhere? Was the suitcase even the point, or was there something inside?

I stepped back for a moment, closing my eyes, letting the drone of the TV and the breeze from the kitchen window centre me. My heart was hammering in my chest, and more than anything, I did not want to open the goddamn suitcase.

Shit.

I stepped forward again, unsteady fingers clasping the metal zipper. In slow motion, I pulled, undoing one short side, then the long edge, then the final side of the suitcase.

Taking a deep breath, I peeled back the lid of the suitcase. There was ... a toy?

A child's stuffed animal. It was a bunny rabbit. A soft blue, with a Quickstop tag still attached. Five dollars and ninety-nine cents, somebody had paid for this toy. It rested upon a thick knitted blanket that was made up of squares in every colour of the rainbow.

I'd seen this toy before.

Guillermo sauntered in, a fresh slice of pizza in his hand. 'You get a package?' he asked, around a mouthful of cheese and dough.

Something about the way the blanket was resting started to make me uneasy, but I pushed the feeling away.

'Emilio delivered this,' I said, pointing at the open case.

Guillermo stopped chewing, but didn't appear alarmed. 'He gave you a suitcase? What, you going somewhere for the boss?'

'I hope not,' I murmured, staring down at the stuffed toy. Maybe it had something sewn into it. Maybe he *was* sending me on a trip. A drug run? I'd done one of those for him before. Christ, I could still taste the thick olive oil that coated the plastic pellets of white powder he'd forced me to swallow, at the very beginning of my complicated relationship with the Il Sangue Cartel.

Guillermo stood beside me, picking up the toy and shaking it. He turned it over, inspecting the stitching. Nothing seemed amiss.

I looked back at the baby blanket. Emilio knew about my miscarriage – there had been no hiding it from him – and the thought that he was taunting me about it suddenly sprang to mind. I swallowed a lump in my throat as I remembered bleeding out on this very floor, at the hands of my lover.

Was that it? Was he reminding me of all I'd lost? Was he that cruel?

If only it had been that. A dig. A taunt. Anything would have been better than what was actually beneath the blanket.

'What's in there?' Guillermo asked. I glanced at him, picking up the edge of the woollen blanket and peeling it back.

I screamed.

'Fucking Christ!' Guillermo yelled, dropping his pizza and backing away. I dry-heaved, sinking to my knees, the reality of my *gift* so horrific, I could barely believe what my eyes were telling me.

I was still screaming.

'Where the fuck – *stop screaming.*'

I kept screaming, only the noise coming from me had turned into more of a low wail. My eyes were blurred from too many tears, hot as they ran down my cheeks and dripped onto the floor. I felt like I was losing my grip on reality, but it was the opposite, really: I'd been thrust violently back into reality. My reality. The one where I was nothing more than a pawn in Emilio's quest for total control over his son.

'Shut the fuck up!' Guillermo hissed, hushing me. He dropped to his knees in front of me, pulling me into his chest, his eyes darting around the room as he clamped a hand over my mouth. I fought for a second, wild with horror and disbelief, clawing at his arms, but he was patient. He was strong. The man bench-pressed more than my weight every day at the gym, and he had no trouble keeping a hold around me.

'Shhhhhh,' he said, low and long. Shhhhhh. Like waves retracting out from the shore. *Shhhhhh.*

I sagged, eventually, and Guillermo raised his eyebrows in question. He was asking me if he could take his hand away. I nodded, and he pulled his palm away from my mouth, ever so slowly.

'Where did it come from?' he asked quietly, his tone deadly serious. I choked, deciding whether to throw up. Nope. I kept my lunch down for the moment as I racked my brain for an answer.

'Emilio,' I croaked, finally. 'It came from Emilio.'

'Why?'

I thought back to the night Dornan had been shot. How he'd almost bled to death in the car beside me, only hours after we'd taken an orphan baby boy to the hospital and dropped him off at the counter, wrapped in a bloody coat.

Emilio's cold hand squeezed the back of my neck as he directed my gaze towards the smallest baby in the line-up.

'I'm taking this boy home,' he promised, his words turning vicious. 'I'll raise him as my own. And if you ever try and leave your post ...'

I sobbed from the pain of his fingers inside my wound. 'I've given you almost ten years,' I whispered. 'You told me you'd let me go once I repaid the debt.'

He chuckled. 'That was before. This is now. Do you have any idea how fucking marvellous you are at what you do? I was going to shoot you that night, and you insisted on coming with me. You've only got yourself to blame, dear.'

I couldn't stop crying. The pain! I just wanted him to get his hands away from me.

'You try and leave, and I'll find you, Ana,' he continued. 'I'll find you and I'll make you watch while I kill that boy in front of you.' He returned his black eyes to me and grinned.

It wasn't over. It would never be over.

Solemnly, Guillermo and I stood over the suitcase; over the dead infant lying on his side in a swathe of blankets, dressed in a pale yellow jumpsuit, already cold, his skin waxy and pale in death, face frozen in an eternal sleep, on his side, as if someone tucked him up in his bed and left him to die.

Only, I know he hadn't just been left to die. He'd been killed. Smothered, probably. And I knew who was responsible.

Somewhere in the background, a phone started to ring. It was mine. In slow motion, I reached for it.

I pressed answer and switched the phone to speaker mode, holding it in front of me so that Guillermo could hear. I didn't speak. I couldn't speak.

'I take it by your screams that you opened your gift,' Emilio said, the only things filling the room his voice, and death.

'Why?' I asked, my voice anguished beyond recognition.

'Your gift, Mariana. A lesson.'

'What lesson?' I cried. 'What lesson!?'

'An important lesson. Are you ready?'

I didn't answer. I was reeling.

'Don't ever try to tempt fate,' Emilio said coldly. His words barely broke the surface of my reality. Because there was a fucking suitcase on my kitchen table with a dead baby inside it.

I dropped the phone, and the screen cracked, turning black. Guillermo's fingers were on my arm, I realised, digging in painfully. I looked down at his hand as if I were moving in slow motion, feeling the way he trembled violently against my flesh.

'I didn't sign up for this,' he said hoarsely. 'Nah, man, no fucking way. I didn't sign up for this.'

I tilted my head to the side, getting a better look at the baby boy.

Button nose.

Dark hair.

Rosebud lips.

Dead.

I reached my hand out to touch his cheek, knowing it'd be cold but unable to stop myself. I was a mother, after all. My instinct said to nurture, to protect, even if this child was too far gone. Guillermo tugged my arm back forcefully before I could make contact.

'What?' I asked dumbly. That ringing in my ears – the buzzing noise that wouldn't go away for weeks after Murphy – it was back. It filled my head with a reverberating whine that was as excruciating as it was bleak.

A car revved loudly outside, and Guillermo left the suitcase long enough to peer out of the window next to the front door.

'He's gone,' he said.

Emilio had gotten what he came for. My horror. My screams. Now he could continue his day, having ticked the box *Fuck with Mariana's head.*

Guillermo slowly folded the suitcase lid shut, the tiny body disappearing from view.

'Wait,' I said weakly. 'We have to call the police.' An image of Lindsay Price floated somewhere in my racing thoughts, the FBI agent who'd accosted me in the women's showers at my gym. I had to call him.

Guillermo glared at me with bloodshot eyes. 'The fuck did you just say?'

'The police. The FBI. We have to call someone. Guillermo, it's a baby!'

He eyed me wearily. 'You want to get killed?' he asked, abandoning the suitcase midway through zipping it up. *There was a baby in there.* Fuck. The room was starting to spin and I wanted to be sick.

'Please don't close it,' I whispered.

'What the fuck is wrong with you?' Guillermo snapped. 'You want to get him out and read him a fuckin' bedtime story before we put him in the ground? He's DEAD.'

I knew it was illogical, but ... 'If you zip it, he won't be able to get any air.'

'Get in the car,' Guillermo hissed. 'Now. Kid's cold. He's been dead for hours. Days, even. He ain't ever gonna need fucking *air*.'

'Wait,' I stalled, desperate. 'Why are we going in the car? Where are we going?'

Guillermo looked like he was about to rip my head off. 'We gotta get rid of this, Ana. Your DNA's all over it. Mine, too. If this is a set-up, then they set us up good. No cleaner purification than fire.'

'We're going to set him on fire?'

Guillermo made the sign of the cross and murmured some silent prayer to the ceiling. 'Crematorium.'

Oh.

'Why would they set us up?' I asked, bile rising in my throat. I put a hand to my chest and made a gagging sound. 'Guillermo, why would they set us up?'

He glared at me as he keyed in the combination for the front door lock. 'Maybe they think we've been disloyal.'

I couldn't be certain, but I was pretty sure the tone in his voice was *accusation*.

I thought about that as Guillermo yanked the front door open with his right hand, the suitcase in his left. I thought about all of the ways I'd been disloyal to the cartel, and there were plenty. A carefully constructed web of deceit. I thought of the blood on my own hands, the blood on John's, the sins we'd indulged in, both collectively and apart.

I followed Guillermo from the apartment, unable to speak, unable to rip the image of the poor child from my mind.

CHAPTER THREE

LINDSAY

Agent Lindsay Price was eyeing a plate of mystery meat when a call came through on his cellphone. He was at the FBI's training facility in Quantico giving a lecture on interrogation techniques, and briefly considered going back into the cafeteria kitchen and interrogating the chef until they told him what he'd be puking up in about three hours.

In the end, he was relieved that he'd gotten the call, for two reasons.

One, because even airplane food was better than this shit, and he'd be calling his day short to high-tail it back to Los Angeles.

Two, because of the reason he was being summoned back to LA.

A body had washed up on the banks of the Los Angeles River – the part that was actually flowing, way up near Long Beach – badly decomposed and virtually unidentifiable.

Except they'd already run a preliminary swab of DNA sample through CODIS and come up with a match.

A DEA agent by the name of Alexandra Baxter.

***

Eight gruelling hours of cabs, turbulence, shitty plane food and LA traffic later, and with a Venti Americano in hand from the Starbucks inside LAX, Lindsay was standing on the edge of the Los Angeles River, watching as police divers searched the bay for anything that might provide clues as to how this woman had come to her end. It was already night back on the East Coast and Lindsay was tired, but giddy, at the same time. He'd been tracking Baxter and her crooked partner, Christopher Murphy, for over a year, their roles in a wider web of corruption and compliance with the Il Sangue drug cartel something he was determined to crack. The problem was, the further he dug into the case, the wider the hole got, filled with tip-offs and trafficked women and missing persons that stretched across the globe. It was a case that saw him come up against brick walls every single day, and so this body was like someone finally taking a sledgehammer through one of those walls and saying, '*Here, step on into this crazy shit.*'

There'd been no leads, save for that one woman. Mariana Rodriguez. She was definitely involved in the bigger picture somehow. Lindsay had spent countless hours combing through her life, her history. Had it not been for the frequent visits Christopher Murphy made to her apartment in the weeks before his death, Lindsay wouldn't have even known she existed.

But she did exist.

And her father had once worked for the cartel, many years ago, before he and the rest of his family turned up dead in a house fire, their hands and feet still bound in death, despite the flames demolishing everything else. Even the walls of their small house in Villanueva hadn't survived the fire, but the bindings on their hands and feet had. A painful way to die.

Drowning was meant to be much more peaceful, but the after-effects on a corpse could be horrific. Lindsay scanned the river's edge, locating a white tent that was no doubt shrouding the body in question.

He made his way over to the tent, the afternoon sun warming his face. Despite being November, it was like a spring day in Los Angeles, much different to chilly Virginia, where he'd been hours earlier. He didn't walk too quickly as he approached the plastic tent the medical examiner had erected. Nobody needed to see what he was about to see a moment sooner than was absolutely necessary.

He was already on good terms with Kathryn Donovan, the city's Chief Medical Examiner, having worked many cases together over the years he'd served with the FBI's organised crime division in LA. Squatting beside the body, she greeted him with a raise of her eyebrows, the rest of her pale face obscured by the surgical mask tied tightly to her head.

'I figured you'd be at the morgue by now,' Lindsay said by way of greeting.

Dr Donovan tilted her head, stripping her gloves and mask off and dropping them into a makeshift trash can as she stood. 'That for me?' she asked, practically prising the lukewarm coffee from Lindsay's hand and pouring a slug into her mouth. Lindsay watched, amused, as she made a face and let the liquid pour back out of her pursed lips and into the cup.

'That's terrible,' she said, handing the now useless brew back to Lindsay as she motioned an assistant for fresh gloves.

She snapped hers on before handing a pair to Lindsay. *No face mask?* he wanted to ask her, but didn't dare. He tossed his beloved Starbucks cup in the trash and pulled his own set of gloves on, finally looking head-on at the long-lost body of Alexandra Baxter.

It wasn't a pretty sight.

'Guess she's not been sunning herself in the Virgin Islands like we thought,' Lindsay mused, standing near enough to Kathryn that their shoulders almost touched. It was close quarters in a small tent like this.

'Nope,' Kathryn said beside him. 'And by the way, the only reason we're not back at the morgue already is because we've been waiting on you. So thank you. I now get to spend all day *and* all night with this delightfully perplexing young woman.'

Lindsay was grateful for the small talk. It distracted from the grisly image at his feet.

Allie had been a pretty girl in life, but death had stripped that beauty away. Her long red hair was missing large chunks, and her face looked as if it had melted like a candle left in the midday sun. Features flattened, merging into one another, lips pulled back over teeth that looked entirely inhuman from the damage the water and elements had done. The clothes that still clung to her body had fused with her skin, and one of her feet was gone. Somebody might've removed it prior to her death, but more likely the fish or some sudden impact would have taken it clean off underwater.

Lindsay had seen bodies pulled from the water before. They often looked intact until you touched them and flesh started to come away in your gloved hands. Water and dead bodies didn't mix well, and nobody ever wanted to attend

31

them. Fishing suicides out of the LA River was something they made rookies do.

But this wasn't suicide.

This was a cop.

A cop who had mysteriously come into possession of tens of thousands of dollars six months ago, and promptly disappeared.

'Sorry,' Lindsay said. 'You know the drill. Federal case, they make me walk the crime scene before the body's allowed to leave.'

Kathryn nodded, crouching again beside the body and motioning for Lindsay to do the same. Reluctantly, he squatted on his haunches, feeling the burn in his thighs from his weight training that morning. 6 a.m. now seemed like it had been years ago.

'You okay there?' Kathryn said, side-eyeing the way Lindsay's legs were trembling.

He nodded. 'Thanks for sticking around, Katie. I owe you hot coffee on the way back to the office.'

'Huh,' she said. 'You owe me dinner at the Roosevelt and a night of mind-blowing sex, at the very least.'

Lindsay stifled the urge to laugh, only for the fact that there was a dead body about five inches from his leather shoe. He'd never slept with Kathryn. She was as dry-witted as they came, as inappropriate as a foul-mouthed teenage girl looking to get a reaction out of her parents. She possessed no filter. The thing about her job, though, was that she didn't need one. It wasn't as if the dead could take offence, much less speak back.

Luckily, she was damned good at her job. Lindsay had long since suspected that her sarcastic, inappropriate comments were a way of trying to lighten the heavy film of death that covered her existence.

Kathryn launched into a long spiel of clinical observations and hypotheses about the body. She lifted one of Allie's arms – gently, so it didn't detach from her bloated corpse – and showed Lindsay just how advanced decomposition was.

Allie had been submerged, or floating along currents, for what looked like several months. It was a miracle she'd remained intact, what with the water and the weather, not to mention the sea creatures that were all looking for a free meal. As if on cue, a tiny crab crawled out of a neat hole in Allie's chest and darted along her collarbone before disappearing underneath her ragged red hair.

Lindsay's stomach turned at the thought the crab had just been eating whatever was left inside her.

After they'd examined the body, Kathryn and Lindsay walked the scene in a grid, starting on the shore and ending up barefoot and wading out into the shallows.

There was nothing, of course. Nothing to signal what had happened, or where. Allie could have been dumped in the water hundreds of miles away, or a few hundred feet. If this had been Florida, Lindsay's last port of call, gators would have found Allie long before any human did. The sneaky fuckers found bodies and stashed them deep underwater, in small caves or under logs, macabre keepsakes until their hunger stirred again and they decided to eat their catch.

But they weren't in Florida, and Allie Baxter had not been made into swamp feed, and now it was up to Lindsay to figure out how this young fellow officer had found her watery grave.

CHAPTER FOUR

MARIANA

'Guillermo,' I said.

He didn't answer.

'*Guillermo.*'

He white-knuckled the steering wheel. 'What?'

We drove along the freeway, windows down, my hair flying around my face wildly in the breeze. It was the weekend and the I-5 was relatively clear, a small mercy.

'I'm going in,' I declared boldly.

Guillermo ripped his eyes from the road and stared at me until I was squirming in my seat, wishing he'd pay attention to where he was driving.

'To Emilio?'

I shook my head. 'With the ... *baby.*'

'To the crematorium? No fucking way.' He slapped his hand against the wheel, agitated. 'My life was never this complicated until you turned up. You got a way of pissing people off, you know?'

I might have grown a skin of steel, but his words found

chinks in my armour and sliced deep. I sagged back in my seat, deflated, feeling the last bits of my strength bleed out through the cracks.

I squinted against the bright sun, a sun that sat bloated and accusing in the sky. I'd forgotten my sunglasses. The sunlight hurt. Everything hurt.

I rested my elbow on the sill of my open window, feeling warm air as it whipped past us. Any other day and this might be an enjoyable outing. Sunday was normally the one day when I could do something outside of the cartel. Go to the beach. Swim. Or, more frequently, lie on my bathroom floor and stare up at the exhaust fan as it turned lazily in the ceiling, for hours, as I recounted every single moment of Murphy's death. The moment he took his last breath, exhaled it, and breathed into me the reality that I was a killer. As the tiles chilled my skin, I'd think about how much blood he'd had inside him, the way it had soaked into my sheets and the carpet on my bedroom floor, his life force, gone, because of me. About how it would look to be slid into an oven, a bloodless corpse, and now I was about to see just what it looked like.

'How could anyone do that to a child?' I whispered.

'He didn't just do it to no child,' Guillermo said. 'He did it to *you.*'

I leaned forward in my seat, pressing my palms against my eyes until it hurt. The physical pain was a welcome relief from the way my heart was shattering into a million bloody pieces inside my ribcage.

'You know,' Guillermo said, 'maybe it's better this way. That kid, he'd be put to work in a fucking kiddie porn house, or worse.'

I took my hands away from my eyes and sat up, facing Guillermo. 'There's worse?'

He fixed me with a stare. 'There's always worse.'

I sagged in my seat, wiping more tears from my cheeks. My pores hurt where the saltwater had seeped in. I'd only been awake a few hours, but I was exhausted. One look at Guillermo told me that he looked how I felt.

***

It took too long to get to where we were going. I counted three police cruisers on our journey and wondered each time if we'd be pulled over. Guillermo's car was nondescript, a late-model Nissan that looked more like a soccer-mom vehicle, but the window tint wasn't quite dark enough to hide the gang tattoos that had been etched across his neck and all over his arms for the world to see and judge. He was like a magnet for attention, and so each time I saw a police car I cringed and waited for the flash of lights to tell us to pull over.

But of course, nothing happened. Nothing ever did when you were expecting it to. It was only when you were caught off-guard that the nightmarish realities happened.

I thought about calling John. Realised that would mean Guillermo would hear. Decided that was too risky.

Shit.

Guillermo pulled into the back of the funeral home and cut the engine, neither of us saying anything for a moment. I kept having paranoid thoughts that I could smell the death that sat on the backseat, encased in a plastic sarcophagus, but it was just my mind playing tricks on me. I think.

'Wait here,' Guillermo said finally, opening his car door and slamming it again.

Like hell. I got out, getting exactly three steps before Guillermo had rounded the car and backed me against it, effectively pinning me in place.

'Am I speaking Chinese? Wait. *Here.*' He stepped back enough for me to open my door again, but I didn't. Emboldened by grief and rage, I reached into my purse and pulled out the handgun I always carried.

'I'm going in,' I said grimly. 'So grab the suitcase and let's go, *ese.*'

Guillermo stepped back, shaking his head as he eyed the gun I was pointing at him. 'Gotta say, my feelings are kinda hurt,' he said, patting his chest with his palm. 'I ever point a gun at your head?'

'I do what you tell me to do,' I said calmly, the gun heavy but also oddly soothing. A mechanism by which I could be heard for once. A tool for controlling a situation that would ordinarily be out of my control.

'So do it now,' Guillermo hissed, looking around to make sure nobody could see our little Mexican/Colombian standoff in the back lot of Budget Funerals. 'Do what I'm telling you. Put that fucking thing away and get in the car before you accidentally shoot me, you silly bitch.'

I shook my head. 'I saved that baby,' I said, my throat burning as a lump grew and grew within it. 'I saved him, and he died because our fucking boss wanted to teach me a lesson. I started this, and I'm going to finish it, Guillermo.'

'Pointing a gun at me ain't gonna bring that kid back,' he ground out. 'Watching him burn ain't gonna do anything except fill your head with more black shit, so black you won't be able to close your eyes at night without seeing it. You really want that?'

I shrugged. 'I can't close my eyes anyway, so it doesn't matter.'

Guillermo made a low noise in the back of his throat. Not a growl, but almost. 'You see some freaky blue eyes when you close yours?'

I swallowed thickly, my pulse pounding in my temples. My grip on the gun wavered. 'What?'

'I'm not an idiot,' he said, his dark eyes shining in the stark sunlight. It was too hot. Too bright. Too loud. Everything was too goddamn loud.

I looked around the lot nervously.

'I know my place,' Guillermo said, his expression tight as he shoved his hands in his jean pockets. 'I'm the thug. I'm the stupid Mexican who does the grunt work.'

'You're not stupid,' I said.

One corner of his mouth tugged up for a second, and then it was gone again. 'No. I'm not. You know who was stupid?'

I wasn't sure I liked where he was going with this. 'Who?' I asked reluctantly.

'That damn DEA agent,' he said, and in that moment, all doubt was gone. Guillermo knew I'd killed Murphy. He knew.

'Guillermo,' I whispered.

'You move the money, too?' he cut in.

I chewed on the inside of my cheek, my arms heavy and tired from pointing the gun at him for so long. I wondered how long I could aim it at him before I'd have to lower it. How long

38

before one of the employees at Budget Funerals came out for a cigarette break and found me bailing up a biker at gunpoint in their parking lot.

'You trust me?' Guillermo asked, his eyes wild as he fixed them on me. It was an excellent question. Did I trust him? Did I trust anyone?

'I killed Murphy,' I said, the gun getting warm in my sweaty hand. 'I killed his girlfriend, too.'

'I knew it,' Guillermo muttered, shaking his head. 'Of course it was you. Look at you. Waving a gun around. Creeping around with the prez like I'm stupid. Of course I know. You've changed, Ana. You finally grew some fucking *cajones*.' He grabbed his crotch for effect. 'If I didn't know better, I'd say your balls are made of brass, *cholita*.'

That saying – my blood ran cold – it's such a cliche. But I swear, in that moment, I felt all of the thick red blood in my veins turn into freezing sludge and sharp icicles that cut me from the inside.

I sagged against the car, all the fight draining out of me. I wanted to cry. *Creeping around with the prez*. Jesus Christ. It was all going to come undone.

'You love him?' Guillermo asked.

'Who, Murphy?' I asked incredulously.

Guillermo rolled his eyes. 'John. You love John.' It was a statement more than a question. It was true.

Yes. A thousand million times, yes.

'Shut up!' I said, launching myself at him.

He stepped back, my show of brute force apparently unperturbing to him, and raked his eyes up and down me. I imagined how crazy I must have looked. Messy hair, cheeks raw from crying and waving a loaded gun around like I was some kind of gangster.

'You got it bad for him, don't you?'

Was I really that easy to read?

'You don't know anything,' I protested. The gun was so fucking heavy.

'Dornan will find out, you know,' Guillermo said.

'Shut up!' I replied. 'I will fucking shoot you, Guillermo!'

I saw the impatience on his face. I felt the trepidation. Any minute now, somebody was going to see us: one woman, holding a gun at one man, as they stood beside one car that housed the body of one infant who'd been inexplicably caught up in a war that was fought with blood and innocents.

'You're not gonna shoot me,' Guillermo said, the self-assured prick that he was.

'Give me this one thing,' I urged.

He glared at me. Neither of us spoke for several long, excruciating moments. Guillermo sighed audibly.

'Put that fucking thing away,' he said finally. 'Don't talk. Don't tell them your name. *Definitely* don't tell them your name.'

I nodded.

'Wait here.'

He shook his head again, apparently very disappointed in my sudden raging psychosis, and disappeared into the service door, carrying the pink suitcase in his arms like it was fragile cargo. For all his bravado, Guillermo was one of the good guys. Well, one of the better guys, at least. I felt guilt at the way I'd just treated him, but I'd been desperate.

Then again, once upon a time I'd believed that Dornan was one of the good guys, and look where we were now. He was a baby trafficker and a fucking murderer.

I waited beside the car, staring at the fire escape door where Guillermo had disappeared. Just when I thought he'd been lying to me, that he'd taken the boy's body and gone on with the plan without me, the door opened a crack.

'Hurry up,' he murmured.

I entered, jumping a little as the thick steel door closed behind me. My eyes took a moment to adjust to the dim inside, as I followed Guillermo blindly through a series of scuffed linoleum hallways. I started to catch the signs as we walked past. There was a viewing room. Then another. A records room full of boxes and files. The further we got into the belly of this place, the more uneasy I became. The staff stared openly, and I guess I couldn't blame them. I didn't belong there. I was dressed for a day on the sofa, watching re-runs on TV, my hair in a messy bun and flip-flops on my feet. I wasn't exactly dressed for a funeral.

'In here,' Guillermo said tersely, ushering me through a door. The smell hit me right away. The stench of scorched bones settled into my nostrils and I wanted to gag, but it hardly seemed appropriate. There was a guy, probably in his early twenties, wearing a white plastic apron and white plastic boots that belonged in mud and dirt, not in a place like this. I studied the boots for a moment. It looked like somebody had tried to scrub blood flecks off them and failed. The apron was the same. Dull brown patches that told a harrowing tale.

I looked from the apron to the boy's eyes and was shocked to realise he was younger than I'd first thought. His light brown eyes looked dulled by life – no wonder, when he was spending his living hours with the dead.

'Hey.' I turned my head to Guillermo's voice, having forgotten him for a moment there. He stared down at something in front of him, pointedly, and my eyes followed his path.

Baby Doe was on a small metal table, lying on his side, just as he'd been in the suitcase. His eyes were closed – a small mercy – and Guillermo was arranging a blanket over him.

I crossed myself, thinking that it had been years since I'd been inside the walls of a church, let alone made the sign of the cross upon myself.

I try to believe that the next part didn't happen, but it did.

I looked away as his bones burned.

I waited while those bones were ground into dust.

It was so *loud*. I hadn't imagined it would be so loud.

***

I carried him away with me in a box.

It was so small. Too small to house the remains of what had once been a living, breathing, innocent human being.

I threw up in the parking lot, feeling the grit of bone dust on my skin, in my hair, and realising that Guillermo had been right – I should never have gone inside.

But nobody, least of all a child, should have to burn alone, forgotten, in a place called Budget *fucking* Funerals.

I wiped my mouth with the back of my hand and got back into the car, staring straight ahead.

'You still with me?' Guillermo asked, putting a hand on my shoulder.

I nodded. The sorrow inside me splintered, became two halves of something that birthed something new.

Rage. The sort of quiet rage that turns men into monsters. I felt it crack apart the grief in my chest and travel like vine tendrils, down my veins, until my fingertips and my toes and my cheeks hummed with a hot fury that felt like a fever.

I vowed to kill Emilio Ross if it was the last thing I ever did.

CHAPTER FIVE

MARIANA

'Where are we going?' I asked Guillermo as we drove.

'Home,' he replied firmly.

Home. I'd had a home, once upon a time.

The small cardboard box on my lap weighed barely a pound, but its weight on my existence was unbearable. This child would never have a home, unless you counted the ground where I would finally bury his remains.

Guillermo handled the car silently and with purpose, occasionally turning his head ever so slightly to look at me. To check on me? I didn't return his gaze; I couldn't. I couldn't do anything except think about the dead baby who had now been reduced to ash and dust and poured into a small box as if he had never existed.

The freeway traffic was heavy, and it took us a long time to go across town to Santa Monica. By the time I'd walked into my apartment I was seething. I was rage personified.

'Hey, we gotta talk about this shit. We're due to see the big man. Where do you think you're going?'

I didn't bother to stop to acknowledge his question. I was on a mission. I stormed into my room, hot tears threatening to roll down my cheeks. I hadn't let myself think about Emilio while I watched the baby burn, because it had seemed disrespectful to be considering my problems when a child was decomposing into ash in front of my very eyes.

Guillermo followed me into my bedroom, and that pissed me off. I couldn't even indulge my rage in private, it seemed. I turned on him, pushing my palms against his broad shoulders.

'Give me five fucking minutes, Guillermo,' I muttered, pointing to the door. He didn't move.

'Get out!' I yelled. 'Just go.' I was going to cry. I was going to cry, and once I started, I wasn't sure if or when I could stop. It was like there was a tidal wave of fear and rage and sorrow that had been building up inside me for ten years, and it had reached tsunami proportions. I was about to lose my shit, and I was about to lose it in a massive way.

But Guillermo didn't *just* go. I pushed him again, hard, and he grabbed my wrists, shaking me. 'What the fuck are you doing?' he breathed, his eyes narrowed to slits.

I couldn't see his face anymore. All I could see was rage. And in my rage, I saw Emilio in my mind's eye, dead on the ground, blood leaking from the hole in his head, the hole that I was about to put there.

'I'm going to kill that motherfucker,' I raged, the answer to all of my problems so simple, yet so profound, it was almost like an epiphany. Guillermo's face fell, his grip around my wrists lessened, and I pulled myself from him, running into the bathroom. I slammed the door behind me, locking it loudly for effect. It had been six months or more, and every time I was

45

alone in this bathroom all I could think of were two things: Christopher Murphy's blood circling down my shower drain, and John Portland's feverish hands as he cupped my face and guided his lips to mine.

I looked at myself in the mirror as Guillermo pounded his fist on the door. I looked fucking terrible. I'd done my make-up extra special this morning, being that it was my birthday and all. But now, my mascara was plastered over my cheeks, my normally bronze skin was pale and blotchy, and the whites of my eyes were so fucking bloodshot, it was like someone had taken a scouring pad to them.

'Mariana,' Guillermo called, 'you're not killing anybody today.'

I ignored him, turning on the cold faucet and splashing my face with water to try and snap myself out of my stupor. That image, that singular image of Emilio with blood pumping out of his head, just the same way Murphy's blood had pumped out of his head, filled me with some kind of renewed hope. I had always wanted to kill him, but I had never really believed that I could.

Now, I knew that it was the only possible thing left for me to do.

The cold water didn't work. It didn't dissipate my rage; indeed, it only grew. Maybe it was because now I was actually a killer. I'd racked up two kills to my name, and ending Emilio would solve every problem that I had in my life. If he was dead, I would be free. If he was dead, I could have my son back.

If he was dead, I could finally get out of this fucking place.

I dried my face with a towel, taking one last look at myself in the mirror. I didn't bother reapplying my make-up. I didn't give a shit what I would look like, because either way, Emilio Ross was going down. It was hardly a fucking fashion parade, shooting somebody square in the face.

I opened the bathroom door, fully expecting to see Guillermo standing outside, waiting for me. But he wasn't there. I heard a soft beeping noise, and suspicion grew in the pit of my stomach. I stormed through my bedroom, the closest room to the front door, to see him tapping something into the security keypad on the wall. He looked up as I approached, guilt written all over his face, as if I had caught him in the middle of something he didn't want me to know about.

My handbag was sitting on the hall table. Inside was my gun. I snatched up the bag, rummaging through it, almost sighing in bitter relief when my fingers touched cold metal. I drew my piece and aimed it at his head.

'Tell me you didn't just change the fucking security code to try and keep me in here,' I said.

Guillermo stood his ground.

'Since when do you think it's okay to keep aiming a motherfucking gun at me?' he mocked. 'I just risked my fucking *dick* by taking you to the crematorium. Pulled it out of my pants and rested it on the fucking chopping block. And this is how you say thank you?'

I could hear the blood pumping in my veins, hot and thick and syrupy. That blood, it needed reparation. It demanded it.

'I don't care about your dick,' I said, deathly calm.

He rolled his eyes, bracing himself against the front door. 'And I don't care about your little revenge vendetta,' he snapped back. 'You stupid girl, you really think you're going to achieve anything by going down to see the boss man, guns blazing?

No. He'll take you back to San Diego and shove you in that dungeon of his so fast, you won't even know what's happening until he slams the door shut on your pretty Colombian face.'

Well. I didn't know what to say to that.

'Think about it,' Guillermo drawled, pointing at his temple. 'He wanted you to react, Ana. He's trying to make you crack.'

I dropped the gun to my side, curiosity winning against the rage, at least temporarily.

'Why,' I asked. 'Why would he do this now?'

Guillermo raised his eyebrows. 'He's trying to get into everyone's heads, isn't he? His right-hand man still hasn't shown up, alive or dead, and Emilio wants to know what the fuck happened to his supposedly loyal prick of a business associate.'

Murphy. He was talking about Murphy.

Guillermo raked his eyes over me. 'Girl, he knows Murphy visited you. He knows ain't nobody seen the man after he left you.'

I swallowed thickly. 'What are you trying to say?'

Guillermo took a step forward. 'Nothing. I ain't trying to say *nothing*. I don't know what happened, and I don't want to know, because knowing anything like that puts me in the firing line, you hear me?'

'You know he's dead. You know I killed him.'

'I know you can be fucking stupid, Ana.'

My anger kicked up a beat. I wanted to kill Emilio. I wanted to feel his blood on my hands. I wanted it to soak into my skin. I wanted his death to become a part of who I was. If that was stupid? So be it.

'Open the door,' I said, my voice hard.

He didn't budge.

'Now, Guillermo.'

He shook his head. Fucking prick. I responded by taking aim at the door, just to the left of his head, and squeezing down three pounds on a six-pound trigger. If I sneezed, Guillermo would be as good as dead.

He just stared at me.

'Open. The. Door.'

'No. Fucking. Way.'

There was a hard rap on the door outside, and it was lucky I didn't blow Guillermo's head off. He stepped to the side and ducked, as I stared at the door, panting heavily. I took my finger off the trigger.

Guillermo glared at me, motioning for me to lower the gun. 'Jesus fucking Christ, I'm on your side, bitch. Settle down.'

I was seething. 'Who did you call?' I demanded. Guillermo ignored my question, tapping a code into the security pad that I didn't quite catch, and opened the door with a heavy thunk.

I gripped my gun tightly at my side, ready to aim at whoever the fuck was daring to come into my house when I was reeling from the events that had happened today. My finger itched against the hard metal trigger, begging for release. I hoped that it was Emilio. In that moment, I didn't even care if he shot me as well. As long as I got a bullet in him first. He needed to bleed for what he had done. For everything that he had done.

But it wasn't Emilio. It wasn't Dornan.

It was John.

Of all the people I had expected to see on my doorstep, John had been the last one. I loved him. And up until that moment, I had truly believed that he and I were the only two that were aware of that fact. Tears pricking at my eyes, I stared at Guillermo.

Could I really trust him?

Was this a test?

Was Guillermo in with Emilio?

I couldn't begin to imagine what he was thinking or who he was allied with, so I turned my attention back to John. He entered my apartment, closing the door behind him and standing silently in front of me. He was a sight to behold – ripped jeans and a tight black shirt that showed off his muscles to fine definition. He looked hot, not just in the sexual sense, but because sweat was beading on his forehead, his shirt sticking to his chest.

'Did you run here?' I asked. *Did you run here?* What kind of stupid-ass question was that?

His expression was grave as he looked at the gun I gripped tightly by my side. 'Heard you weren't doing too well. You know me. I can't help myself.'

I didn't know whether to laugh or scream.

CHAPTER SIX

JOHN

He'd been smoking on the back porch when the message came through from Guillermo.

Get here now. M is going fucking crazy.

John had peered into the house to see Juliette talking on the phone, like she always did these days. Caroline had bailed a couple of days earlier, and John was beyond taking to the streets of LA to look for his drug-addled wife. His stolen moments with Mariana had made him realise that the only person who could really help Caroline was Caroline herself.

Plus, a very tiny part of him – the part that he liked to pretend didn't exist – imagined a day when the police would turn up and inform him that his wife had finally taken too much heroin, or crossed the wrong dealer, and ended up dead in a ditch.

One could always dream, right?

'Julie!' John hollered at his daughter through the screen door, making sure to hold his cigarette away from the mesh so that smoke didn't seep into the house. 'I'm going out for a little while. You okay here?'

'Yeah, Daddy,' Juliette's voice filtered back to him. 'I'm on the phone!'

John rolled his eyes. She was on the phone to that kid again. Long-lost son of Dornan. The kid who'd had to discover his own mother dead in a bathroom covered in her blood, before meeting his father – her murderer – for the very first time. A terrible feeling swept over John as he locked the door. They lived on a quiet street, safe enough, but you could never be too careful when you were the president of the Gypsy Brothers MC.

Truth be told, that sinking feeling he lived with these days wasn't because he was worried about the neighbourhood he lived in. It was the constant recall of the casual manner Dornan had displayed in the wake of murdering Stephanie, the woman he'd once loved above everything else.

It was the abject terror that Dornan would find out that John was fucking Mariana. That John loved Mariana.

It was the way his imagination presented Mariana's death to him in countless grisly ways.

John checked the locks three times before he felt confident enough to leave his daughter alone.

**

Ten minutes later, Guillermo was letting him into Mariana's apartment in Santa Monica.

'He told me you weren't yourself,' John said, hoping those words were benign enough to appease her.

'Not myself,' Mariana snapped, her eyes flashing with what looked like rage. Oh, shit. He'd never, not in ten years, seen her like *this*. Mariana Rodriguez was poised, she was controlled, she was almost annoyingly detached unless you pressed her in just the right way. Usually up against a wall, with three fingers and a tongue. That was the thing that inevitably made her icy exterior melt away, the thing that made her turn to butter under John's touch.

But he could hardly fuck the rage out of his little spitfire in front of Dornan's lackey. Guillermo didn't know about their relationship, and John very much wanted to keep it that way. Keeping his head attached to his body was high on his priority list, and if Guillermo ratted him out to Dornan, he'd likely cut John's head off and have it mounted on the wall at the clubhouse as a trophy. Disturbingly, he and Mariana had spoken at length – more than once – about how Dornan would choose to kill them if he ever found out about them. Decapitation always seemed to be at the forefront of their predictions.

Shaking that image from his mind, John focused on the woman he loved. She was shaking, pacing, tapping a gun against her leg. In some terrifying way, she reminded him very much of Dornan.

She looked like she'd finally lost her mind.

Maybe she had.

'Will somebody please tell me what the fuck is going on?' John asked, making sure to use his pleasant voice. Unlike Dornan, who liked to ask questions with his fists, John always opted for tact and friendliness as a first resort. Sometimes it worked. Sometimes it just bought an extra five minutes before shit got crazy and fists became essential.

'A dead baby,' Mariana was muttering as she paced. 'He killed a baby!'

John glanced at Guillermo, remembering the day just months ago when he'd come back to the apartment to check on Mariana and found her in a pool of blood, miscarrying Dornan's baby, thanks to those very same fists Dornan used to fight his way through life. Seemed Mariana had argued with Dornan about how unhinged he'd become, and earned herself a beating and a brush with death as thanks for her concern.

Was that what she was talking about now? Her dead baby?

John saw that Mariana's finger had crept back onto the trigger of her gun, and that was dangerous. He'd seen grown men blow holes clean through their feet by accident before, just because they'd been too itchy with a trigger as they bounced about.

'Hey,' John said, his voice sharper this time as he tried to snap Mariana out of her trance. 'Ana. What's happening?'

Mariana glared at Guillermo, who, for once, wasn't cracking jokes. And that was deeply troubling to John.

'Guillermo?' John said. 'Want to fill me in?'

Guillermo's eyes darted about the apartment, first to John, then Mariana, then to a cardboard package sitting on the kitchen countertop.

'That something I need to be worried about?' John asked, suddenly alarmed. He'd seen his fair share of suspicious packages. Severed fingers. Dirty bombs. You never knew what the new day was going to bring when you were a Gypsy Brother.

'I need to get out of here,' Mariana said, that damned gun still in her hand. She wielded it like it was a lifeline.

'Guillermo!' John yelled. 'Fucking *talk*!'

54

Guillermo cleared his throat. 'Boss man sent a package today. For her birthday.'

John used the distraction to step nearer to Mariana, closing his hand over hers and squeezing tightly. 'Gun, please,' he said, feeling her bones crunch under his grip. He didn't want to hurt her, not one little hair on her head, but more than that, he didn't want her to shoot him by accident. Mariana might have been small – five two to his six one – but she was strong. It took some serious force for her to concede, dropping her grip on the gun so that it fell neatly into John's other hand.

She stared at him with what looked like bitter rage. Funnily enough, it didn't make her look any less beautiful. Her dark blue eyes were like twin storms on the horizon, threatening to destroy everything in their path.

John rolled his eyes, emptying the bullets from her gun and pocketing them. The gun went in the back of his jeans, where it rested in the small of his back.

'This better not be a bomb,' he said, shoving past Guillermo and Mariana to pick up the box on the counter. He shook it gently, surprised at the sound it made. It was like someone had filled it with gravel.

He wasn't entirely surprised when Mariana snatched the box from his hands.

'Don't,' she said.

'Tell me what it is, and I won't have to,' he countered.

They stared off for a moment until Guillermo's voice broke through the tense silence.

'They're ashes. Emilio delivered a body this morning. A fucking kid.'

John stepped back as if he'd just touched a live wire. He immediately felt regret at having shaken the box so casually. His palms burned accusingly, glowering hot with shame.

'What? Whose kid?'

Mariana slid the box back onto the counter, the mention of a dead child apparently having snapped her out of whatever psychotic break she'd been experiencing.

'Remember the woman I told you about? She was meant to be delivered to a buyer,' Mariana said, 'but she was pregnant. She gave birth in the truck. It was the night Dornan was shot. We took the baby to the hospital, the same hospital where Dornan ended up after – well, you know.'

John remembered all too well. The night Dornan had been shot by a cop, a vengeance shooting after Mariana had killed the cop's partner, Murphy. The guy had been dead for months and he was still causing fucking problems.

John nodded, feeling his teeth grinding in his mouth. It was as if a dark cloud had settled over the room, and everyone was stuck in its shadow. Something was very, very fucked up, and John wasn't sure if he wanted the whole story now that he'd heard the teaser reel.

'Emilio knew what we'd done, how we'd saved the baby and taken him to the ER. He found me at the hospital, watching the baby through the nursery window. He threatened me. Said if I ever betrayed the family in any way, he'd take the baby and ...' She trailed off, her eyes lingering on the cardboard box.

John's stomach squeezed painfully, and all the air went out of his lungs as if somebody had hit him with a baseball bat. He glanced at Guillermo in horror, and then back at Mariana.

'Do they think you've betrayed them?' John asked, choosing his words carefully. He kept giving Guillermo surreptitious glances, wondering if the guy was even remotely trustworthy.

'Don't look at me, man,' Guillermo said, shaking his head. 'I ain't no baby killer.'

'I didn't say you were,' John snapped.

Mariana's eyes darted towards John, and in that moment, he saw the uncertainty that *maybe somebody knew about them.* The moment passed between them silently, swiftly, until John blinked and it was gone.

'I haven't done anything,' Mariana whispered.

'Apart from take out Emilio's best inside man.'

John and Mariana both snapped their attention to Guillermo, who held his palms up in a sign of submission. 'Hey, whoa, you all think I'm some dumb fuck, but I live with her.' He pointed at Mariana. 'I was ninety per cent sure one of you had something to do with it. Can't say I'm disappointed. It's been peaceful these past months, without that Murphy motherfucker following you around all the time.'

John clenched his knuckles until they made several faint popping sounds. Guillermo shifted on his feet uneasily, glancing down at John's balled hands.

'You can trust me, Prez,' Guillermo said. 'Six months that asshole's been missing, and I ain't said a word to nobody. This situation?' Guillermo gestured to Mariana, to the apartment they were standing in. 'It suits me. This girl?' He put his hand on Mariana's shoulder. 'I like this girl. Not like that. She's like a sister to me. Like a daughter.'

'The same way Dornan's a brother? The same way I'm your brother?'

Guillermo chuckled, but there was no joy in the sound he made. 'Man, you know my deal. I'm a hired fucking thug. I wear the patch, I look out for my boys, but I would shoot any one of them, you included, if she needed me to.'

John felt his eyebrows practically hit the roof. He hadn't known that Guillermo could speak that many consecutive sentences, let alone have an opinion on something that didn't involve free pussy or cheap beer.

'How'd the ... package get here, anyway?'

'Emilio called me this morning,' Mariana said quietly. She was as removed now as she had been fiery, not five minutes earlier. 'He told me there was something waiting outside the front door for me, and I knew he was outside watching. I had this weird feeling that he was going to shoot me or something. But instead, I found this big box.' She was gesturing with her hands the size of the box. 'I brought it inside and locked the door again, and I opened it. It was a suitcase. And inside ...' Her chin wobbled, tears welling in her eyes. 'When I saw the box sitting outside, I thought ... I thought it was a computer. To replace my old one. I didn't think–' She made a little gasping sound, holding her chest with her hand. She looked so young when she was terrified. She looked like the girl Dornan had first ushered into his office ten years ago, instead of the steely woman she'd been forced to become.

John stood there helplessly. All he wanted to do was kill somebody. Rip them apart, limb by limb, until this pressure in his chest went away. This throb in his skull. This desperation that sat in his stomach like lead. He'd always known what kind of men he worked for – was controlled by – but this? This was something else. In that moment, John's thoughts flashed to his own death, and part of him knew there was almost no chance they were going to escape with their lives. It was just that cut and dried, that fucking sure. He loved this woman more than he'd ever loved anyone, and as she wept in front of him he could already see how the blood would look when it seeped from her nose and her mouth, the way she would cry as her life bled away. As she *died*. John ground his teeth together hopelessly. He just wanted to be with her. More than that, he just wanted her to be free. He just wanted her to be able to see the son she'd had ripped from her as a teenager, the son she hadn't seen since he was hours old, the son who was waiting for her in Colombia until it was safe enough for them all to leave Los Angeles.

An unbearable sadness fell upon John. He didn't want to die. Didn't want Ana to die. Didn't want to leave Juliette with the likes of Caroline to guide her through life.

We could just get in the car now, John thought. Knock Guillermo out – hell, shoot him dead – get the car, get Juliette, and drive across that border. It was only three hours from LA to the Mexican crossing. They'd get over there, get some fake IDs and disappear. Shit, they didn't even need to go to Mexico. LAX was a thirty-minute drive away if the traffic was favourable. They could ask for the first flight to England, or Australia, or fucking Antarctica.

She wouldn't do it. She wouldn't leave without Jason. And John wouldn't leave without her. So they were all stuck.

'Show her some fucking comfort, man,' Guillermo said, his words cutting through John's vortex of thoughts as he gestured to a sobbing Mariana.

'You're the one who lives with her,' John said gruffly.

'You're the one who's in love with her,' Guillermo shot back.

Well, he didn't know what the fuck to say to that, but he did briefly regret emptying Mariana's gun of bullets. He'd very much have liked to empty the thing into Guillermo's face right now.

'What the fuck did you just say?' John asked.

'You think I can't hear you sneaking around in here?' Guillermo shot back.

That was it. Prick was practically begging for it. John launched at Guillermo, one hand grabbing his T-shirt in a fist, the other reared back and ready to slam into the fucker's meaty face.

How was Guillermo still *smiling*?

'Hey!' Mariana said sharply, her fist closing over the one John was about to eviscerate this motherfucker with, punch by bloody punch.

John turned his head to where Mariana stood. 'Let. Go,' he growled.

She didn't.

'He's not our enemy,' Mariana whispered, her long nails digging into his arm. 'He's our friend. And right now, we can use all the friends we can get.'

John took a ragged breath. Let go of Guillermo. Took a step back, running a hand over his head.

'Does Dornan know about what happened today?' he asked finally.

Mariana just stared at him.

'Nope.' Guillermo glanced at Mariana before returning his attention to John. 'He's not in a good place, man. Not after Colorado. If he sees her like this ...'

So Guillermo knew about Stephanie.

'No shit,' John replied.

'I'm right here,' Mariana muttered.

'And you're hardly giving me straight answers,' John snapped at her, looking back to Guillermo. 'Anything else I should know?'

He shrugged. 'Nothing that comes to mind right now.'

Jesus, fuck. Things were unravelling faster than John had anticipated. He felt hollow. Tired. Fucking worn out. Like someone had taken an ice-cream scoop and carved out his insides.

He closed his eyes for a moment, pressing the fingers of one hand against his eyelids for a brief reprieve. Dead babies and boxes of ash were more than he'd been wanting to deal with today. Any day.

It was in that moment that he realised, with absolute fucking clarity, that despite everything he'd promised Mariana, this life was almost certainly going to kill them all. If Guillermo knew about his relationship with Mariana, then who else knew? Granted, it was almost impossible for John not to openly stare at Mariana whenever they happened to be within shooting distance of each other. He knew that Dornan knew something was up. He'd been banking on the fact that Dornan probably thought John's hostility was because of the way he had brutally slain Stephanie back in Colorado and then asked John to do the clean-up, just months beforehand.

Did Dornan know?

Was this child's death some kind of message?

Were he and Mariana deluding themselves that they could run from these people?

'It's almost twelve,' Guillermo said, pointing at the small digital clock on the microwave. 'We're gonna be late for church if we don't hustle.'

Just like that, his words seemed to close the conversation. Church, just another word for the weekly meet at the Gypsy Brothers clubhouse, was something none of them could miss, unless they were dead. John stared at Mariana pointedly as he slipped the empty gun back into her handbag and held it out in front of her. She took it, looking a little calmer than she had when he'd arrived.

'I gotta change this fuckin' shirt,' Guillermo said. 'I smell like barbecue.'

Mariana flinched, and John glared at Guillermo's back as he disappeared into the second bedroom he'd claimed as his own. Even alone, he daren't put his hands on Mariana. She looked like she might scream if anyone touched her.

'I should change, too,' Mariana said quietly. She disappeared, returning a few moments later in a plain black dress and heels. She looked ready for a funeral.

'We going?' she asked.

John could feel grit on his skin, like fine beach sand, and though it was likely psychological and not from the box of some kid's ashes he'd just inadvertently manhandled, he still wanted to wash his hands with some boiling water. 'Let me just use the bathroom,' he said, heading for Mariana's bedroom at the front of the apartment, and the ensuite that was attached. As he went to pass her, she grabbed onto his forearm. 'Can I have my ammunition, please?'

John stopped, raising his eyebrows as he stared down at the woman he loved more than he loved almost anything.

Something in her eyes unsettled him deeply. 'Can I trust you to keep your finger off the goddamn trigger?'

She rolled her eyes. 'Yes, John. I'm angry. I'm not an idiot.'

'You sure about that?' John asked. 'Because you look like you're about to murder somebody.'

'I'm fine,' Mariana said, waving her hand dismissively. 'Just change the code back so we can go to the clubhouse together.' Guillermo re-entered the kitchen, looking exactly the same as he had before he went to change his clothes. 'It's zero-six-six-six,' he interjected.

Mariana stilled briefly, car keys in her hand as she stood by the front door. 'The devil's number. How appropriate.'

'Wait. I need to talk to you,' John said, taking Ana's elbow and leading her into her bedroom. She followed him without a fight, and closed the door behind her.

'I'll just wait here then, shall I?' Guillermo hollered, rummaging around in the kitchen.

John rolled his eyes. He still didn't trust the guy. Had never had the greatest feeling about him. Maybe because of the way Guillermo had dealt with his own wife and the guy she'd been fucking in secret, blowing their house to smithereens and reducing two humans to pieces of charred flesh that had to be scraped off what remained of the walls. Technically John was a cheater, and he wondered what Guillermo would do to him.

'Ana. Look at me.'

After a few seconds, she made eye contact. Her dark blue eyes were clouded, and she looked like she might cry again. He hated it when she cried. Made him feel fucking powerless.

'We're leaving,' John said resolutely.

'What?' Mariana said. 'What are you talking about?'

'You wanna bring the kid, we'll bring him. The four of us. Me, you, Juliette, Jason. I'll organise new papers for all of us. Passports. Birth certificates. We are not hanging around here until we find ourselves in the firing line.'

'John–' Mariana started.

'Don't *John* me,' he cut her off. 'I know why you're packing that gun. You're going to try and kill Emilio? You know that's exactly what he's expecting of you today, right? Jesus Christ, it's like he's chumming the waters with blood and you're swimming up, thinking you're about to get your teeth into something.'

Mariana looked at the ceiling pointedly.

'Promise me you won't do anything stupid.'

She narrowed her gaze on him. 'I won't do anything stupid.'

She went to pass him, heading for the door. Without thinking, John's hand shot out, pulling her back to him. He took her shoulders and turned her so that she was up against the door, squeezing her chin so hard he was probably hurting her.

'We're getting out of here,' he murmured against her lips. 'I promise you.'

'I don't need a man to save me,' she whispered, her eyes wet.

John kissed her, long and hard, pressing his body against hers until he was practically grinding her into the bedroom door.

'Good,' he said. 'Because I need you to save me.'

And he did need her to save him from this.

There was a rap of knuckles on the door.

'We rolling?' Guillermo hollered.

With great reluctance, John peeled himself from Mariana's slight form, swiping a thumb across her face to erase the smear of red lipstick he'd just kissed halfway across her cheek.

'Gimme five,' John yelled back, finally letting Mariana go. 'I'll meet you out there.'

She nodded, straightening her clothes before she opened the door and stepped out into the hallway.

John felt strangely out of place as he wandered through Mariana's bedroom – a place where he'd fucked her countless times behind the security a locked door afforded – and into her bathroom. He had an eerie feeling of deja vu that he couldn't quite place. That sinking feeling again. That inescapable reality.

He went into the bathroom, and by the time he heard Guillermo yelling and bashing his fists against the front door not thirty seconds later, Mariana was long gone.

John burst out of the bathroom, almost bowling Guillermo over. The Mexican's face was red, his fists white as he clenched them tight, raining down blows on the locked front door.

'She changed the fucking code again!' Guillermo said.

John looked up at the ceiling, taking a deep breath, hoping Guillermo was just clumsy-fingered. 'Here, let me try,' he said, shoving him aside and entering the code. Zero-six-six-six-hash.

Nope. Nothing.

More alarmingly, he knew that if they entered the wrong code more than five times, an alarm would be triggered remotely and the security company would call Dornan. Not a great idea to have him turn up with armed guards to find his girlfriend missing and John and Guillermo standing sheepishly in her foyer.

'I'll try her birthday,' Guillermo said, reaching his hand out to hit the keypad next to the door. John caught his hand mid-air. 'Don't do that.'

Guillermo looked surprised. 'Huh?'

'If you do that enough times, the alarm gets triggered. Dornan gets a call. How the hell are we supposed to explain us being stuck in here?'

Guillermo sagged against the door. 'Well, how the fuck are we supposed to get out? We don't turn up to church, Boss is gonna notice that, too, send out a fucking search party to cut our nuts off.'

John was already dialling Mariana's cell. She answered on the second ring, and he heard the noise of the highway in the background.

'What the hell do you think you're doing?' John asked, trying to keep his voice as steady as possible. He didn't need her hanging up on him.

'I'm meeting with Emilio,' she said, her voice sounding far away. He imagined the way she'd balance the cellphone on her knees while she drove, her hair blowing around her face as she cruised down the freeway. She always drove with the windows down, no matter what the weather was like outside. Said it made her feel alive.

Well, she wouldn't be alive much longer if she was going to pull shit like this.

Guillermo leaned over towards John and yelled, 'You'd better let us out of this fucking place, now!'

John narrowed his eyes at Guillermo, as if to say, *what the fuck?* He purposefully took three steps away from him, staring at the tiled floor as he pinched the bridge of his nose.

'Just tell me what you're doing,' John said wearily. 'Tell me why you've got a gun and six bullets and don't want us to come with you to your meeting with Emilio.'

'She took the box,' Guillermo said. At first John was confused, until he looked to where Guillermo was pointing at the kitchen counter, where a box of human ashes had sat just minutes ago.

'And a box of ashes,' John added, a feeling of utter dread forming in the pit of his stomach and travelling like icy tentacles to every part of his body, until he was consumed by the feeling. His heart beat faster as he imagined the countless horrible fates that would befall the woman he loved, should she try anything so stupid as to murder Emilio Ross in his own building, surrounded by security and family and no doubt his own fucking son across the desk.

Mariana's voice came through clearly. 'Emilio needs to die. Then we can all be free.'

She ended the call. John looked at the screen in disbelief.

'Call Dornan,' John said to Guillermo, as he pocketed the phone and picked up a heavy brass vase that sat in the foyer.

'And tell him that Mariana's on her way to kill Emilio?' Guillermo asked in disbelief.

John looked at the floor-to-ceiling window that butted up against the front door and prayed it wasn't bulletproof. 'No,' he said, gripping the neck of the vase with two hands and rearing it back like a baseball bat. 'Tell him you got clumsy again and broke the fucking window.'

Guillermo looked up from his phone. 'Huh?'

John swung.

CHAPTER SEVEN

MARIANA

I'd put on my best calm voice on the phone, but as soon as I'd ended John's call, a mile from the Gypsy Brothers clubhouse, I had started to shake. I drove down Abbot Kinney and turned onto Venice Boulevard, passing tourists and moms pushing strollers with one hand, Starbucks firmly gripped in the other. People liked to think of Venice as a hip, grungy place, but if they knew what happened inside the nondescript warehouse I was pulling up to, they'd drop their pumpkin spiced lattes onto the pavement and run.

I parked in front of the clubhouse and gripped my steering wheel, trying to catch a breath. Dark desires stirred within me, ones that had lain dormant for years, the spark of the girl I had been when I was first thrust into this life. The girl I had been forced to be when I killed first Murphy, then his partner, Allie.

Breathe in.

I was probably going to die in the next thirty minutes.

Breathe out.

I was going to die because my shock had worn off, and in its place, a violent rage had taken hold of me. I was its willing hostage, its dutiful foot soldier, its vengeful lover.

Breathe in.

It spread through my veins like poison, an elaborate network of arteries and organs that ached for reprisal. My pale shocked cheeks were now flushed with anger as I placed a palm on the office door and pushed, not bothering to knock.

***

Emilio Ross sat behind the great wooden desk in an office he occupied for two hours every week. He didn't need anything so elaborate, but he insisted for the other 166 hours a week, that this room was off-limits. Normally, I knocked and waited for his gruff invitation to enter.

This time though I walked right in, shoulders squared, eyes steeled, every ounce of me screaming with silent rage.

I didn't even glance at Dornan, who'd replaced Murphy in these financial meetings we had every Sunday. No, in that moment, he didn't even exist. I went straight for Emilio, who didn't look at all surprised that he'd finally hit a nerve in me that I couldn't ignore.

'Mariana,' Emilio greeted me, amusement written all over his face. 'You're late.'

I smiled thinly, the box in my hands far heavier than its actual weight. 'I am. I had a very busy morning.'

In my peripheral vision, I could see Dornan staring at me, and I knew he was probably dying inside that he wasn't in on whatever Emilio and I were discussing.

'I suppose I should be lenient, since it's your birthday,' Emilio said sweetly, his sugar-laden words failing to cover the poisonous barbs that lurked beneath. 'I trust you got my gift, darling?'

Darling? He'd never called me *darling* in ten years. The word sounded like cursing coming from his mouth.

I dropped my smile, but didn't turn my gaze away. To be able to out-stare a powerful man is a very rare gift, and I intended to use that gift. I stared at Emilio Ross until my eyes were burning, begging for me to blink, or look away, but I refused.

I'd assumed that I would place the box neatly in front of him and step away, but in that moment, the way his cold eyes surveyed me with an almost amused look, that shock I'd been experiencing subsided. In its wake, a tsunami of rage swelled through me, unbidden, uncontainable.

'I got your gift,' I replied, opening the cardboard box. 'I'm returning it.'

I said a silent prayer, an apology for the child whose remains I was about to use to prove a point. He shouldn't have had to bear the weight of my anger, but it was too late. I'd tried to save his little life once, had held his newborn flesh against mine and warmed his body as his mother lay dead in the car seat behind us. He'd survived being born in a tiny cell in the back of a truck, he'd survived the cold and the dark as his mother bled to death beside him, and he'd survived the precarious months since then. But he had not survived ultimately. He was dead, and Emilio had killed him. His death could not be in vain. An innocent child didn't deserve this ending, not after he was already dead. He didn't deserve to be disrespected. But in what

I did next, I hoped that I would be standing up to his killer, to make sure his death didn't mean nothing. *I'm so sorry,* I offered up to his poor tiny soul, as I did what I did next.

I tipped the box upside down over Emilio's ridiculous fucking desk, sending pieces of ash and bone in a pile that gave off grey dust, enough to choke a person. Emilio closed his mouth as soon as he realised what it was I'd just deposited in front of him. Something about the look in his eyes tantalised me – he was surprised. Not angry. Just shocked.

'I'm impressed,' Emilio said, pursing his thin lips together as he looked down at the ashes in front of him. 'I didn't think you had this in you.'

'Neither did I,' I replied.

Beside me, I heard Dornan clear his throat. 'Will somebody please tell me what the fuck is going on?'

Emilio's eyes were on the ashes in front of him, and it was then I realised I'd won. I'd out-stared him. Out-manoeuvred him. Question was, how was he going to punish me for it?

I turned my cold gaze to Dornan. It was almost comical how much he looked like his father – the Italian features, the dark eyes, their identical cheekbone structure. I marvelled momentarily at how I could have fallen so hard, so fast, for a man who looked eerily like the person I hated most in this world.

'Your father delivered a package to me this morning,' I said, my voice monotone. 'He even called me to make sure I personally unwrapped it.'

Dornan shifted uneasily in his seat, looking between me and his father. Emilio wore a smirk as he looked between the mess on his desk and me. It was almost as if he were pleased that I'd done this. Maybe he was.

'And?' Dornan pressed. 'What was in the package? What is that?'

'A dead baby,' I said flatly.

Dornan raised his eyebrows. '*What!*'

'The baby we took to the hospital the night you were shot. We tempted fate.' I looked back at Emilio, who couldn't wipe the smile off his smug fucking face. 'Luckily, your dear father was here to restore the balance in the world. Make sure nobody got away unaccounted for.' My words were dripping with sarcasm, and it was a wonder Emilio didn't stand up and slap me from across the table. He was oddly removed, and I realised how much he was enjoying this – watching my reaction unfold.

I would give him nothing. Not a single outcry, not a single tear. I could be a blank slate, a monster, just like the two men I was currently sharing oxygen with inside this stuffy room.

I heard footsteps in the hallway come closer, rapidly, as if someone were running. I had two guesses as to who they belonged to. Sure enough, the door burst open to reveal Guillermo, his round face shiny with sweat as he held on to the door handle, panting heavily.

'Get out,' I said to him. 'We're not finished yet.'

Guillermo looked like I'd shot him, he was so surprised. Glancing at Emilio, who tipped his chin in a gesture that said he agreed with my sentiments, Guillermo closed the door again.

I could feel Dornan's presence beside me. He was bewildered. He was angry. Most of all, he was afraid. I didn't even need to look at him to know that he was terrified for me. Because if his father could kill an innocent baby, what would he do to me?

'Pop, tell me she's wrong.'

I side-eyed Dornan, a little surprised that he'd found his voice. He was a man who could intimidate anybody except his own father.

Emilio leaned back in his chair. 'She's not wrong,' Emilio countered. 'You two left quite the mess for me to clean up. You should be thanking me for tying up your loose ends.'

I laughed mirthlessly. 'Are you fucking kidding me?' I exclaimed. 'Seriously. We should thank you.'

Emilio didn't respond. His smile started to shrink a little. His amusement, it would seem, was turning to displeasure.

'How did you do it?' I asked, smacking my palms down on the desk as I stood over the man I'd once feared too much to even look in the eye. 'Did you even do it yourself? Or did you make somebody else, you fucking coward!' I picked up the closest thing to my right hand – ironically, a framed photograph of Emilio with several of his grandchildren, Dornan's sons – and drew my arm back, aiming right for Emilio's face. I was going to smash that framed photograph into his face so hard he'd see stars. He'd need stitches from where the glass shattered and cut his face. He'd probably kill me for my transgression.

I no longer had the capacity to care if I lived or died.

But somebody else did. Out of nowhere, Dornan was behind me, his hand around my wrist, twisting painfully so that my grip on the photo frame faltered. With an angry cry, my fingers loosened and the photo fell to the floor, bouncing harmlessly.

Dornan pulled my arm, hard enough that I was forced to face him. 'Hey!' he said. 'Look at me. What do you think you're doing?' His fingers were squeezing my upper arms so hard, it ached. I struggled in his grip, my eyes only for Emilio.

'Look at me!' he roared. It was like time stood still for that moment, our tragic tableau representative of our entire lives – Emilio, smirking as he crossed his leather shoes on the edge of the desk where a dead child's ashes lay scattered; Dornan, hurting me, always hurting me. And me. Useless. Pathetic. Emilio had killed a baby. He was a human trafficker. He dealt in women and children like it was nothing. I'd known the depths of his depravity for almost a year now, ever since that night when Dornan had been shot, when he'd revealed to me the cost of keeping me alive was to do his father's bidding – transporting human beings across state lines, across countries, stealing people and selling them. Selling them! And I'd sat on my hands and blamed my need to protect Luis and done nothing.

In some ways, I was just as bad as them. Worse. Because I couldn't help feeling – knowing – that if I'd done things differently, the nameless baby Emilio had killed would be alive right now. Maybe even his mother, if we'd taken her to a hospital instead of Dornan shooting her in the back of his truck to relieve her suffering as she slowly bled out after giving birth. I could have done something, anything, and I'd been sitting on my hands for a year, hell, for ten fucking years, and I had nobody to blame but myself.

'Look at me, goddamn it,' Dornan muttered. I did. I raised my eyes. I could only imagine what they looked like. Wild. Empty. I was empty inside. Dornan's dark eyes widened a little when he saw my gaze. I think I must have repulsed him, then. With my face twisted into a mask of rage and grief, my eyes blank and hollow, it was a wonder he recognised me at all.

'It was easy, really,' Emilio said. I didn't look away from Dornan as Emilio continued to speak. 'I used a pillow. Didn't take more than a few minutes. He struggled, a bit, but then he stopped. He looked so peaceful, Mariana. It made me wonder what your child would have looked like if it hadn't died inside of you.'

I saw the light die in Dornan's eyes as his father spoke so casually about murdering an infant. The subtle way his broad shoulders curved inward, the way his whole body seemed to deflate. He took his hands off me, let them hang at his sides.

'Go home,' Dornan bit out, his eyes pained. He put his hands on his hips, shaking his head as he finally broke our gaze.

'We still have our meeting,' I replied, feeling like my insides had been hollowed out with a melon scoop. Like someone had taken out every bit of energy and life inside me, and left a vacuous nothingness in its wake.

'The meeting is cancelled,' Dornan said, the first trace of decisiveness I think I'd ever seen him display around his father. Dead kids brought out the rebel in him.

'Good,' I replied. 'It's my birthday. I'm taking the day off.'

Without looking back at Emilio, I slung my bag over my shoulder and brushed past Dornan without giving him eye contact.

My hand was on the door handle when Emilio chuckled. It was a noise that made me want to go on a murderous rampage. I felt the weight of the gun in my handbag and briefly contemplated if I could get off a couple of bullets before Dornan could stop me. He was, after all, blocking my aim.

I swallowed down the need for immediate violence and turned on my heel, my eyes landing directly on the man I most hated. 'Do I amuse you?' I asked softly.

Emilio grinned, wiping some of the ashes off the desk and onto the floor as he held my gaze. 'I've finally driven you mad,' he whispered, the delight – the wonder – clear in his raspy voice.

I stilled. Was he right? 'I was mad when I met you,' I said bitterly, opening the door. 'No sane person would have agreed to *this*.'

CHAPTER EIGHT

DORNAN

Mariana slammed the door so hard, it was a wonder the fucking thing didn't fall off the hinges. He listened to the click of her high heels as they disappeared down the hallway, away from them.

And then he turned and faced his father, and whatever the fuck it was that was on the desk in front of him.

'I should follow her,' Dornan said, his eyes lingering on the closed door.

Emilio slapped the desk, making little pieces of bone bounce in the shockwave of his gesture.

'Sit. Your goon will watch her. If he can move his fat ass fast enough to catch her.'

Dornan sat in the chair across from his father, his fingers itching for a cigarette. Fuck it. Why had he quit smoking again? It was something he'd done just recently, after Mariana had lost the baby. If he wanted to get her pregnant again, he couldn't be going around smoking all the damn time and snorting flake off strippers' tits. He needed to take care of himself so they didn't lose another pregnancy. Somehow, in his mind, this self-enforced penance made it easier to believe that she'd forgive him one day, that they'd have a family of their own. In the wake of his divorce from Celia, marrying Mariana was something he was determined to do.

Fuck it. 'You got any cigarettes?'

Emilio watched his son wordlessly, dragging a packet of expensive-looking Italian cigarettes from his top pocket and sliding them through grimy ash towards his son. Dornan picked up the packet gingerly, shaking off ash before he opened it and withdrew a smoke. Placing it between his teeth, he took the lighter from inside the packet and lit up.

It tasted good. So good. Emilio raised his eyebrows as if to say *What about me?* and Dornan slid the packet back, making sure to avoid the mess Mariana had made on the table.

'She didn't call you,' Emilio said, lighting up his own cigarette. 'I'm surprised. If not you – who?'

Dornan had to think about that for a moment. Who had Mariana called when she'd received a dead child on her doorstep? The thought of her in that moment was horrifying to Dornan. He loved her more than almost anything. He loved her so fiercely, sometimes it scared him. And she hadn't called him when something so monumental had happened.

Dornan knew what his father was doing. Trying to drive a wedge between them, to make him distrust Ana. And even though he knew this on an intellectual level, it was still impossible not to let that question burrow into his head like a fat worm and sit there, in the middle of his brain, burning him. Who had she called?

'Guillermo was already there,' Dornan said dismissively. 'That's what I pay him for. To be with her. Always.'

'Where you'd like to be, no doubt,' Emilio mused. 'Ana's a very beautiful woman, son. Beautiful women have needs. Do you really think it's a wise idea to have a thug like Guillermo living with her? On her couch. In her kitchen. Maybe even in her bed, who knows? You think he's licking that Colombian kitty of hers while you're hard at work, earning the money for your family?'

It took every ounce of self-control that Dornan possessed to keep from flying across the desk and smashing his fists into his father's face, but that self-control unfortunately didn't extend to the visual image Emilio had just implanted into Dornan's mind. Guillermo's fat fucking bald head perched between Mariana's thighs as she moaned and writhed on the bed. Whether it was true or not was completely irrelevant. Just the act of imagining the scene was enough to make Dornan want to go to Ana's apartment and put a bullet between Guillermo's eyes.

He needed to talk about something else before he killed somebody, right now.

They observed each other for a little while, Dornan smoking angrily, Emilio puffing away leisurely, as if the remains of a dead kid weren't right in front of him.

It was Emilio who finally broke the silence.

'You broke procedure when you took this kid to the hospital.' He gestured at the ashes for effect, then tapped his own cigarette ash on the top of the kid's remains, making Dornan's stomach turn violently. It just kept getting worse.

'We should never have been transporting somebody that pregnant in the first place,' Dornan replied, unable to tear his gaze from the spot where Emilio's light-grey cigarette ash had crumbled on top of the darker, sandier remains. He sucked desperately at his own cigarette, knowing that wasn't what he needed, but utterly bereft at the thought of what he did need. He needed some fucking peace. He needed to not be doing this shit anymore. He needed his father to either stop what he was doing, or die, neither of which was likely to happen any time soon. The old bastard would outlive all of them. Of that, he had no doubt.

'That's not your concern,' Emilio replied, waving his hand dismissively. 'Your concern is to get the package from A to B. Your concern is to do what you're told so I don't have the fucking FBI breathing down my neck.'

Dornan baulked. 'The FBI aren't after you because I let some kid live after I shot his mother. The FBI are after you because your fucking business partner double-crossed you to go sun himself in the fucking Bahamas with his new piece of ass and a bunch of our money.'

Emilio's smile had dropped completely. 'Are you quite finished?'

'The mother was dead,' Dornan continued. 'The kid was still worth something. I did what I thought best at the time. Dump the kid, let the hospital do their thing, and then go in and get the kid back once we knew it was viable.' It was a lie, but one he'd had plenty of time to construct. 'I didn't know I was about to get fuckin' shot, did I?'

'The kid would have been fine,' Emilio replied. 'You should have called me.'

Dornan itched to get up and leave, get away from the oppressive stare his father was beaming down on his face like twin fucking laser beams that were burning holes in his skin.

'The kid didn't look right. He would have died. I made an executive decision. That *kid* was worth a lot of money.'

Emilio brushed some of the ash away from where he'd been resting his clasped hands. 'Come on, son. We both know you didn't take pity on that child because of money.'

Dornan didn't respond. Of course he hadn't. He'd taken the kid to a hospital because he wasn't about to kill an innocent fucking baby that had just been born.

At least, not purposely. An image swam in his vision – Mariana's pale face as she sat on a hospital stretcher, her accusing eyes, the blood that still stained her thighs. He'd accidentally killed his own unborn baby, so why not somebody else's?

Emilio let his previous words hang in the air for an excruciating moment before he cleared his throat, pressing on again. 'Here's what I think happened,' he said. 'I think your pretty little whore batted her eyelashes at you – and, son, they're powerful fucking eyelashes, I get it – and you handed her your dick, and you let her wrap her fingers right around the shaft and *lead you astray*.'

'You're wrong,' Dornan snapped. 'That bullet fucked things up.'

Emilio raised his eyebrows at the sudden rise in Dornan's voice. 'Speaking of that bullet. Any ideas on who fired it?'

'No,' Dornan said warily, 'but I'm betting you have some.'

Emilio opened the drawer in his desk, pulled out a specimen jar, and slid it across the dark mahogany surface to his son.

'Somebody wanted you dead, my boy.'

My boy. His father hadn't said that since Dornan had been an actual little boy. When his brother had still been around.

81

Before he was gunned down in front of their house and Dornan had been left all alone with an unhinged mother and a megalomaniac for a father.

Something about those two words hurt more than that damn bullet had.

Dornan picked up the small jar, marvelling at the piece of twisted metal within. It no longer resembled a bullet. It had punctured his chest cavity and exploded inside him, blooming fatal shards of metal that shredded his insides like ribbons. It was ironic that something that started out smooth and oval-shaped spread into something that looked eerily flower-like when it pierced flesh. This had been *inside* him. Dornan's chest ached as he remembered the shot, out of nowhere. He'd been so confused, the pain not beginning right away. It had felt more like somebody had punched him square in the middle of his chest, like some kind of pressure had exploded inside him. He remembered the broken glass all around his face, in slow motion. The rain, as it battered them inside the car.

He remembered Mariana, her small hands pressing over his bloody chest as she tried to stop the bleeding. He remembered voices, even after he'd lost the ability to keep his eyes open and he'd tasted his own blood bubbling up in his mouth, drowning him from the inside. He'd been too far away to understand what the voices were saying.

He remembered a second gunshot. Mariana had shot somebody, or at least, she'd shot at somebody. The memory jerked him out of his daydream with a violence that was as unsettling as it was fierce. Fuck. Mariana had shot at somebody? He'd never remembered that before.

Did she know who had tried to kill him?

No, it couldn't be possible. She'd told him, in the hospital, that she had driven him to the hospital as soon as she'd managed to move him out of the driver's seat of his truck. That John and Viper and some of the other brothers had met them there, taken care of the surveillance footage.

He had almost died – half an inch to the right and the bullet would have hit his heart – but he hadn't died, and *did she know who had shot him?*

'I want you to take care of that little bitch for me.' Emilio's words roused Dornan from his macabre reliving of his near-death experience. He pushed those thoughts away, struggling to focus.

'You want me to kill her?' Dornan asked, confused. 'The best money launderer we've ever had? Because she didn't like that you delivered a dead baby to her doorstep?'

Emilio laughed, grinding his cigarette butt into the pile of ash on the desk in such a casual manner, it made Dornan cringe.

'I don't want you to kill her,' Emilio replied. 'She's far too valuable to me. She may be fiery, but she's a good girl with my money. Such a good girl.' Emilio's smile bared his teeth in a way that was entirely unsettling to Dornan. He'd always been afraid of his father, especially when Mariana was involved.

'Well?' Dornan pressed.

'I want you to marry that little bitch,' Emilio said, staring at Dornan until he wanted to squirm. 'Fuck her. All day and all night, you fuck her. Get her pregnant again. I want that cunt barefoot and compliant, you hear me? The FBI is breathing down my fucking neck, and the last thing I need is for them to cherry-pick your little whore out of our organisation and turn her against us.'

Dornan got lost somewhere between the words 'barefoot' and 'whore', but he got the general gist of what his father intended. It was shocking. It was oddly exciting. Still, Dornan didn't want to just act like he was excited at the prospect of trapping the woman he loved so that she could truly, irrevocably, never leave, by sealing their fate together with a child he could use as leverage. That would be wrong.

It sounded like a great fucking idea, though. Now that Celia was gone, he'd fuck Mariana until his dick was raw, come inside her until he was empty, and have so many babies with her she'd never even think to leave his side.

Dornan cleared his throat, shooting for an expression of amusement.

'You think sticking a ring on her finger and knocking her up will make her less likely to turn on us? It's been ten years. If she were a traitor, she would have gone by now.'

Emilio steepled his fingers in front of him. 'Are you saying you don't want to *finally* marry the woman you've been pining over like a pathetic fucking dog for the better part of the last decade?'

'No–'

'You're saying you don't want to kick that Mexican schmuck out of that apartment – your apartment, don't forget – and move in there with her? Don't you want to control her, son?'

'I do control her,' Dornan replied, perhaps a little too defensively. 'I know where she goes. I know her every move. Marrying her wouldn't change that.'

'You know her every move, huh? You know where she got a cremation, last-minute this morning?' Emilio picked up a handful of the ashes and let them spill through his open fingers, back onto the desk. 'Because I'm pretty fucking sure she didn't just burn this kid in a fireplace.'

Dornan's heart sank at that thought. Why hadn't she called him this morning? He would have helped her take care of the kid. But maybe that was the whole point. His father had done it, so indirectly it was Dornan's fault, because he refused to forsake Emilio. And by cutting Dornan out of the equation completely, Mariana was making sure he knew that she would not tolerate Il Sangue's bullshit forever. She had never been totally complicit, one of the many reasons Dornan loved her so much, but she had never been this defiant. Reckless, even.

'She was in my car when I dropped off the mother's body that night,' Dornan said. He sounded a hell of a lot more self-assured than he felt. 'Before this fucking bullet happened.'

Emilio seemed curious. 'She ride along with you a lot?'

Dornan knew what he was really asking. Emilio was asking how much Mariana had witnessed. How much the FBI could potentially get out of her.

'Never. This was different.'

'How so?'

'Nothing. It was ... Nothing. I took her with me. It was a mistake. It won't happen again.'

Emilio rattled off some more instructions, but all Dornan could think about was that fucking cellphone he'd found hidden in Mariana's kitchen all those months ago, and whether she'd betrayed him already. He stared at the tiny, blossomed bullet that had once lived inside him for a brief spell, and a wave of pain touched his chest sharply, suspicion and regret all wound up in one imaginary stab to the heart.

'Son,' Emilio said sharply. Dornan raised his eyes from the bullet to meet his father's gaze – cold, almost reptilian. He'd always been terrified of the man. Dornan Ross loved his mother, but *love* was not an emotion he'd ever associated with the man who gave him life.

'Has she said or done anything to make you believe she could be involved with Agent Murphy's disappearance? Think, son. Cast your mind back. It's been a long time since that girl made her way to us. And Christopher always had a certain obsession with our Mariana, didn't he?'

Dornan nodded. 'Yeah. You could say that.'

Emilio brushed his palms off. 'Think. And think some more. You can love somebody and still find the weak spots in their armour. You understand?'

'Yeah.'

Emilio slammed his open palm on the table, making Dornan blink. 'You're not getting it, boy.' It was funny being called a boy at forty-odd years of age, but damn if it didn't make him feel like he was seven again.

'I'm not asking you if you want her to be a part of this. I know you don't. I don't, either. Because if your little girlfriend is in on this – if she's planning something with my fucking money – I go to prison.' He pointed at himself, jabbing a finger into his own chest as his face flushed with anger. 'You go to prison,' a jab at the air in front of Dornan, 'and the house of cards burns to the ground. You'll last a day in prison before Sinaloa, or Medellin, or hell, the fucking FBI kill you to shut you up. Think of your *sons*. Think of your *club*. Do not think of her and how well she sucks your cock. Am. I. Clear.'

Dornan nodded. 'Crystal.'

'Right,' Emilio said, apparently satisfied. 'Let me ask you again. Do you think there is *any* chance Mariana is in on Murphy's disappearance? Do you think she's been talking to the FBI behind our backs? I will not act until I have proof, out of respect for you and only because of you.'

Dornan laughed. 'You expect me to believe that?'

Emilio ran his tongue over his teeth, fiddling with his deep crimson tie. 'You are my only son. I'm not getting any younger. All of this will be yours soon, and you'll have to decide who you can trust to love your sons.'

A flash of Jason and Juliette came to him then. The girl he'd helped raise as if she were his own, and the boy who really was his own, but he'd never known existed. Of all his children, he thought of them, his son and John's daughter, falling in love, and the thought gave him a small amount of comfort. At least out of the seven sons he had, he could trust one of their girlfriends. Even with the way he and John had grown distant over the years, he still thought of Juliette as one of his own.

'You didn't trust Celia,' Dornan said wryly, referring to his ex-wife, freshly divorced and back in New York now with her family on an extended 'trip'.

'You didn't love Celia,' Emilio replied. 'You love Mariana. Love is the thing that messes everything else up. Love makes us blind. Love makes us foolish.'

You got that right, Dornan thought.

'One last time. Do you think Mariana has been compromised?'

Everything inside Dornan wanted to scream no. But he remembered the cellphone he'd found hidden in a bag of flour in Mariana's kitchen cupboard, smeared with blood. How enraged he'd been at the fact she'd hidden it from him. Who had she been calling? Why didn't she want him to know? He'd been in such denial that she could betray him, he'd never looked at the spot in her kitchen again to see if the phone was still hidden in there. He'd never checked the outgoing calls. Never tried to trace the phone back to a supplier, or a call list, or even asked her about it.

Because the moment he'd been about to ask her was the moment he'd instead lashed out with his fists, beat her until she was knocked out on the floor, and then he'd gotten the call that she'd lost their baby.

The secret phone had been relegated to an uncertain fate. He hadn't wanted to deal with it. If it were bad? He'd kill her. He'd wrap his hands around her neck and fucking kill her. He'd watch the life drain out of her face, squeeze harder as she choked and begged silently for him to stop. It was a fact that if she'd betrayed him by fucking somebody else, or by feeding information to the FBI, or by funnelling money to Murphy – he would destroy her.

But if Dornan destroyed Mariana, then he'd be all alone. So he didn't ask about the phone.

Now, though, now it was time to get some fucking answers.

'I don't think she's been compromised, no,' Dornan said to his father, choosing his words carefully.

Emilio nodded. 'Thinking is one thing. I want you to know one hundred and ten per cent, son. Will you do that for me?'

'Yes,' Dornan replied, his chest feeling like someone had parked a truck on top of it.

'Tell me if you can't,' Emilio persisted. 'Right now. There's no shame in honesty, my boy. If you can't do this – beat the answers out of her, if you have to, violence goes a long way in drawing out the truth from a woman – then I'll step in and I'll be the bad person.'

'No,' Dornan said quickly, imagining all of the horrible torture devices he'd seen his father employ in the past. He'd once seen Emilio hammer nails into a woman's forehead while she was fully conscious, in an effort to torture the truth out of her. No. Emilio could not have his twisted way with Mariana.

'Give me a couple of days,' Dornan said, standing quickly. 'I'll prove she's not a threat.'

'How's the sex?' Emilio asked suddenly.

'What?'

'The sex. She still a little whore for you in the bedroom? Because if she's not, she's getting it from somewhere else. Question is – is she getting it from our friend Murphy?'

Dornan just blinked at that question. He imagined Murphy's stupid grin as Mariana bobbed in his lap. No. He'd kill them. He'd slaughter the pair of them.

'She has never betrayed this family,' Dornan said defiantly. 'She's loyal. Always has been.'

But the phone, his mind urged. *Why does she need a secret burner phone? Is it to call Murphy? Is it?*

Is she in with the FBI?

Has she been tainted?

Is Mariana a fucking snitch?

'Loyalty doesn't always last, son,' Emilio added, on a more serious note. 'They might be loyal at the beginning, but it doesn't mean they'll be loyal until the end. Beat a dog and that dog will bite you, given the chance.'

He took the vial containing the bullet between his thumb and forefinger and held it up for Dornan. 'Beat a woman like Mariana, kill her unborn child, and who knows what she'll do to make you pay?'

Emilio grinned, flesh pulled back over pointed teeth as he shook the bullet in the vial for effect. *He's a sadistic fuck*, Dornan mused to himself. And then he thought, *but so am I.*

CHAPTER NINE

LINDSAY

Somewhere close by, another man was studying another bullet. But the body that had held this bullet hadn't survived the impact. Allie Baxter's cold, dead corpse lay naked on a metal gurney, the flesh around her hairline slipping from her scalp as the medical examiner sawed off the top of her skull.

After dropping his suitcase back at his apartment in Silver Lake, changing into a fresh shirt and making the obligatory pre-autopsy stop for coffee, Lindsay had walked into the deserted LA County Department of Medical Examiner-Coroner. For such a long name, the place was depressingly simple – it was the place where dead people kicked around, for a brief period of time, where they were sliced and sawed and sewn back together, before they were either reduced to ash or interred in the ground, or sometimes both.

From the outside, the building itself was quite beautiful – old, rendered with limestones and reds, not quite Spanish architecture, but close. It annoyed him that he couldn't place the name for such a building. Lindsay Price liked to think he knew a little of everything.

It was after hours, and he'd had to be buzzed in. A guy dressed in janitorial garb led him through a maze of corridors, down a tiny elevator, and into the partially submerged basement that housed the city's morgue.

Not all bodies came here, of course. Just the suspicious deaths. There were already too many suspect deaths for the building to accommodate, and large refrigerated shipping containers sat in the parking lot out back, housing the overflow in neatly stacked shelves. Lindsay had spent a lot of time in these walls over his career, and he was always glad to leave.

It was going to be a long night.

The janitor guy pointed to a small room and Lindsay grimaced internally. He'd been in this room only once before – a shady guy, small-time drug-dealing type, had died in his apartment and nobody had noticed the stench of decay for months. It was only when the neighbours started hearing strange noises – what turned out to be swarms of blowflies battering the windows, trapped – that the police knocked his door down and discovered the guy face down at the dinner table, gun still beside his head, as his flesh broke away from his face and started to puddle on the table in front of him, like rancid candle wax. This particular room had been installed with a sophisticated ventilation system meant to draw out gases and odours, but some deaths just insisted on overpowering all your senses, no matter how well the fans extracted the rotten air.

Lindsay had never been able to forget that guy, but he had a feeling this was going to be much worse.

As if on cue, the door opened an inch and a gloved hand came out.

'Detective,' a female voice called out. 'You want to see this?'

Not really, Lindsay thought, steeling himself as he entered the small autopsy suite. He almost gagged when the taste of rotten flesh stuck to his tongue like glue. A smell so bad you could actually taste it in the air. Lindsay mentally calculated how many years until he could retire.

'Here,' Kathryn said, handing him a surgical mask. It was lined with scented cotton, unlike regular masks, the eucalyptus smell masking about three per cent of the stench that filled the room like poison. Kathryn was good about things like that. Some other medical examiners were known for their penchant for making cops throw up.

'Coffee's outside,' Lindsay volunteered. 'Extra hot, extra cream.'

Kathryn nodded, not wasting any time as she began cutting a Y-shaped incision into Allie's bare chest. The image of the crab came into Lindsay's mind again, and he wondered if it was still burrowed into her hair.

'Any idea on cause of death?' Lindsay asked. Kathryn nodded, lifting her scalpel long enough to gesture to a small vial on the counter behind Lindsay. He turned, grateful to put space between himself and the body, and picked up the small evidence jar carefully.

'Somebody shot her?' Lindsay asked.

'At that angle, she didn't shoot herself,' Kathryn replied, resuming her incisions. 'The decomp's too advanced for me to tell if she was still alive when she was put in the river, but the bullet was in one of her lungs. So either she drowned in her own blood from being shot, or she drowned shortly afterwards in the water.'

Lindsay nodded. 'You mind if I call one of my guys in ballistics, get an early report on this bullet?'

Kathryn nodded. 'Go for it. Miss Baxter and I need some girl time to bond, see if I can't get any more secrets out of her.'

Kathryn powered up a Stryker saw and brought it down to Allie's skull. Lindsay's shock was still fresh. Whenever he'd imagined that skull over the past months, he'd always imagined it lying on a beach somewhere tropical, its owner grinning smugly as she sipped from a cocktail and leaned back on her hand. He'd seen the money in her bank account, watched as withdrawals were made over and over again. He'd genuinely believed that she was alive and sticking the middle finger to every law enforcement agency that existed as she lived on her drug cartel money with her equally corrupt partner.

Lindsay swallowed thickly, adjusting his plastic goggles as bits of skin and skull made a sheen of dust in front of Kathryn's intensely focused face.

This part was always the *worst*.

He had to wait, staring at the wall, as Kathryn cut the top of Allie's skull clean off. How somebody could do that to another human being – even a dead one – was beyond him. Lindsay could reach into a person's past, into the darkest recesses of their mind, and figure out what they'd done. But he couldn't reach inside their bodies and figure out how they'd met their maker.

After what seemed like an eternity, the loud whining noise stopped. Kathryn placed the saw on the bench beside her and used two hands to gently wiggle the top of Allie's skull free. That was the moment Lindsay decided he had about three minutes in him before he needed to puke.

Lindsay made a face under his mask, pocketing the vial that held his precious bullet of evidence. He stripped his gloves off, trying not to look directly at the hideously decomposed brain Kathryn was lifting out of Allie's open skull. *Now. Got to leave, right the fuck now.* The worst part of leaving this room was knowing his clothes would still smell like death long after he'd left the building. He should have thought ahead and changed into a less expensive suit.

'Next time, don't wear your Armani,' Kathryn said, apparently reading his mind.

'I'll call you from the lab,' Lindsay replied, swallowing back coffee and stomach acid. 'Have fun.'

Kathryn snickered.

Lindsay was about to high-tail it when he noticed the two cups of coffee sitting on a filing cabinet in the hallway, probably stone cold by now.

'Your coffee's going cold out here,' he called through the remaining crack in the door.

'It always does,' Kathryn replied. 'You enjoy yours.'

He wouldn't; he left it where it sat, a sacrificial lamb left on a filing cabinet altar. He rushed outside, taking the stairs two at a time, and just made it to the bottom and outside before he heaved his stomach up, all over a rose bush that was thriving despite the dry Los Angeles climate.

***

95

Back at the Bureau's main office downtown, Lindsay lucked out. It was late, but a ballistics tech was still kicking around the lab, blasting some pop shit at a volume that made Lindsay want to jump out of a window, or smash the computer it was coming from, all distorted and tinny. Nobody appreciated quality these days. They didn't even buy their music, just downloaded it from torrent websites, and they were the fucking FBI.

Nothing was the way it used to be. Lindsay was only forty, but he felt old. Worn out. Twenty years in the force kind of had that effect.

'Hey,' Lindsay called from the doorway of the laboratory. He didn't want to walk in unheard and spook the lab tech – this was a room full of guns and bullets, for Christ's sake – but the dude working at his computer was totally oblivious.

Lindsay rolled his eyes, marched in and slammed the specimen jar on the desk so hard the whole thing rattled.

The guy jumped so high, Lindsay was surprised his head didn't hit the fucking ceiling.

Lindsay blinked, his patience fraying, as the lab tech scrambled for the mute button.

'I need a bullet run.'

The guy started typing, barely glancing at Lindsay. 'I'm off the clock in five,' he said. 'I've got a booking at Romera's. Leave it with me and I'll add it to the pile.'

Lindsay ran his tongue over his teeth, tasting the faint remnants of coffee and vomit. No. He would not add it to the pile.

'A cop was killed. She washed up in Long Beach this morning. This bullet's the only thing we have. I guess Romera's is gonna have to wait.'

The tech paled, his eyes meeting Lindsay's as he held out his palm. Lindsay smiled congenially, smacking the jar into his hand.

'Give me thirty minutes,' the tech said.

Lindsay nodded. 'I'll be back in ten.'

Time enough to get coffee from the Starbucks down on Westwood and drive around in the peace that one could only enjoy in downtown LA in the quiet of the night. He drove as he sipped his Americano, all the while theorising how Alexandra Baxter had met her death. He was betting on a certain DEA agent called Christopher Murphy, who hadn't been seen or heard from in the same time that Allie had been missing. Had he killed her? Dumped her body and fled, keeping their shared steals to himself?

Or was it just a matter of time before his body washed up, a matching bullet hole for a crab to burrow into and make a home?

***

Fifteen minutes later, Lindsay was carrying two cups of coffee back to the lab. He'd decided to be nicer to the lab tech, in hopes that it'd speed up the process. At first, when he walked in, the lab was empty, and Lindsay almost threw his second cup of coffee at the fucking wall. That bastard had left? Gone to keep his dinner reservation?

No. He hurried back into the lab a few moments after Lindsay, skittish and almost excited. He was waving around a printout that looked like a series of lines and going on about striations and barrels.

'Here,' Lindsay interrupted, handing him coffee.

'Is it black?' the guy asked breathlessly. 'I'm vegan.'

He frowned. 'Romera's is a steakhouse.'

The guy tore the lid off the coffee – which was black and steaming hot, luckily for him, the *vegan steakhouse frequenter* – and started pouring sugar packets into the brew. 'My girlfriend likes to eat dead animals. I see enough dead people to never eat meat again.'

Lindsay thought of Allie's skull. 'Fair call.'

The lab tech handed Lindsay a piece of paper with those irregular lines again.

'You want the good news or the bad news?'

'Just start talking.' *Before I throttle you.*

'See these striations? They're rare.'

Lindsay's ears pricked up. 'How rare?'

The guy grinned. 'Only four hundred and twenty of this model were ever made with the extended barrel.'

It was like fucking Christmas.

Lindsay almost forgot to ask. 'What's the bad news?'

'They're made in Italy. There's only ever been a few recorded in the United States. Course, doesn't mean it didn't come here illegally.'

Like Christmas and a blowjob all at once. He knew a man who favoured Italian weaponry. His name was Emilio Ross. Could it really be that easy?

Il Sangue. *Of course.* The very people who'd no doubt been depositing money into Allie's bank account.

A quiet sense of excitement began to build in Lindsay's chest; the thrill of the chase in these cases was addictive. It was what he lived on. It was the thing that kept him going through the long nights and the harsh realities and the midnight autopsies.

Having someone to chase.

'What does the gun look like?' he asked, almost breathless.

The tech clicked around a few more pages and pulled up a picture that made Lindsay's dick want to go hard.

The bullet striations. A rare handgun with a wooden inlaid grip. The Il Sangue Cartel.

Lindsay Price knew exactly where he'd seen a gun like that before. In a gym locker in Santa Monica.

Seemed a visit to Mariana Rodriguez was long overdue.

CHAPTER TEN

MARIANA

'You ever think about leaving?' I asked Guillermo, as we sped down the freeway some twenty minutes later, headed back to the apartment minus a box of ashes, a funeral procession without a body.

Guillermo reached a hand out without warning, grabbing my upper arm. Not rough, but insistent. *Stop.* I felt his fingers dig into my skin as I squinted against the harsh sunlight, trying to make out his expression.

'These are dangerous times, Ana,' Guillermo said, his expression grave as he watched the road in front of him. 'Dangerous times. He's testing you, don't forget. He wants you to fail. He wants you to run, so he can aim at your back and pull the trigger.'

I nodded, crossing my arms against my chest as I remembered the box of bones and ash. It was sad, how little remained after you burned an infant child to cinders. It was barely enough to fill a box the size of a coffee mug.

'Where's John?' I asked.

'Being the fucking prez, now that he knows you're okay. I had to stop him from coming in and getting himself killed by your beloved.'

I snorted. 'Who, Dornan? He's hardly my beloved anymore. Not after everything he's done.'

He must have heard the violent reality behind my words. 'It was bad, huh? In Colorado?'

I opened my mouth to answer him and a sob came out. Just one. An overflow of emotion, and then I caught it and shoved it back down where it needed to stay. 'He's not the man he used to be,' I said, staring out of the window as Los Angeles passed by in a blur of asphalt, overpasses, and randomly spaced palm trees. 'There's killing someone and there's murdering someone. You know?'

Guillermo nodded, and I suddenly remembered what he had gone to prison for. Killing his wife for betraying him. 'I didn't mean—'

'It's okay,' he said, cutting me off. 'Don't worry about it. I don't.'

'Did you know Stephanie?' I asked him. I thought of her, the woman I had never known except in myth, as the woman Dornan had first loved, and then in death, as I greeted her bloody corpse in a bathtub in Colorado.

I'd never seen Dornan so indifferent in the face of death. When he'd killed the woman in the backseat of his truck, he had cried. Wept as he pulled the trigger and delivered the bullet that ended her life. I'd seen the anguish in his eyes, seen the devastation that engulfed him. Now he seemed almost bored with the fact that he'd just killed someone. And not just anyone. He'd loved her, once. That was the part I found the hardest to accept. He'd loved her, and she'd left, and this was what happened when you left a man like Dornan Ross and never came back.

Eventually, he found you, and then he slaughtered you.

Guillermo nodded. 'I did know her.'

'Do you think she deserved to die?'

He frowned. 'I didn't even know she was alive.'

I thought back to my ill-fated pregnancy. How I'd given myself two choices – get an abortion, or run. I'd wanted that baby. A daughter. I wasn't going to erase her. I was going to *run*. And then, before I could, he killed her while she was still in my womb.

'He killed Stephanie because she took his son. He killed her because she wanted a better life for her child. He beat her until her face was ...' I couldn't even think of an adequate way to describe it. Pulp, maybe. 'Until it was *gone*. It was just a mess. You couldn't even tell who she'd been.'

'She was a pretty girl when I knew her.'

I'm sure she was,' I replied. I remembered Dornan's hands on me after he'd murdered her, the way he held me down and forced himself inside me. It hurt. But him – he *liked* it. He was turned on by my begging. The way I fought him off excited him. That was not the man I'd fallen in love with.

'So you're not going to run, are you?'

Guillermo's eyebrows were raised, the prison tattoos on his neck slick with sweat despite the AC blasting in our faces. His sudden question snapped me out of my macabre rerun of that night in the motel room, when Dornan began his systematic destruction of anything good I'd ever seen in him. The night he'd turned into my nightmare. The night I started to be more afraid of him than I was of his father.

The night my lover became my nightmare.

'No,' I said softly, tucking my long hair behind my ears. As Guillermo drove, I rested my head against the window, my throat thick, my eyes burning behind my dark sunglasses, my black clothes like magnets attracting heat. I felt like I was burning up, but inside I was so cold.

I opened my mouth, my breath hitching in my throat. Closed it again. I didn't want to breathe in the tiny particles of bone dust that had somehow attached themselves to my shirt, to the seat I was sitting on. There was already enough death inside me without swallowing more.

'Don't ever pull a fucking stunt like that again, you hear me?' Guillermo said. 'Don't ever change that code on me.'

'Don't ever change it on *me*,' I shot back. 'You know how long I was stuck in that goddamn apartment before you came along. I refuse to be trapped in there for one more minute of my life.'

Something in my words appeared to get through to him. He sagged a little in his seat. 'Sorry.'

I don't think he'd ever apologised to me in all these years. Suddenly I felt shame at the way I'd effectively trapped him and John inside the apartment.

'Me too,' I muttered.

We drove in silence for a bit. The sun was filtered by the traffic haze that always seemed to hang in Los Angeles. On the freeway at this time of day it was brutal. We sat in a crawling procession of cars, everyone poisoning the air together as we fought each other to get where we needed to be. I'd grown to hate this place. The place that had represented freedom to me as a child growing up in Colombia had inadvertently become my prison cell. I couldn't wait to put my bare feet in the dark soil of the jungle in some lush locale in South America, or maybe it'd be white sand in some tropical paradise. Whatever, it didn't matter, because it would be somewhere other than here.

I dared to consider John's words from earlier. At the time I'd still been too focused on Emilio and the baby to think about what he'd been saying, but now I couldn't stop thinking about it.

'Can we stop at the beach on the way back?' I asked quietly, my throat aching at the sudden exertion. Guillermo looked at me oddly, but he didn't argue. 'Sure,' he grunted. 'Why the fuck not.'

***

It was hot and crowded at the beach, but I found a small stretch of sand that wasn't taken over by towels and kids. I didn't even undress. I kicked off my shoes and walked into the water fully clothed, painfully aware that the remains of an infant child were now on Emilio's desk.

I waded into the water quickly, deeper into the waves, letting my arms float away from my body, fingers outstretched. The waves helped me, dragging me deeper as they pulled back from shore. I cried. I cried for that baby. I cried for my son. I cried for Dornan. Why couldn't he be good for me? Why couldn't he take me away from this? Why, in saving me from Emilio's plans to sell me all those years ago, had he brought me here, to *this*?

I felt like I was losing my mind. I wondered, briefly, how hard it would be to drown myself without Guillermo saving me.

I let myself sink into the water. It felt delicious, like a balm against my skin that burned in the Californian sunshine. My Colombian skin wasn't used to the sun anymore, and though it was still milky brown, it didn't like being outside. A decade of closed rooms and no windows will do that to a person.

The water rushed around me, my long dark hair floating wildly in the waves. I lifted my feet from the sandy ocean floor and let myself float.

Let myself sink.

It was quiet down here. Peaceful. As peaceful as you could get when you'd just waited while a child's body burned to cinders.

I opened my mouth and screamed silently against the safety of the waves. As loud as I could, knowing nobody would ever hear how much sorrow tore at my throat as saltwater rushed into my mouth. It made my eyes sting, but I didn't care. In the silence and the cold, I felt so ... *free*. I imagined opening my lungs and taking in a mouthful of saltwater. Just breathing it in like it was air, until it filled me up. It would hurt, no doubt. My body would try to fight it. My survival instinct would kick in.

Luis. I could never kill myself, knowing my son was alive and waiting for me to come to him in Colombia. Never.

I kicked towards the surface with great reluctance.

I felt Guillermo beside me, and then his strong arm was hooked around my chest and under my own arm, pulling me close. I glanced over, seeing that he'd walked into the water, jeans and all. At least he'd taken his shoes off.

'They say drowning is a peaceful way to go,' he said, a knowing smile on his face as he dragged me closer to shore, his kick strong. I felt like I was a wet blanket. I wasn't even strong enough to pull away and slip beneath the water's surface. I was too much of a coward to even figure out how to drown.

'Sorry, baby,' he said, treading water in front of me, holding my head above the surface by cupping his hand below my chin. 'Today's not your day.'

I nodded dully, looking at a couple of surfers who were paddling past us, giving me strange glances. I suppose I did look a sight, fully dressed and crying my eyes out while I half-heartedly tried to drown myself in Santa Monica Bay.

Guillermo's grip eased, and he stood next to me, the water up to his shoulders. He was pretty much the same height as me, and I let my feet drop to the sandy ocean floor.

'You love him?'

I refocused my gaze on Guillermo as his words pierced my fog. 'Who?'

'Prez. John. You never answered me before. Too busy with your pretty little gun. So tell me. You love him?'

I nodded, shivering. I don't think I'd let myself believe it until that moment. But I did. Oh, how I loved that man. I didn't want to be here, metaphorically and almost literally drowning. I wanted to be with him. I wanted to be tucked underneath his chin as he told me everything was going to be okay. I wanted to be in a car with him, flying down the freeway, breaking the speed limit as we left every single Gypsy Brother and the Il Sangue Cartel for dust, never to be seen again.

'You got shitty luck with men, honey,' Guillermo said, trying to make me smile. 'Shitty, shitty luck. Remind me never to get involved with you, yeah?'

I smiled a watery smile that matched our surroundings.

'I'm tired, Guillermo.'

'I know. Me too.'

I saw the Ferris wheel in the distance, and behind it, my apartment. 'I miss my family.' *I miss my boy.*

We stood in the water, as it gently rocked us from side to side.

'Come on,' Guillermo said, putting a hand on my shoulder. 'We got things to do.'

I nodded, wading to shore with him.

'You gonna call John?' Guillermo asked, as we walked along the sand, headed for the car.

I stopped in my tracks. 'Yes. No. I don't know.'

'He'll pull the trigger, Mariana. *Think.* He'll do something drastic. Kids are sacred to him. Kids are the one thing you don't mess with.'

I swallowed thickly.

'Just make sure you got your shit in a row before you start plotting with him, girl, because he's going to snap, and you'll be the one in the firing line when Emilio comes looking for penance.'

'Hard to keep track of all the lies, isn't it?' He gave me a knowing smile.

I nodded.

CHAPTER ELEVEN

John Portland hated lap dances. Despised strip clubs.

It was an odd fact for a man like him. A biker. A president. A criminal. A murderer. And, ironically, a man who ran a strip club. It was funny, he could stare into the eyes of his victim and pull the trigger, cold as ice, but when a woman lowered her ass into his lap, he suddenly burned up like he had a fever. He didn't want hands touching him, clammy hands that had touched everybody else. He didn't even like his wife's hands when they reached out to him.

He liked Mariana's hands, though, and that was a problem. A big fucking problem.

She'd almost gotten herself killed today, and only escaped by·some survival instinct she possessed, the thing that had carried her through a decade with the cartel. She should have died a hundred times by now, but she wasn't dead. She was alive. She was beautiful. She was somebody else's.

Dornan Ross was not like John. Dornan very much enjoyed the attention of women, and their clammy hands. He had a decidedly different way of looking at the world, a more fluid appreciation of relationships and monogamy. He could touch a stripper or a whore, stick his dick inside them, snort flake off their tits, and it didn't *mean* anything aside from a good time. If anyone looked at his women sideways, though, he would kill them.

He never used to be like that. John used to like him, trust him. Christ, Dornan was the only one John had trusted with his own baby daughter, fifteen years ago, when he was in prison and Caroline ran away from the screaming newborn who was already a tiny little addict.

Time had worn them both down, two brothers in arms, complete strangers. Now John despised Dornan.

Sometimes, when he was screwing Mariana, he'd fantasise about a world where Dornan Ross did not exist.

His lines had been clearly drawn. But the years and the bodies and the lies wore everyone down in different ways. They were no longer the brothers in arms they'd been as teenagers, setting off on the open road, criss-crossing the country with abandon. They were prisoners of fate now, soldiers of a fortune that they could never have foretold.

Or, perhaps they could have foretold it.

Perhaps they should have.

John had never wanted to be a biker. Fuck! He'd never wanted to kill a man with his bare hands. Had never wanted to be involved in the shit that came with being indebted to a cartel like Il Sangue, carved and sculpted from the ruins of Dornan's father's enemies. John was a simple man and he'd wanted simple things. But once you were in with a man like Emilio Ross – just one time, one job, one task, one loan, one favour – before you'd even finished striking the deal with him, he'd already sucked your soul out of your body and put it in his cabinet with the rest of his trophies. Sometimes he did it literally – displaying a photograph of you with your family, with anyone you loved, under the guise of affection and concern; and sometimes he just told you that he owned your ass from now until the day you died. By his hand, if you fucked up.

And now John did want to die. There was a stripper grinding on him, trying to push one of her fat nipples between his lips. He kept turning his head, trying not to offend her, but in the end he had to stand up and grab her by her shoulders. 'How much do I have to pay you to go away?' he asked, fishing a twenty out of his wallet. The blonde didn't smile, but she plucked the money out of his hand and tottered away on her six-inch stilettos.

John turned his attention to Dornan, who was sitting on a low armchair to his left, seemingly fascinated as another stripper shook a line of white powder onto his cock and then snorted it right off. Dornan caught him looking and it seemed to amuse him. He fisted a hand in the woman's hair and squeezed her cheeks with his other hand. 'You gonna pay for that?' he asked, guiding her mouth to his erection. Dornan stared at John as the woman made a gagging noise.

John wanted a fucking drink. Beer wouldn't cut it, he needed something stronger – like maybe bleach, so he could pour it into his eyes and pretend he'd never seen what he'd just accidentally glimpsed.

'I can see the cogs turning in your head, Johnny boy,' Dornan chuckled. His teeth gleamed in the oscillating light, his grin too big and bold to be anything but artificial. He looked like he wanted to lean over and start eating the girl who was gagging painfully on him, and not in a good way. He looked like a wolf. He looked like his father.

'You celebrating your divorce?' John asked, his fingers itching for a drink. Whiskey, vodka ... anything, Christ. He was the president of the Gypsy Brothers and why wasn't somebody bringing him a fucking drink already?

'Hey!' John barked over his shoulder, towards the bar. 'Two whiskeys. On the rocks.'

He held up two fingers briefly before turning his attention back to Dornan. He focused on his face, not on what was going on in his lap. Because Jesus Christ, *could he not get a room?*

'You must be happy,' John said, choosing his words carefully. 'To be away from Celia.'

Dornan shrugged, accepting the whiskey that a waitress was holding out to him. John did the same, closing his eyes briefly and tipping the amber liquid down his throat, enjoying the delicious burn that took the edge off his frustration, his terror. 'Sure. Yeah. I don't want to talk about Celia right now.'

'What do you want to talk about, brother?'

That word. *Brother.* It sparked something in Dornan's eyes. Something wounded. He stared down at the stripper on his cock and then pushed her away with force. She landed on her ass, hard, but she was too high to be offended. 'Go,' Dornan barked, zipping his jeans as he turned his full attention to John.

'I figured you'd be celebrating with Mariana,' John said, and didn't the shit hit the fucking fan right then.

'Did you have anything to do with the shit she pulled this morning?' Dornan asked.

Get straight to the point, why don't you?

John clenched his teeth, suddenly itching for a cigarette. 'No.'

Dornan held his eyes for a few moments before he seemed satisfied.

'What the fuck is going on, Dee? Kids? A *baby*?'

Dornan took a swig of whiskey and slammed the glass down on a table beside him. 'It wasn't fucking me, okay? You think I'd do something like that?'

John apparently took too long to answer, because Dornan's entire demeanour changed. 'Fuck,' Dornan muttered, looking to the ceiling. He was like a tightly wound coil, about to snap. About to explode.

'You need to do something about your father,' John said in a measured, controlled voice that belied his utter rage. 'Now.'

Dornan gave John a withering stare. 'You might be the prez, big boy, but don't ever think you get to tell me what to do.'

'I'm not telling you as the prez, you fuck, I'm telling you as your friend. Your father murdered a KID.'

Dornan pounded the table with his fist. 'Don't you ever fucking say that. Not here, not anywhere. You hear me? Don't talk about my family.'

'For fuck's sake, how many of these things does Mariana have to deal with before you do something about him?'

Dornan went very still, his eyes far away for a brief second. And for a moment, the aura of anger that surrounded him was gone, replaced by an unsteady silence. 'I'm going to make things right with Ana,' he murmured, spinning his empty glass with two fingers. 'We'll have another baby. I'll marry her. Things will be made right again.'

John felt like he'd been punched in the fucking heart. He would kill Dornan before that happened. Even if it meant he died with him. If anyone was marrying Mariana, it was John.

You have a daughter, John. Calm your shit. Get it together.

It wasn't easy to be calm around a storm like Dornan Ross. He made you see the worst in yourself, like a mirror, held up to expose your dirtiest truths. He was like poison.

'You really think that's gonna fix what's done? You think that'll make up for the shit you've done to her? You think she'll ever forget that the only reason she isn't fat and pregnant right now is because you beat that baby out of her?'

John couldn't take any more. The club suddenly felt too small, like the walls were closing in, squeezing the air out of him. He stood, and that would have been fine, except that Dornan stood too, his face in John's.

'This conversation isn't fucking finished,' Dornan seethed. 'Sit your ass down.'

John held his ground. He even laughed, because it was really this absurd right now. 'You know who you're acting like right now, don't you? I mean, I don't even need to say it.'

They were starting to attract attention from other Gypsy Brothers. Viper, sitting a few feet away with a topless brunette, watched the scene unfold as he pushed the woman away. There was a thick tension in the air. John didn't need a sixth sense to tell him that something bad was about to happen.

'You should say it,' Dornan said, throwing his empty tumbler at the floor so that it exploded in a mess of glass shards.

'You're acting like your father, Dee. You're acting like you've lost your fucking mind.'

John had been anticipating the swing, yet it still came as a surprise. In twenty-odd years they'd never come to blows. Not once. But as Dornan's fist came at him, John knew with a certainty that lived in his bones that one day very soon, one of them was going to kill the other. It was the only way.

John jerked his head back in time to lessen the blow, but not avoid it completely. Dornan's fist connected with his jaw, and he felt his teeth move in his mouth. It was like poking a sleeping snake. John attacked, a hand on each of Dornan's shoulders as he smashed the hard part of his forehead into his nose. It hurt, but it'd hurt Dornan more. Sure enough, Dee stepped back, blood exploding from his nose as he held a hand to his broken face.

And then Dornan pulled a fucking gun on him.

'Put that away, shithead,' John said, suddenly aware that Dornan was unhinged enough to actually shoot him right now. Goddamn it, why'd he have to open his mouth?

Dornan grinned, blood seeping from his nose and down his chin, staining his teeth a ghoulish red. It gave him the appearance of a vampire, one who'd just been feeding on some poor victim.

Dornan didn't put it away. He stepped into John's space, so their noses were almost touching, and he rammed the barrel of the gun underneath John's chin. It was hard to breathe with a metal gun barrel pressing against your windpipe, but it wouldn't exactly be the first time John had been at gunpoint. It was, however, the first time he'd experienced it at the hands of one of his own men.

John was aware of the crowd gathering around them. Nobody spoke. Over Dornan's shoulder, John saw Viper, an original Gypsy Brother, circling behind as if to offer assistance. John gave him a sharp look that stopped him in his tracks. He didn't need assistance. He would beat down this motherfucker for his transgression all by himself.

'You've lost your fucking mind,' John said to his oldest friend, his voice barely above a whisper. Dornan stared at him, his pupils and irises the same black in the low light of the club. He looked possessed. Demonic. John suspected both were true.

'You gonna shoot me?' John asked, bringing his hand up and tightening it around Dornan's wrist. 'Your oldest friend. The one who would do anything for you. If you shoot me, who would ever have your back?'

'I don't need anyone to have my back,' Dornan seethed. 'I got my back.'

John smacked the gun away, taking Dornan by surprise as he grabbed his throat. He had always been an excellent hand at poker. Maybe he should have played more, gotten a nice stash of cash happening so he could get out of this fucking place.

Hindsight's a cruel bitch.

John tightened his grip around Dornan's neck and drove him into the wall, hard. He heard his skull hit the brick wall with a loud *thwack*, and took the opportunity to bend Dornan's arm until it was almost at breaking point. The gun dropped out of his grip, and John kicked it away, using both hands to grab hold of Dornan's shirt.

'Don't you EVER pull a fucking gun on me!' he roared. Dornan shoved him away, throwing him off balance. He was heavier than John, higher than John, crazier than John. Insanity seemed to breed a strength that normal men could not possess. Dornan kept coming at John, who'd now lost the element of surprise. He charged John, tackling him around his waist as they both slammed to the floor. Dornan straddled John, bloodthirst in his eyes, as he rained blows down on his face.

Nobody was stepping in to stop this, and John understood why. For a club that had always prided itself on being a singular organism, two factions had slowly started to emerge. Without voicing it, people were starting to bleed towards one side or the other. Towards John, or Dornan.

Their club was falling apart at the seams.

Dornan was still hitting John, but the blows were less forceful now that he had him pinned. Almost like Dornan thought John had given up.

'Apologise,' Dornan ground out, his bloody face hovering above John's. 'Now.'

Something old and forgotten was unleashed in John. The part of him he tried to hide. The part that enjoyed blood and violence as much as Dornan did. John lived by a different set of morals than Dornan Ross, but that didn't mean he didn't take great delight in beating down somebody who had it coming. And Dornan had it coming.

This was overdue.

John's adrenaline spiked, and he flipped Dornan easily. The tables were suddenly turned, but John wasn't going to settle for a few punches. No, he wrapped both hands around his best friend's throat and squeezed hard enough that Dornan was actually scared. He heard Dornan's breath get stuck in his throat as he struggled beneath him. Whatever Dornan had been snorting off that stripper's skin might've made him feel invincible for a short sprint, but John was filled with enough rage and contempt for a fucking marathon.

'I will never apologise for telling you the truth,' John said, his teeth about to shatter they were clenched so tight. 'You killed Stephanie. The woman you've been looking for for fifteen fuckin' years! Because you were still in love with her! And you killed her, Dee. Why?

'You tie your own kid up and drug him and dump him in your trunk and leave him there so he pisses himself. He didn't do anything to you. He didn't even know you.'

'Shut up!' Dornan managed, his words barely audible. He started to prise John's fingers from his throat, but John wasn't finished yet. He picked up Dornan's head with very little effort, slamming it back into the ground. Once. Twice. Three times. Dornan stopped fighting.

'You beat the woman you say you love until your baby was dead. You say Juliette's the daughter you never had, but that's not true, is it? You had a daughter. She was alive. And you beat her mother until you killed the baby inside her.'

Dornan snapped. Perhaps he had seen himself in the mirror John was holding up and decided he didn't like what he saw. Whatever it was, he managed to break free of John's grip and then they were on their feet somehow, throwing punch after punch.

John still hadn't gone for his own gun, but it was only a matter of time. Something had to put an end to this shit. As Dornan punched John in the jaw, he staggered back, the fight clearly wearing on him.

'Don't ever fucking talk about Stephanie again,' Dornan said. 'About any of it. Do you understand?'

John used the segue to get down low, to kick his leg out and sweep Dornan's feet from underneath him. He went down hard, making a sound as the air knocked out of him again.

The time for games was over.

John pulled his gun, cocking it as he stepped over Dornan. He planted one foot on either side of Dornan's torso, aiming the gun right between his fucking eyes, and everything in him screamed at him to pull the fucking trigger and end this. Kill the motherfucker, save the girl, and everyone could live happily ever after. Only, it was never going to be that easy. John knew only too well how surrounded he was by people who were firmly in Dornan's allegiance, people who were probably aiming their guns at him right now. Instead of unloading a round of bullets in Dornan like he wanted to, John changed his grip on the gun and brought the butt down straight into his forehead. Dornan's eyes rolled back in his head momentarily, before they refocused on John, the fight completely gone.

'I buried Stephanie!' John roared, spittle landing on Dornan's cheek. 'I will talk about whoever, whenever, because I dug her grave with my bare hands and I fucking buried that poor bitch myself!'

The place was as quiet as the dirt grave John had lowered Stephanie into, back in Colorado. Nobody moved a muscle. Jaws were on the floor and somebody had turned the music off completely. Even the girls who were supposed to be dancing onstage were motionless, their eyes bugging out as they took in the scene unfolding.

Anarchy like this had never existed within the Gypsy Brothers before. The brotherhood was bleeding away in front of everyone, replaced by mistrust and greed. And in Dornan's case, by a darkness so black he couldn't even see his way back to the light.

Selfishly, John wanted to reach through and pull him back. To go back to a time when things were simpler. To know who was a friend and who was an enemy.

But it was too late. He'd seen too much. The blood. The death. It was all just too fucking much.

'Let me tell you what happens if you stay on this road, brother.' John's eyes burned, his throat thick. Dornan had been his only true friend. What had gone so colossally wrong? When? Where? Before Mariana, before any of it, where had their paths diverged so violently?

And then, John understood. An epiphany that lay beneath him, beaten and still. Dornan had been born on this road. Naked, bloody, screaming, a pawn in a game much bigger than him. A chess piece that belonged to Emilio Ross, in blood and in name.

John could run.

Mariana could run.

But Dornan would never be able to run from the thing he came from. The thing that created him. The darkness didn't just exist within him.

He *was* the fucking darkness.

CHAPTER TWELVE

DORNAN

It was quiet as John left. He didn't go without leaving his mark – in this case, spitting his own blood on the floor of the strip club before he smashed the doors open and disappeared.

Dornan stared at the ceiling for a minute. A fleeting moment of peace after he'd just had the shit beaten out of him. He didn't know whether to feel embarrassed that John had at times overpowered him, or victorious that he was still here while John had walked away. As he was lying there, catching his breath, a female face appeared in his vision. The stripper who'd been grinding on him just a few minutes ago was now ashen, her eyes big and alarmed, her tits still shiny from where he'd sucked on them.

How quickly things could go from good to terrible.

'Are you okay, baby?' the stripper asked, reaching a hand down to him as if she were going to pull him up. A waifish thing, all skin and bone and tits, and she was offering to help him up. Dornan would have laughed had the situation not been so dire. As it was, he got to his feet and smacked her hand away. 'Scram,' he said, and she did.

A lot of the club members were in this place. A lot of customers, too, and they'd seen the entire thing. Dornan looked around at the tight faces, the stares, and he laughed.

'Hasn't anyone ever seen a scuffle before? Get back to your fucking drinks!'

And just like that, the place thawed. The music was turned back up, the girls onstage grabbed at the nearest pole and started grinding, and most of the onlookers dispersed to other tables. A few customers left, casting worried glances behind them. They were probably tourists. Regulars didn't usually get their panties in a knot when things got ugly.

Viper approached Dornan carefully, a look of unease on his face. He was a tall skinny thing, with a deadly bite if you messed with him – hence, the name Viper. He was also called Viper because he liked to bite the women he fucked, all over their bodies, but that was an aside.

'What was that?' Viper asked, cool concern masking the worry Dornan could see in his eyes, clear as day. Dornan wiped blood from his nose, leaving a sticky trail of the red stuff up his arm.

'That was John signing his ticket out,' Dornan said, placing his fingers between his lips and whistling, short and shrill. The rest of the Gypsy Brothers who'd witnessed the fight drifted over to him, drinks and women forgotten. There were over a dozen core club members present, and they formed a loose circle around Dornan and Viper.

Dornan looked at each of them, right in the eyes, before he delivered his proclamation.

'He's done.'

The music was loud in the club, the flashing lights bright, but their focus on Dornan was so absolute, he could have whispered and everyone would have understood.

'We have to make it official,' Viper said beside him. 'A vote.'

Dornan nodded. 'We do.'

He let the silence stretch on until it became uncomfortable. He grinned, his teeth still bloody, and for that he was glad. It made him look more commanding to be covered in battle blood.

'I look forward to your votes,' Dornan said finally, again making eye contact with each of the Gypsy Brothers in front of him.

He left before anyone started asking questions. Took himself off to his motorcycle and tried to call Mariana. He was going to need stitches in some of these cuts on his face, a hot shower, and then he was going to need to have his dick sucked.

He called her three times. She didn't answer. Santa Monica was only ten minutes by car at this time of night, faster on a motorcycle, but if she wasn't there Dornan would be pissed.

He tried her one more time. It rang out. Dornan smiled as he thought about who else lived nearby. Somebody who could tend his wounds. Somebody who John loved above all else.

He shoved his cellphone into his jeans pocket and pulled on his helmet, gunning the engine before he roared down Venice Boulevard.

CHAPTER THIRTEEN

JOHN

He drove around in circles after smashing his fists into Dornan's face; windows down, radio blasting. Anything to drown out the blood that roared and pulsed at his temples, in the tips of his fingers, that steady smash of blood around his heart as rage pumped through him, alive and bright red. Red stoplights and red road signs and red gas station signs, Dornan's red blood splashed across John's torn knuckles, the world a haze of John's anger and Dornan's violence. The old Dornan never would have killed Stephanie. The old Dornan would have thrown himself off a roof sooner than laid a hand on a woman, his pregnant mistress at that.

He had changed. Embraced his darkness, gone full circle. He'd pulled away from his father in the early days, resisted his vacuous demands for bloodshed and absolute loyalty – loyalty he had given, bloodshed he had kept to a minimum – but now it seemed Dornan Ross relished the hunt of bloodletting as much as his soulless father.

After driving aimlessly for what seemed like an hour, John pulled in to Redondo Beach and parked on the shoulder of the road. Hands shaking, he took out his cellphone and called home.

He called twice, each time getting the red 'busy' symbol flashing up on the screen. More red.

His daughter was probably still on the phone to that fucking kid, the one she and Mariana seemed obsessed with. Dornan, too, for that matter. Everyone was so concerned for this kid who'd found his poor mother dead in a bathtub full of blood, but nobody seemed to care that John had had to dig her goddamn grave in the dirt behind her house. Nobody seemed to care that he'd had to spend hours wiping down every surface for prints and possible DNA, especially when he was a mechanic and most definitely not a crime scene cleaner.

Then he felt like shit, because of course poor kid. John felt bad for him. He was so young, and he'd just been stolen from the only life he'd ever known. Of course John's sweet daughter was going to try to help him. She was a little naïve when it came to club matters, his Juliette, and he had to wonder if protecting her from the worst of his role as president of the MC had unwittingly sheltered her from being safe in the midst of monsters and killers. The body count around a Sunday church meeting at the Gypsy Brothers clubhouse was in the hundreds. Thousands if you counted all the deaths from the drugs they'd sold over the years. From two guys – himself and Dornan – making some shit up on a road trip on their motorcycles, John could never have imagined that this would end up their fate.

The red tinge started to dissipate a little from John's view of the world, and with that he pulled back onto the road and pointed his car home. He'd have to sneak in, get his face sorted and wash off the bulk of all this blood before Juliette saw and freaked out.

About thirty minutes later, he turned into his driveway, uneasiness pooling in his gut, thick and anxious, as he observed his dark, quiet house. Julz always left a light on for him.

The engine had barely stopped when John was out of the car, his legs burning as he scaled the stairs up to the front door two at a time. He burst into the unlocked door to absolute silence.

'Juliette!' he yelled, checking the kitchen. Empty. Living room – empty. Every room was empty.

Fuck.

She was fifteen. Sometimes she did things like ride her bike to the gas station a couple of blocks away for milk or candy, but she always left a note.

A note. Yes. It'd been dark in the kitchen – had he missed a note from her? John left his daughter's bedroom, sensing movement as he passed his own. He stopped, pivoting and gripping the two sides of the doorframe.

A familiar sight, but one that never ceased to terrify him.

His wife, Caroline, was in the throes of a heroin high. It wasn't hard to tell. She was on her back in the middle of their bed – a bed he hadn't shared with her in months, opting instead to crash on the couch with a gun beside him – and she was laughing. There was something invisible on the ceiling, and it was fucking hilarious.

'Caroline,' he hissed. She didn't flinch. John took a step into the room he'd long since abandoned and was immediately hit by the smell of junkie. It was a unique smell – body odour, but mixed with some kind of sweet scent, sickly, like rotting oranges. Maybe it was Caroline's perfume. He'd never lived with another junkie to compare.

'Hey,' John said, more forcefully this time. He reached out to touch her arm and recoiled when he saw the fresh needle still hanging from the crook of her elbow. Fucking hell. John had no idea where she'd gotten the money for a hit. He didn't want to know. He didn't want to have to imagine his wife doing all manner of terrible things – fucking, stealing, bribing – to get the white powder she so viciously craved. He didn't have to worry about other Gypsy Brothers, who all respected John and had far more desirable options to choose from on the female menu at the clubhouse. But there were plenty of men in Los Angeles who owed John no respect, or Caroline, for that matter. Men who would pay good money to disrespect her. All of these things crossed John's mind as he watched Caroline laugh, her eyes rolling back in her head every so often.

He'd liked to have thought that his next move was unconscious, but it was a very deliberate one. He reached behind his back to the gun tucked snugly into his waistband and pulled it out, resting it against Caroline's forehead. If she felt it, or even knew he was there, she didn't show it. She was too busy focusing on something over his shoulder, something that only existed in her opiate-soaked haze.

He looked at the fit still around her arm, the needle that hadn't quite been emptied still resting in her vein. If he pressed down, would she die? Would it be too much? Or what if he shot her in the head and made it look like she'd shot herself?

The woman whose only service to John Portland in their entire time together had been the child she bore him chose that exact moment to start a high-pitched giggle. It was loud. Frenzied, even. But her eyes weren't laughing. They were vacant. Haunted. He didn't need to put a bullet in her to send her to hell. She was already there.

Taking a deep breath, John put his gun back into his waistband. 'Caroline,' he barked, flicking his wife's forehead with his thumb and middle finger. 'Hey! Where's Juliette?'

Caroline finally seemed to hear him. 'School,' she muttered.

John ground his back teeth in frustration. 'It's fucking night time, Caroline,' he said. 'She's not at fucking school. Did she come see you before she left?'

Of course she would have. She was a good girl. She'd always check with whichever parent was home before she went anywhere.

Caroline sat bolt upright in bed, reaching for John's belt buckle. 'Twenty,' she said. 'Twenty.'

John had the sudden urge to smash his fist into her head so hard she'd be decapitated, but he suppressed that urge, because he wasn't Dornan and he didn't hurt women, even when he thought they well deserved it.

'Dornan,' Caroline said, and the hairs on John's arms stood up.

'Dornan *what*?' John ground out. *Dornan's been giving you twenty dollars to suck his dick?* John highly doubted it, but then he'd also doubted Dornan was capable of cold-blooded murder of a woman he'd once professed to love.

Caroline flopped onto her back again. 'Julie's at Dornan's,' she whispered, and then she passed out cold.

Fuck. Double fuck. Of all the places in the world, the one he least wanted to find his daughter was anywhere near Dornan

Ross. John sped the whole short drive to his house. It was only a couple of blocks, but it felt like an eternity.

Take my cunt wife, he mused as he walked up to Dornan's front door and knocked sharply, three sharp raps that shook the door. *Burn my house to the ground. You can have everything of mine, but you cannot have my daughter.*

Or my Mariana, he realised a moment later.

Dornan's oldest son, Chad, answered the door. He opened it without a word, and John noticed his knuckles were raw and bloody. He nodded in greeting, walking past Chad and down the long hallway that demarcated the rooms in Dornan's Spanish-style abode. So many rooms for so many sons – six there had been, and it seemed once you had six, you got one for free. At least that was the way it had gone, with Dornan stumbling upon his unknown son, his seventh progeny, the secret John had kept for sixteen years as he broke his ass sending Stephanie money to keep them from starving and losing their goddamn house, far away from Dornan's lethal lifestyle.

John wondered how long it would be before Dornan figured out that he'd known of this seventh son all along, from the moment he'd personally purchased the pregnancy test and made Stephanie take it in a McDonald's bathroom in West Hollywood. He couldn't remember what the fuck he'd been doing all the way up in Wankville that day – no doubt something to do with drugs or cash or beating somebody up for payments owed – but he did remember how pale Stephanie's face had turned when she handed him the piss stick with two lines in it. And he *did* remember shelling out three hundred bucks in twenties, a greyhound ticket to Colorado purchased with a fake ID, and a promise that he'd help her if she decided not to come back.

Dornan had blamed Stephanie for stealing his son away all those years ago, but if he found out his best friend was the instigator of the entire 'Get the fuck away from the Ross Family' plan, John knew he'd retaliate. Painfully. And Dornan knew Juliette was John's entire existence. He'd give anything, kill anyone, for his only child.

His only child, who right now was applying an ice pack to Dornan's nose as he sat and smoked and drank whiskey at his dining table. He grinned when he saw John, but it wasn't a friendly gesture so much as a warning.

'Juliette,' John said, aiming for casual yet loving father, but ending up sounding strangled. She turned sharply, her face drawn, concern etched in her features.

'Hey, Dad. I'm just helping Uncle Dornan.'

John nodded, circling the pair as he moved closer. No sudden moves. What to say? He could blame their need for a hasty departure on Caroline.

'Sweetheart, that's nice of you, but we have to go,' John said, his eyes never leaving Dornan's.

Dornan smirked, putting his hand on the ice pack and pulling his head back slightly. 'It's okay, darlin',' he said, motioning towards John with a tilt of his chin, 'your daddy seems upset.'

John ignored him. 'Your mother's not good,' he said. 'She's sick. I need to get back to her.'

He noticed, for the first time, the kid sitting on the other side of the room. The refrigerator had been obscuring his presence, and since he hadn't moved a muscle since John had walked in he'd attracted zero attention.

'You been there the whole time?' he asked Jason, who nodded. 'Jesus. This kid here's like a goddamn ninja.'

Juliette glanced at Jase as she dabbed antiseptic ointment onto a piece of gauze and continued to tend to the wounds John had inflicted on Dornan's face. A cut right above his nose looked red and angry; purple shadows were starting to appear under his eyes. It wasn't a pretty sight, but it didn't seem to worry his psychotic brother in arms, who sat still like a kid waiting for their lollipop at the fucking doctor's surgery, getting their shots.

'That's my boy,' Dornan said evenly, glancing at Jase and then back at John. 'Stealthy, like his brothers.' He smiled at Juliette, and it was the first gesture John had seen that seemed genuine. 'You didn't have to do this, sweetheart. You're a good girl. Good to our family.'

Sweetheart. Please.

'Juliette,' John said. Forceful, this time. He'd rather she hated him, as long as she still listened to him. There was no time to play soft cop right now, not when Dornan could reach out and pluck out her eyeballs before John could so much as clear the space between them. Not that Dornan would hurt Juliette. She was like a daughter to him. Had been his daughter, really, for the first few months of her life, until John had been released from prison and was able to get back to the new family he'd unwittingly created when he screwed Caroline in a haze of weed and booze. He didn't really drink anymore, because he sure as shit didn't want to end up making that mistake twice. Having one daughter – one beautiful, smart, perfect daughter – to keep tabs on in a vicious underworld where the things you loved became your weaknesses, was hard enough without adding more to the mix.

'Did I ever tell you the story about when you were born?' Dornan asked Juliette, his eyes all for John.

Juliette looked kind of confused, but she could stay confused. She didn't need to know this asshole was responsible for her survival in her first six months while her mother sold herself for blow and slept in gutters.

'We're going,' John said, stepping forward and tugging Juliette's elbow.

'Dad!' she protested, stumbling a little as she followed him. John turned towards the hallway and the exit it promised, but suddenly he was blocked.

By Jason.

Little bastard.

'Did he hurt you?' Jason asked Juliette, alarm in his eyes.

Juliette shrugged John's hand off, wrapping her arms around herself. 'What?' she asked. 'No. I'm fine. I'll call you later.'

Mercifully, she headed for the front door.

'Move,' he growled, but Jason stayed put. John's eyebrows practically hit the roof. 'Really, kid?' he asked without thinking. 'You don't think that maybe you're barking up the wrong tree if you're worried about violence against women?'

Jason sagged immediately, letting him pass. John felt shitty for delivering such a low blow – the poor kid – but desperate times and all that. By the time he got outside, Juliette was already sitting in the passenger seat, her arms folded tightly across her chest and her eyes shiny with tears. She always got upset if she saw John hurt. It frightened her, and rightly so.

She shouldn't have to worry about her parents not making it home. Shouldn't have to be tricked into leaving the house with Dornan, an obvious and cruel move to fuck with John. His heart was torn up at how Juliette was worrying in the seat beside him, yet wouldn't say a word.

John made the quick decision not to go straight home – in his fantasy, Caroline might have more time to miraculously die before they arrived to find her – and instead drove towards Hermosa Beach. It was a little over thirty minutes to get there with no traffic, and thankfully there was none this late at night.

He could tell that Juliette was too cut up to ask where they were going. John said nothing. Eventually, after about fifteen minutes of silence, she cleared her throat.

'Where are we going?' she asked quietly.

'For a father–daughter drive,' John replied. 'Humour your old man.'

'You're not even that old,' Julz said, fiddling with her jacket sleeve. 'I don't know why you always say that.'

He snorted. 'It's all about how old you feel. I feel like I'm about a hundred right now.'

Juliette seemed to digest that. 'It's because you never get any sleep, Daddy,' she said quietly. 'You're always busy worrying about everybody else.'

She was a smart girl. It broke his black heart that she noticed so much.

'Don't worry about me,' John said, making the turn that would take them to Hermosa. It was utterly desolate on the streets of LA tonight. He hadn't seen it this quiet in forever.

'You hungry, kiddo?' he asked. He hadn't taken her shopping for groceries in a week or so, and they were down to pop tarts and long-life milk. Juliette never complained, and John barely remembered to eat these days.

'Starving,' Juliette replied. 'Your face, though.'

John waved his hand dismissively. 'We'll get a booth in back.'

He cleaned his face up as best he could with some water and napkins before he headed into the diner. It was one of those old mom and pop style diners, covered in a layer of grease, and with management who had seen John come in bloody and hungry more than once. He led Julz straight to one of the booths in back – dark, away from the windows.

They ordered quickly: a steak for John, who was still feeling off after the whole fight and only picked at his food, and apple pie with ice cream for Julz. As she was shovelling pie, John set his knife and fork down and tried to formulate a question that wouldn't make her shut down.

'Did you hit Uncle Dornan?' she asked around a mouthful of pie, before he'd even decided what to ask her.

His mouth opened, but no words came out. He wasn't quite sure what to say to that. 'Yeah,' he said, finally. 'I did.'

Juliette nodded. 'He must have deserved it,' she said, taking another bite. 'You only hurt people if they deserve it.'

John scrubbed his palm across his mouth, his brain screaming for words that would divert the attention from what he was. A lowlife fucking criminal.

'Was it because of what happened in Colorado?' she asked softly, not looking him in the eye this time. 'With Jase and his mom?'

John's stomach knotted painfully. 'What do you know about that?' he asked. 'You shouldn't know anything about that.'

Juliette placed her fork on her empty plate and straightened in her side of the booth. 'Jason told me,' she said. 'He needed to tell somebody, Dad.'

She was right. The poor kid did need somebody to confide in. But why did it have to be *his* daughter? Why couldn't it be anyone else?

'You'd think he would be talking to his brothers,' John said tightly, gripping his steak knife so hard he had to set it down. Juliette went quiet.

'What?' John prompted.

'The boys aren't nice to him,' she said to the table.

Jesus. Open a can of worms and watch them wriggle out. 'What do you mean?' John asked tiredly. He couldn't believe he'd disassociated himself from the boy's plight so brutally, but he was just trying to survive here. Dornan's youngest son was a liability. John might've funded his survival for the better part of sixteen years, even as he grew in his mother's womb, but he was terrified at the thought of taking the boy when they left LA. Almost like Dornan would be able to seek out his own blood, his DNA, easier and more swiftly than if the boy was not an issue.

'The boys have always been good to me,' Julz said softly, referring collectively to Dornan's six other sons, who ranged in age from seventeen to twenty-four. 'But they're really scary, Dad. They hung Jason off a bridge by his feet and he says he almost fell.'

'What kind of bridge?' John asked.

'The I-5,' Juliette replied.

'Shit!' John said. 'They hung him over the fu– the goddamn freeway by his feet?'

134

'Yeah. He could've died, Dad. I wish he could come live with us.'

John made a growling sound under his breath. 'No daughter of mine will ever be living with one of Dornan's sons.'

Juliette settled back in her seat, a wry smile on her lips. 'You won't say that when I marry him,' she said, and John didn't know what to say to that.

CHAPTER FOURTEEN

MARIANA

Dornan had tried to call three times.

Each time, I'd let it go to voicemail, but then I realised that if I didn't call him back and talk to him, he'd damn well show up at the apartment.

I couldn't bear for him to be in the apartment with me. He was still living between two houses, spending most nights with his sons in the house he'd shared with his wife, and even though she'd moved out, I had definitely not moved in. With all of his kids there – he had seven, all boys, a number that still made me cringe – I refused to move into a mad house filled with teenagers and testosterone. And so far, he'd acquiesced. Hadn't packed my stuff up and told me I didn't have a choice. I think, after Stephanie's death, Dornan Ross had decided that walking on eggshells was going to be the way to win me back.

It wasn't, because nothing was going to win me back, but he didn't need to know that.

It was late. Almost midnight. I wasn't even going to attempt to sleep after the day we'd had. Instead, I was sitting on a stool, tucked into the kitchen counter as I smoked cigarette after cigarette, lighting one off another. Beside my hand was a tumbler of vodka and melted ice, a half-empty bottle reminding me it was time to replenish my stocks. It had been full when I'd started a couple of hours earlier. I preferred wine, but wine led to a messy kind of drunk. Vodka was the perfect thing to dull the ache in my skull, while letting me stay in control of myself. The last thing I needed was to start mouthing off to Emilio, or worse. Guillermo and John had both been right. I should have listened to them.

I was going to be severely punished for my reckless show of defiance in Emilio's office. And although I didn't regret doing it, I was so annoyed at myself for having acted so impulsively after almost a decade of careful, measured steps. Things were starting to unravel, fast, and I needed more time. Before we made a run for it. Before I got my boy back. *Luis. Baby. Mama's coming for you.*

With much reluctance, I called Dornan's number. He picked up after the first ring.

'Thought you might be dead,' he said, his annoyance coming loud and clear over the line. It was noisy in the background, music and voices clamouring to be heard.

'The night's still young,' I said, not liking the way my words slurred ever so slightly at the ends. I stared into the bottom of my glass of vodka and had the unbearable urge to scream.

'What's that supposed to mean?' Dornan said sharply. 'Are you okay?'

'I'm fine,' I said, taking a gulp of vodka and enjoying the way it burned on the way down. 'Don't worry. I'm not about to slit my wrists just yet.'

'Don't joke,' Dornan said. 'Why the fuck didn't you call me this morning? I had to find out in a meeting with my father?'

I heard the hurt in his voice and chose to push it aside. He didn't get my sympathy anymore. 'I'm sorry,' I snapped back, pouring more vodka into my glass. 'I wasn't really thinking about your feelings when I was trying to deal with a dead kid delivery in my fucking *kitchen*.'

I heard a female voice, the titter of laughter, a squeal. 'Where are you?' I asked. 'Are you at the clubhouse?'

'Where else would I be?'

His voice sounded … strange. 'Are you *high*?'

'Are you drunk?' he shot back, the cruelty clear in his deep voice.

'Absolutely,' I answered, unashamed. 'If you can't get drunk on your own birthday, when can you?'

That floated in the air between us for a moment. I heard Dornan make a sound in the back of his throat. 'Fuck. I'm sorry.'

'Don't be,' I replied, watching the untouched cigarette in my hand as it burned down to the filter. 'I'm not in the mood for company right now.'

'Right,' Dornan said. 'Well, I'll see you later.'

He ended the call before I could make a bitchy remark. I knew exactly where he was, and it wasn't the clubhouse. They didn't play stripper music at the Gypsy Brothers HQ. They played death metal and old eighties classics that made me cringe. I'd distinctly heard sexy music in the background, and I knew exactly what it was from. My office was in the back of the club, for Christ's sake. I knew the music playlist by heart.

I wondered if he was cheating on me. If he had his dick in somebody else right this minute.

I decided I didn't care. I was cheating on him, after all. And if some stripper could buy me a few days without having to fuck the man who'd decided raping me and beating our unborn baby to death was the right way to love me? I'd pay her myself.

It was only when I'd set the phone down that I realised it was technically still my birthday. At least for another seven minutes. I texted Guillermo. *Where are you? Bring birthday cake / vodka.* He replied almost immediately. *Sorry, got a situation. Be back in the morning.*

I slumped over the counter, burying my face in my arms. I closed my eyes for a second, my fingers still around the bottom of the vodka bottle. I just needed to rest, just for a few minutes, and then I'd resume my pity party for one.

***

'Ana,' a voice murmured in my ear. I sat bolt upright, one side of my face cold and squished from where it had lain on the countertop.

'Huh?' I said, my voice still thick from sleep and all the vodka I'd just downed. My eyes felt gritty, like I'd just taken a face full of sand.

'John? What are you doing here?'

I looked at him again. In the bright light of the kitchen, he was an apparition. He had a swollen lip, and had he split his forehead open? 'What happened to you?'

He raised his eyebrows. 'More like who.'

My heart sank. 'What happened?'

John shrugged. 'I don't even know,' he said, running his hand through his dirty blond hair. 'Dornan and I ... Ana, we can't save him. He's too far gone.'

'I know that.'

'So what the fuck are we waiting for? Waiting around to die?'

'I don't know, you tell me.'

He looked at the floor. 'When I got home, Juliette was gone. He'd picked her up and taken her back to his place to fix him up. But really, to get at me.'

My stomach roiled at that knowledge. Dornan had taken John's teenage daughter, at night, without asking him, as a warning?

'Is she okay?'

John waved his hand dismissively, but there was hurt in his eyes. Anger. 'I picked her up, took her for a drive. She's at home now, hopefully asleep.'

I exhaled a sigh of relief.

'Come with me,' he said. 'Hawaii. Miami ... Fuck, Australia. I know people. Good people who'll help us.'

I looked around my empty apartment. 'Where were you when you were fighting?'

John looked at the floor again.

'I called him,' I said, eyeing off the vodka again. My head felt like it was going to split in half, and my mouth was unbearably dry. 'Dornan told me he was at the clubhouse, but last time I checked, you don't play stripping music there.'

'He was at the strip club,' John confirmed. 'We were supposed to be having a meeting.' He gestured to his face. 'I don't think he liked what I had to say.'

'Was he high? He sounded high.'

John nodded. 'He's developing quite the taste for his daddy's product.'

I scrunched my face up. 'That sounds disgusting.'

John laughed. 'You should have seen him snorting it. It *was* disgusting. That stuff'll make your nose bleed like a goddamn faucet.'

'Like your head?' As if on cue, the split on his forehead was open again, blood streaming down his face. 'Shit,' he muttered, and before I could think to get up and get a towel, he'd taken his T-shirt off and had balled it up, pressing it to his bleeding forehead. I swallowed, my eyes drifting down his chest, past chiselled abs and a smooth, tattooed chest. His jeans were slung low around his narrow waist, and I found myself staring at the top button of his fly, almost like I could use the force to unbutton it from three feet away.

He gave me an odd look, and I tore my gaze away from the clothing I would have liked him to remove, motioning for him to move the T-shirt from his forehead. The cut continued to bleed heavily.

'Let me help you,' I said, hearing my words as they came out a little thicker than normal, muffled by exhaustion and too much alcohol. I was dying for a drink of water, but I needed some steri-strips first. 'Wait there,' I said. 'I've got a first aid kit somewhere around here.'

I rummaged in a few kitchen cabinets, finally finding the kit under the sink. I grabbed it and turned back to John, noticing where his eyes had been – squarely on my ass. It was nice to feel wanted without any strings attached. Nice to feel desired. I tried to push that away, my nipples hard enough to cut glass as I thought of the last time John and I had been together. The way he'd made me cry out beneath him.

Jesus, woman. Get a grip. He'll have bled to death from this cut by the time you get your shit together.

'Sit down,' I said, patting the stool. 'So I can reach better.'

He did, and I got to work, washing my hands with alcohol sanitiser, before setting up my tools – gauze, steri-strips, cotton balls and alcohol solution. The strip club was dirty. If you shone one of those luma-lights down there, it'd light up like a fucking Christmas tree in Times Square, all body fluids and blood from old fights.

'I'm not used to people helping me,' John said, keeping perfectly still as I dabbed the alcohol solution around his cut.

'This is deep, John,' I said, trying to focus but suddenly aware that if I was just a tiny bit closer, I could rub one of my nipples against his lips. Stop. Fix him first, and then figure out a way to screw him without getting killed.

'That's what she said.' That glint in his eye, and I couldn't help but laugh.

'I'm serious. You need stitches.' *I'm serious. Deep sounds exactly like what I'll say when you ask me how I want it.*

'No time for stitches,' he said, waving a hand dismissively. 'Unless you've got a needle and thread?'

'A needle and thread,' I repeated, taking a steri-strip and closing his wound as best I could. 'You'll have a scar on your head the size of Tennessee. I mean, I'll love you anyway, even if you're horribly disfigured.'

'What?' He sucked in a breath, and my chest tightened.

'I was kidding,' I said, pressing another steri-strip to his cut. 'You won't be disfigured. It'll be a little line.'

His hand shot out, fingers wrapping around my wrist and squeezing. 'That's not what I meant.'

Oh.

'You … love me?' He said the words like they were in another language and he wasn't quite sure how they fit together in a sentence.

I stopped what I was doing, meeting his gaze. 'Of course I love you, you idiot,' I replied. 'You think I'd risk my head for somebody I just kind of thought was okay?'

He smiled, teeth and all, and it was like the sun was beaming directly onto my face. I felt blood rise in my cheeks as we digested that reality together. Had I really never told him that I loved him? Had he never told me? It was just something that I knew, at a cellular level, something that I didn't ever have to question, not after that first night we'd spent together. I loved him as ferociously as I had ever loved anyone.

'You hungry?'

I nodded. I wasn't offended that he hadn't said it back. I wasn't a teenage girl with stars in her eyes. John loved me, whether he said it or not. He'd risked everything for me, more than once. The way he stared at me when he thought I wasn't looking was not the stare of casual affection. He loved me so much, I was afraid when we had to associate with each other in front of other human beings, because couldn't they see how bright we burned for each other?

'Come on. I'm taking you out. He can hardly be suspicious if I take you out for the birthday he forgot.'

I glanced at the clock. It was almost 2 a.m. 'It isn't my birthday anymore.'

John shrugged. 'And?'

'Okay,' I said. 'Give me a minute.'

I changed into a tank top and a skirt that hung loose over my hips. You know, just in case we stopped off on the way. It's not like we were going to fuck in a restaurant.

We went to Denny's, over in Burbank, where nobody would spot us. I was already experiencing the hangover from hell, and I ordered the biggest cup of coffee they had. Strong. Black. When it arrived I dumped my body weight in sugar into it, gave it a stir and mainlined it as quickly as I could.

I had waffles and bacon. John had eggs. 'Next time I'll take you somewhere a little more upmarket,' he said, drinking his coffee.

I shrugged. 'I love diners,' I said, stabbing a piece of waffle with my fork and drizzling maple syrup all over it.

John laughed, his eyebrows raised in that adorable way. 'You love *diners*,' he repeated dubiously.

I winced as I saw the gauze on his forehead redden. 'Don't smile,' I said, gesturing to his wound with my fork. 'In fact, no facial expressions from now on, okay? Or I will take you to the hospital and make you get stitches.'

He arranged his face into a perfect blank stare. 'Yes, ma'am,' he said, dissolving into laughter. I made a disapproving sound in my throat. 'You're opening your wound again, silly. You're gonna bleed all over the place.'

The gauze was steadily getting redder. 'Jesus, he really got you good,' I said. After the words had left my mouth, I winced, realising how stupid they sounded. He'd just brawled with his best friend, my lover, and from the sounds of it, he'd been lucky to walk away.

He didn't take offence, though. He smirked, and that

fucking dimple in his cheek was enough to make a woman orgasm just by looking at it. He had that playful twinkle back in his bright blue eyes, almost like the fight with Dornan had woken him up or something. Given him some motivation to make a move.

'You think this is bad?' he said, spinning his coffee cup around and around. 'You should see the other guy.'

I sat back in my side of the booth, raised one eyebrow. 'Oh, yeah?'

'I'm pretty sure his nose is broken,' he said.

I smiled wryly, thinking about how it was about time somebody knocked some sense into Dornan, even as my chest tightened at the thought of him being hurt. Old habits died hard. He'd hurt me so much, I should've been numb to his suffering. And yet I found myself hoping that he was all right. *Did he need me?*

On a practical level, I was also thinking about whether he was at my apartment right now, wondering where I was, waiting for me to patch him up. Then again, he was impatient. If he arrived and I wasn't there, he'd call me. My phone had lain on the table beside my breakfast the entire time, silent.

'You must have been mad,' I said, 'to break his nose.'

John's playful expression dropped away.

'What?' I asked.

'He pulled a gun on me,' he said, making his hand into the shape of a gun and wedging it beneath his chin, his fingertips – the make-believe barrel – pressed into his throat.

'He pulled a gun on you?' I echoed. Suddenly, I wasn't envisioning a testosterone-fuelled fracas, but a full-on vicious cage fight to the death.

'He didn't like some of the things I called him out on,' John said, pressing his fingers to his forehead. They came away red, the gauze pad taped to his skin completely soaked through. A waitress came over, barely glancing at John's wound. For all she knew, he was an extra from one of the nearby studio lots. We were in television city, make-believe land, and our oddness made us blend in, in a way.

John paid the waitress and she took my waffles to box up. I'd barely touched them, too busy talking, but I might want them after a couple of hours' sleep.

'You got a bathroom?' John asked her. The woman looked at him like he was an idiot. She didn't even respond with words, just pointed to a door in the back.

'I'm gonna go get this cleaned up,' he said.

I held up my purse. 'I'll come with you. I brought extra gauze. Since you insist on not getting stitches.'

Luckily there was a staff bathroom and changeroom that nobody seemed to be using. John held the door open for me and then locked it, testing it to make sure it couldn't open. We were good. He leaned down while I took off the old gauze and tried my best to clean the wound again. It was deep, and looked nasty.

'Does it hurt?' I asked him.

He shrugged. 'I've had things hurt a lot more.'

'Like what?'

He licked his lips, put his hands on my waist. 'Like my cock right now.'

Lust dragged through my belly like wildfire and I swear, I *felt* my pupils dilate.

'Oh, yeah? Your cock needs medical attention, too?'

146

He smirked, pulling me close with a forceful jerk. I could feel his hardness against my belly, and I wanted it all to myself. An empty ache throbbed between my thighs, demanding to be filled.

He brought a finger to my chin, tilting my face up to his. One kiss. That was all it took for my lamb to become a lion.

'Take your fucking panties off before I rip them off.' His eyes burned with desire and I felt my heart skip a beat.

Shit. I was about ready to come just from his words.

I hitched my skirt up, making it a show for him as I hooked my thumbs into the edges of my panties and slid them down my thighs. I was wearing white panties, and there was a clear wet patch on the inside. John saw it as I stepped out of the panties and he made a growling noise in the back of his throat, snatching them from me.

He fell to his knees before me, prising my thighs apart. I had to shuffle my feet wider apart to accommodate him. His tongue touched me, ever so gently, and it took everything inside me not to scream.

'John,' I begged. I wasn't even sure what I was begging for. I just knew that I needed him, desperately. He slid a finger inside me and I tightened around it, involuntary, pulsing with need. A finger wasn't going to be enough. I needed him. Inside me. Now. I squeezed his head, my hands fisted in his hair. Every time his tongue touched me, it was like a fucking inferno lit up inside me. Every time he pulled away, I pressed my hips forward, seeking that wet caress that was threatening to bring me undone in a Denny's bathroom stall. Of all places.

Guess I'd been wrong. Seemed we really were going to fuck in a restaurant bathroom.

When he pulled his face away, I just about crumpled over on myself. I caught a look at myself in the mirror – clumped mascara from the nap I'd taken on the kitchen counter earlier; my cheeks flushed.

'Somebody might catch us,' John said, that teasing glint in his eye.

I held onto his arms, my legs still shaking from the way he'd cruelly taunted me until I was almost coming. 'Let's shoot everyone on that bridge when we come to it,' I said, pulling my tank top down to expose a nipple. I pulled his hair, and he went with it, bringing his mouth to my pebbled nipple and sucking hard enough that pleasure hummed dangerously close to pain.

He pulled his mouth away and picked me up effortlessly, his hands cupping my ass cheeks. 'Wrap your legs around me,' he murmured. I did, breathless with anticipation as he walked me backward to the sink. He dropped me onto the edge, and luckily the thing was built solid enough, because he hitched my skirt up and slammed into me so hard, my head went back into the mirror and left a little crack in the glass. Not enough to draw blood. Not even enough to see stars. But enough that I hoped I'd be driving past this Denny's with Dornan one time, and have to stop off, and come in here to relive this moment, one crack in the mirror and John's hand over my mouth as he made me come so hard, I drew blood along his arm with my fingernails. Especially when he pulled back and with every insistent thrust inside me, he told me he loved me.

I love you. Fuck. *I love you.* Fuck! At one point, I thought his love was going to send me through the wall and into the next room. With my free hand I gripped the edge of the basin, as hot, wet kisses trailed up my neck, one thumb on my clit, making me come so hard I bit down on his shoulder without thinking, and John shuddered forcefully as he came inside me.

I felt bruised inside. I'd be sore for days after that. Some very sick part of me wondered if I'd still feel like this, raw and tender, the next time Dornan put his fingers or his mouth or his cock near me.

I hoped so.

I know, it's not right. I never said I was a good person, did I? Part of me was already looking forward to the bruised places Dornan would touch inside me, the map John had made when he'd fucked the shit out of me, to put it plainly, and that Dornan would never know I was feeling John's touch when he was inside me.

It made me want to fuck again just to feel that rush of illicit love.

***

The drive home took time. John took the scenic route, which meant he drove all around LA. Trying to avoid having to drop me off. I got inspired halfway home and opened the container that held my leftover waffles, dipping my finger into some of the syrup and smearing it all over his cock. I licked it all off as he tried not to crash. I think he liked that. Sure sounded like it, and by the way he was pressing his hips up, his cock bottoming out at the back of my throat, I think I was doing just fine.

'I meant what I said,' I murmured, just as we were rounding the corner to my apartment block, John's maple-syrup-covered dick securely back in his pants and my own panties back on under my skirt. The clock on the dashboard said 3:48 a.m. I was into my first full day of being twenty-nine. So far, it wasn't so bad.

I'd already kissed John goodbye in the parking lot of the diner. This close to home, it'd be foolish to do something so obvious. Emilio haunted these streets. Dornan lived here half the time. And while Guillermo might in theory be accepting of some relationship between me and John, I still didn't want to give him, or anyone else, a reason to tear us apart before we'd even had our chance to get away from them all.

CHAPTER FIFTEEN

MARIANA

I was in the shower when I had my near-death experience. I mean, I almost had a goddamn heart attack. Washing shampoo from my hair, I closed my eyes for the briefest of moments, letting the suds wash down my face until the water ran clear.

When I closed my eyes, I *swear* he wasn't there. But when I opened them again, I jerked back in shock, my ass and palms hitting the cold wall tiles behind me as Dornan stood in my bathroom, watching me like a fucking creeper.

He seemed slightly amused by my *Psycho* victim rendition. All that was missing was the shower curtain to wrap around myself while Norman Bates went to town. My bathroom was all tile and glass, but besides that, I hoped Dornan wasn't in here to murder me.

'Sorry,' he said, a faint smile playing on his lips.

Jesus, John hadn't been wrong. Dornan looked like someone had run him over, thrown the car in reverse, and driven over him again, paying particular attention to his head.

I shut the water off, taking the towel Dornan offered me.

'What the hell happened to you?' I asked, feeling genuine worry for Dornan in the sea of bitterness that was getting higher and more treacherous to navigate with every passing day.

'John happened to me.' He paused for a beat. 'Did you speak to him?'

Well, damn. It wasn't worth lying. I'd only be found out, wouldn't I? And lying about John was going to arouse a whole lot of suspicion. I wondered, briefly, if Dornan could see the cogs turning in my mind the way I sometimes saw them in his.

'He came around asking for a first aid kit,' I replied. 'His head wouldn't stop bleeding.' I drew a line down the middle of my forehead with my index finger. Fucking fuck fuck, it was harder to lie when you hadn't come up with the lie in the first place. Could he tell? Dornan was as sharp as they come, but as I studied his bloodshot eyes, it was pretty clear that there was enough of something bubbling away in his veins to dull his ability to read me.

Dornan watched as I wrapped the towel around my torso, tucking it in tightly. Normally this was the part where he'd rip the towel from me and fuck me up against the wall, but tonight he made no such move. I knew my suspicions had been right. He was getting it somewhere else. So was I, so I didn't exactly judge him, but it was one more nail in our coffin.

My hair hung around my face, soaking wet and straight. I stepped out of the shower, taking the hand that Dornan offered me. It was an odd gesture, almost gentlemanly. And my Dornan was anything but a gentleman.

'And?'

'And ... he said you guys got into an argument,' I continued. Jesus, the circles under my eyes were getting darker. Too much stress. Not enough sleep. The bottle of vodka probably hadn't helped, either. 'He didn't really seem in the mood to talk.'

'And?' Dornan pressed.

Shit, shit, shit!

'I asked him to take me to pick up waffles,' I said. 'I don't feel safe by myself at night, and Guillermo said he was busy. And I wanted birthday waffles.' *And I'm so fucking sick of having to explain my every move to you.* What had once been concern and an overprotective instinct had morphed into an absolute need to control and micro-manage every facet of my life under the guise of making sure nothing bad happened to me. When the plain truth was, Dornan and his father WERE the bad that happened to me.

Dornan went to open his mouth again and without thinking, I pressed a finger to his lips. 'Please,' I said quietly, 'do not say *and* again. It's been a long day. Days. It's a new day now, right? And I'm going to finish my birthday waffles.' The birthday guilt trip was effective, at least. I walked past him, looking back as he stood mute. 'You coming?'

He nodded, his dark eyes hooded, drawn. 'Give me a minute.'

He closed the bathroom door until just a sliver of light could be seen at the sides, and I heard water running. I used the alone time to lose the towel and throw on the first nightgown I could find – something long, beige, and definitely not sexy. It was like a potato sack, only softer. I scooped up my wet hair, piling it into a messy bun on top of my head and using hairpins to keep it there. I padded into the kitchen, barefoot, and what I

153

saw took my breath away, replacing it with something between a hiccup and a sob.

There were candles everywhere. Dozens of them. They smelled like vanilla, the entire kitchen and dining area smothered in candlelight. I felt my chest crack open as I saw the way he'd arranged them. There were flowers in the middle of the table, white lilies. Something turned uneasily inside my stomach – they were death lilies. They were for funerals, not birthdays.

'I'm sorry I wasn't here,' Dornan said at my back, his voice like gravel, even more hoarse than normal. I glanced at his throat, seeing red marks, wondering if they were from John's hands. Funny how hands were so versatile. They could take you to the brink of death, or the brink of orgasm, just with the way you used them. He stepped closer, wrapping his arms around me, and a hard rock rose in my throat, refusing to budge. I looked up, tears burning my eyes and blurring the room into a garish caricature of candles and stucco ceiling.

He kissed the top of my head, one palm smoothing down the hair at the crown of my skull. Just like my mother used to do when I was a girl, but I wasn't a girl anymore, and my mother was dead. The hard lump in my throat turned into a moan; the threat of tears spilling over became twin tidal waves pouring down my face. It had been less than twenty-four hours since the suitcase baby had been delivered. It played on a loop in my mind, no matter how hard I tried to switch it off. I couldn't even replace the image of the little boy with one of Murphy's face after I'd shot him. It wouldn't go away.

'Hey,' Dornan murmured, one hand coming around to my chin and tilting it so I was looking at him over my shoulder. 'Talk to me. You never talk to me anymore.'

I turned in his arms, resting my face against his chest for a second. His heart thrummed along slowly, evenly. In my mind, I'd already said goodbye to him a long time ago, checked out of the relationship the moment I woke up in the hospital, my pregnancy over, my baby scraped away. I'd gotten used to the idea that Dornan Ross was no longer the great love of my life, but the heart is a fickle thing. My heart still remembered his concerned eyes, his insistent touch, the way he'd always kept me safe. My heart was a goddamn traitor.

What about John? It's possible to love two men at once, you know. I wouldn't be the first woman torn between obligation and desire.

I wanted to take him by the shoulders and shake him. I'd managed to push everything away for months now, to forget the man he used to be, but suddenly I was overcome by the memory of the first time I ever saw him. Sadness engulfed me and my eyes started to fill with fresh tears. I wouldn't blink, didn't want to let them fall down my cheeks and give them to him. They fell, anyway. Gravity is strange like that.

'What happened to us?' I whispered against his neck, just loud enough for him to hear. 'We used to be different.'

A different question. *What have we done to each other? What have I done to you?*

He tucked a stray strand of hair up on top of my head, winding it around a hairpin so it stayed put. 'It's not too late,' he murmured, his hands on my neck, firm, but gentle. 'We can start over. I'll get us a new place. A real house. We can have a baby.'

I turned my head away, covering my mouth with my palm so I didn't cry out. 'We had a baby,' I whispered, my teeth gritted as grief was replaced by rage, my tears falling of their own volition. 'You never hurt me in ten years,' I seethed. 'Why'd you have to hurt me like that when I was carrying our *baby*?' I stepped back and shoved him as hard as I could, barely moving the solid mountain of muscle.

'I'm sorry,' he said, digging his fingers into my hips as he knelt in front of me. He lifted my nightgown, and I tried to push him away, until I realised he wasn't trying anything sexual. He rested his stubbled cheek against the bare flesh beneath my belly button, moving his head back and forth ever so slightly, rubbing against my skin. His fingers dug into the backs of my thighs as he pulled me as close as possible, and I had to steady myself on his shoulders so that I didn't fall.

'Why are you doing this?' I whispered. 'Why now?'

And no, I wasn't perfect, and no, I hadn't even been sure about keeping the baby Dornan and I had conceived unknowingly. But in the end, by his act of violence, he'd taken that choice away. He'd ended a life that was yet to begin. And although he'd said the words, he had yet to show me that he was ever truly sorry. Mostly, I think, he just wanted to forget about it and move on. A dark few days in the evolution of him, of us. In the space of three days, he murdered his son's mother, raped me while her blood was still all over him, and then punched me so hard for questioning him about said murder that our baby died.

Before then, I would have said there was hope for him. For us. We'd walked a dark road, Dornan and I, months and years of violence and suffering and compromise, thanks to our fathers and the choices they'd made.

'Why am I doing what?' he asked me slowly. And truth be told, I didn't even know what I was trying to quantify. What was he doing? Begging for my forgiveness, on his knees, the both of us surrounded with enough flickering candles to wipe out half the apartment building.

He straightened, my thighs aching from where his fingers had been as he towered over me once more. He bent his head down to mine and kissed me, taking me by surprise. He tasted like whiskey and cigarettes. His kiss was soft, almost hesitant. He kissed me like a boy would kiss a girl on prom night, one hand at my waist and the other cupping my chin. It was the sweetest gesture he'd ever made, and something in my chest expanded painfully, a supernova that stretched insistently, ready to shatter me.

How could I feel anything for him?

He broke the kiss, another anomaly, and pulled his head back so we were eye to eye. 'I wish I could take it all back,' he said, his eyes glassy.

Damn him to fucking hell. I had to hate him. I couldn't love him.

My heart was a fickle bitch.

He picked me up like I was weightless, gripping me so tight it was almost painful. I wrapped my legs around his waist, my head burrowed into the space between his shoulder and ear, almost like a child, my breath and his neck creating a warm pocket of air that I stared into vacantly.

He laid me down on my bed, and softness enveloped me. It felt blissful, to sink into downy blankets as hands stroked my face. I was shivering despite the heat, burning up with a fever that no medicine could fix. Heartsick and confused, as the man who professed to love me the most, for once, touched me with loving hands.

'You remind me of her,' he whispered, his thumb tracing my bottom lip. 'Stephanie. She had a fire inside her, like you. You would have liked her.'

I stared at the ceiling, remembering *Stephanie*, who I'd met only in death. The memory was anything but pleasant.

'You can't say that,' I choked. 'You murdered her. You can't *say* that.'

Dornan's palm wiped the tears away from my cheeks, but more streaked down to take their place. 'Shhhh,' he said. 'It's okay. It's okay.'

I shook my head. 'It's not okay.'

He kissed me. His mouth silenced me, drowned me out. He ground his hardness against my thigh and I remember wondering if I'd go to hell for fucking two men in the space of a few hours. A whore. That's what I'd been labelled as. Might as well enjoy the benefits.

I felt guilt, thick and swirling in my belly, as I pictured John's face. If he saw this, he would kill Dornan. But he was the other man, and he knew it. He had no say, and for that matter, neither did I.

Dornan hitched my nightgown up over my knees, bunching the material around my hips. The air on my stomach and thighs was cold, despite the night heat. I think it was being exposed like this, a gentle caress, a loving touch. Two hands, one on each of my knees, and then I was open, my hips protesting at how wide he'd parted them, his cock heavy as it rested against my pussy. My nipples were hard pearls beneath my thin nightgown, the material deliciously rough as it rubbed against them. I throbbed with desire – I still possessed desire for this man, somehow – and shame blanketed me like fog.

It was so much easier to detach when you were thrown onto a bed and fucked without any tenderness. When you weren't given a chance to say yes or no. When it was mechanical, going through the motions.

Love made things ... complicated.

What would he do if I said I didn't want this?

'Stop,' I said, pushing his hands away. He gave me an odd look, his cock in his palm, the blunt tip glistening with pre-come. We regarded each other silently, my hips arching of their own accord as he slid his free hand up the inside of my thigh and slipped a finger inside me.

'That doesn't feel like stop to me,' he murmured hoarsely, lowering himself, my eyes glued to the bruises blossoming on his neck. John's hands had made fine work of Dornan's flesh, before they'd made fine work of mine.

'Fuck,' Dornan groaned, pushing inside me so tenderly, it was as if he were another person. He'd never been gentle with me, not once in ten years, and I hadn't asked him to be. But something had possessed him. He rocked his hips against mine, slow and soft, his cock stretching the bruised parts of me that John had been anything but *gentle* with when he fucked me against a bathroom sink in a diner not three hours earlier. I cried out when he touched the spaces inside me that John had already punished. It hurt. I liked that it hurt. Above me, moving faster, it was clear that Dornan liked my pain, too.

We'd been together ten years, Dornan and I, and I can safely say that this was the first – and last – time we'd ever made love.

It was tragic. He was trying to start anew, a fresh beginning, and I was opening, yielding my flesh to him one last time to say goodbye to the man who saved me all those years ago.

And neither of us was brave enough to admit what we were doing.

CHAPTER SIXTEEN

The ring had been burning a hole in his pocket since he'd gone home to get it that afternoon. At the same time, one singular thought had burned in his head.

Had the woman he loved turned her loyalties against him?

It had gone something like this: His father had given his macabre version of a blessing to a Dornan-Mariana marriage, as well as a warning about where her allegiances might lie; Dornan had walked out of the meeting, and straight out onto Venice Boulevard. He didn't pass go. He didn't collect two hundred dollars. All he did was get on his motorcycle, speed home and find the ring his grandmother had left to him when she died.

He'd considered asking her properly if she'd marry him, but *what if she said no?*

She hated him for what he'd done. For everything. And he couldn't even blame her, because she was right to hate him. To fear him.

None of that mattered, though. She was his. She would always be his. Since the moment he'd laid eyes on her in that motel room in San Diego, he'd known.

Ten years. She'd be fine. She'd be happy again.

Was she fucking somebody else?

'Pack a bag,' Dornan called into the bedroom.

Mariana appeared in the doorway, wearing nothing except panties and a confused look on her face. Her hair was wild, from where he'd ground her into the bed, and her nipples still glistened from where his mouth had just been.

Dornan groaned, pressing his palms into his eyes. His dick hurt at the thought of fucking her again, yet, of its own accord, it stirred to life once more. She was the only woman in the world capable of killing him via sex. She'd literally suck the life out of him if he wasn't careful. He could fuck her all day, every day, and still the itch would not be scratched away.

'Where are we going?' she asked.

'Can you please put some fucking clothes on,' Dornan asked, squeezing his cock through his jeans. His clothes were already in the trunk of the car that waited for them downstairs – one small bag and a pair of shoes, enough for a quick jaunt out of LA.

Mariana raised one eyebrow, her lips tugging upward in the closest thing he'd seen to a smile in a while. 'I don't think you've ever said that to me before,' she said, leaning against the doorframe that led to the bedroom.

In the hallway, Dornan slipped his boots on, then his leather jacket. His fingers smelled like sex, and that was okay with him. There would be a lot more sex where they were headed.

Was she fucking somebody else?

'Where are we going?' Mariana called from the bedroom. 'I'm kind of tired. Can we just stay here?'

No. They could not just stay here. *Fuck.*

Dornan strode back into the bedroom to see Mariana on her back in the centre of the bed, again, with nothing on except those damn lace panties that left nothing to the imagination. Her legs were parted enough that he could see her pussy through the fine material.

Who else had seen her like this?

Without thinking, he yanked the edge of the comforter up and threw it over her, so she was sandwiched like a burrito.

The post-coital calm disappeared from her face and she sat up on the bed, alarmed. 'What's going on?' she asked. 'Is it bad? Are you taking me to Emilio? He's going to kill me, isn't he? *Motherfucker.*'

The motherfucker didn't seem to be directed at his father specifically; rather, it sounded like Mariana chastising herself, her voice ringing with disbelief.

'Hey.' He touched her thigh; she was shaking. 'Stop.'

'Fuck!' Mariana yelled, hitting the bed with her fists.

Something about her anger made him feel calmer. Almost like a transference. She was terrified, staring down at the comforter like it might offer up an answer to her problems, and he felt soothed by her desperation. Probably because the more desperate she was, the more she had to rely on him to survive.

'I'm just taking you somewhere because I fucked up your birthday. Okay? Don't ruin the surprise.' He softened his words for her, slowed them right down. Like soothing a child.

Her eyes lifted to meet his. 'Your father sent me a surprise for my birthday. I don't want a fucking surprise.'

Well, shit. 'We're going to Vegas. The Wynn. Room service and champagne. You'll like it.'

Her shoulders fell; she exhaled a breath that she'd been holding in for a while. 'What did Emilio say?' she asked breathlessly.

'About Vegas? Nothing. I didn't tell him.' It was true. Pop could hold the fort down for twenty-four goddamn hours.

'Not about *Vegas*, Dornan. What did he say about what I did?'

He licked his lips. 'Nothing much. I think he's more impressed than mad. But I get the impression if you ever pull that shit again, he'll shoot you in your fucking face. So maybe call me next time you decide to stage a coup.'

Her eyes were like fucking laser beams slicing him to bloody ribbons. 'Maybe tell him the same thing,' she said, and just like that, their connection was broken. She got up off the bed and started opening and slamming cupboards, her tits bouncing as she stomped around the room in her little panties and nothing else.

Who else has seen her like this?

Dornan thought it wise to shut up. He waited patiently until she had ventured into the bathroom, probably to pack make-up or something, and then he took the opportunity to rummage through her closet as quietly as possible. He knew what he was looking for. And when he found it, he smirked. He pulled the dress out, slipped it from its hanger, and rolled it up into a ball, shoving it into her bag underneath the rest of the clothes she'd packed.

'Let's go,' he called into the bathroom.

They were already going to hit traffic, at this rate.

CHAPTER SEVENTEEN

MARIANA

Ten years in America and I'd never set foot in Nevada. Sure, I'd seen it in movies, read about the place, but driving into Sin City in the back of a pimped-out limousine was something entirely different to experience. The place was alive and dying all at once – the towering hotels, the decaying storefronts, the shells of high-rise buildings long since abandoned and waiting for their date with the demolition crew.

It was a place of extremes, more so than Los Angeles could ever be. It made me realise how out of my comfort zone I felt in this foreign city. It was only a five-hour drive, even with the traffic we'd hit on the highway, but it was another universe. The sun had risen while we were driving, or rather, while we were being driven. Dornan spent the majority of the drive on the phone to various club members. Viper called about a shipment of weapons, then Chad called his father to let him know about a deal going down with another club. I caught snippets of each conversation but tried to ignore it for the most part, thankful for the distraction that business afforded Dornan.

And then there was John. He called a few times before Dornan answered. Their conversation was brief and to the point; from the sounds of it, they were going to deal with things like adults and pretend nothing had ever happened. Fucking males and their inability to figure shit out. Not that I particularly cared. After the sex I'd just experienced underneath Dornan's greedy hands, I was feeling exposed. Vulnerable. Memories of the good times had started flooding back to me. I'd never forgive him for the things he did, for the death and destruction he'd brought upon us, but I was starting to feel an aching void inside me that was the space he used to occupy. The darkest recess inside my treacherous heart muscle called out for Dornan Ross to put me back together again, to hold me close, to cradle me safely in his strong arms.

He hadn't been that man in a long time, but then, I hadn't been that girl in years, either.

Driving down the main street in Vegas was ... interesting. I wondered why Dornan had chosen this place, of all places. When I asked him, he shrugged, a hint of something in his eyes. *Don't ruin the surprise*, he kept telling me, and I just prayed that the surprise wasn't my own violent death in a Vegas motel room at eight in the morning.

If I died here, I'd be so fucking pissed, I'd haunt Dornan and his father until their last breath. I made that vow, just as we pulled up in front of a swanky building, its gold mirrored windows reflecting the desert and surrounding buildings with a brilliant sheen.

I found myself marvelling at the change in Dornan; the rough biker carried himself like a businessman going to a high-powered meeting where he would call the shots. He was dressed up more than normal, even though he was still sporting his uniform. But the leather jacket bore no insignia, his hair was neat instead of mussed up by the wind and his helmet, and his black T-shirt looked like it came from an expensive store, hugging his broad chest in all the right places. His dark denim jeans were a slimmer cut than usual, his boots were new, and goddamn it, my lover looked like he'd just entered the WITSEC program for former bikers and drug cartel members. He looked like sex on a stick, his stubble neatly trimmed and sculpted around his chin, his dark eyes flanked by thick eyelashes that most females would be envious of, and the salt-and-pepper at his temples softened his dark brown mop of hair. The one tell-tale sign that he was a criminal was the slight bulge at the spot where the waistband of his jeans gripped his lower back, a gun neatly stashed against his skin, should we encounter any trouble. Oh, and the fact that he had two black eyes and a broken nose. *Thanks, John.*

We didn't need to check in, a private butler whisking us straight from the limo to our room. It was a penthouse suite overlooking Vegas. The city was a mess of contradictions – who the fuck thought it was a good idea to put a city in the middle of a desert, anyway? So many buildings. So many billboards, each screaming about a two-for-one seafood buffet, or a shooting range, when they weren't loudly advertising their respective casino floors. It was overwhelming, suddenly being thrust into the artifice of it all. I hadn't had any time to prep. I didn't even know what the hell I'd packed in my bag, though I suspected it was mostly summer dresses and flip-flops. This was something entirely different. This was about Dornan and Mariana and nobody else.

And yet, when I locked myself in the bathroom to freshen up, I stared at the edge of the basin and remembered John.

This was my first time in Vegas, and it was likely also my last, because I was either about to be killed, or, if I survived this 'surprise trip' and John and I managed to get away, we'd be going a little further afield than the next state over.

When I was done, the image of that Denny's bathroom still visceral and unrelenting in my mind, I headed back out to the suite. It was bigger than my apartment, and looked like something out of a *Vogue Living* magazine. Dornan was standing at the window, his hands folded across his chest as he watched the city stir into action below. For a city that was switched on twenty-four seven, it sure seemed sluggish on a Monday morning. Probably everyone was hungover, or broke, or both.

'What are we really doing here?' I asked, joining him at the full-length window.

He turned to me, his face impossible to read. 'Brunch. You should wear the white dress.'

Oh.

Shit.

How fucking stupid was I? I caught my reaction before my face conveyed it, tamped it down quickly and trapped it.

The *white* dress.

The trip to Vegas.

The last-minute plans.

'Why are we here?' I repeated, my chest a carved-out hollow because I already knew the answer. Dornan didn't answer. He opened my overnight bag and pulled out the white dress, handing it to me with an air of finality.

The dress in one hand, I stared down at Las Vegas Boulevard and wondered, if I ran at the glass hard enough, would it break and let me fall to my bloody death fifty floors below? I handed it back. Dornan laid the dress out on the bed instead, smoothing out the creases.

'Your father would never allow this,' I said, staring at the dress Dornan had arranged. I didn't have my burner phone with me. I couldn't call John. Fuck! I needed to call John.

Right.

Now.

Dornan smirked, standing before me and tugging the hem of my dress. I resisted, holding on to that hem with everything I had. Dornan raised his eyebrows and took hold of my wrists, squeezing them just enough to show his strength.

'Allow what?'

I rolled my eyes, trying to shake his grip off, but he was having none of it. He tightened his fingers around my wrists, and they throbbed in protest.

'A trip to Vegas. A white dress. Look at what you're wearing!'

He shrugged. 'Maybe we're going to have a nice dinner.'

'It's the middle of the morning,' I shot back. My wrists were on fire. There'd be marks on them tonight.

'Maybe we're going to have a nice *brunch*,' Dornan said, his jaw tensed, his demeanour no longer amused. Now he just looked fed up.

'I'm not marrying you,' I said, the words out of my mouth before I could think twice.

He slapped me across the face so hard I tasted blood. My wrists were free, though, and purely on instinct I punched him in the face, as hard as I could.

Right in the nose.

The nose that John had broken the night before. *Teamwork*.

Blood exploded from his face and he stepped back, cupping his hands over his nose. All I could see were his eyes – black, cold, determined. The pain of my blow hadn't angered him, or so it seemed. No, it seemed that the violence had only strengthened his resolve.

He took his hands away and blood dripped onto his shirt, a chilling grin spreading across his face. His nose was bent slightly, and red.

Oh, Jesus. I was going to pay for that.

He came at me like a fucking CIA operative: blunt, fast, effective. He grabbed my hair and yanked, spinning me until I was in his arms. Before I could break free, he had his arms locked around my neck, squeezing against my carotid artery, and within a matter of seconds, the room went black.

***

I woke up on the plush carpeted floor of the limousine we'd travelled in to Vegas. I had no idea how I'd gotten there, or how long I'd been there. I had some drool on my cheek. I wiped it away, craning my head to take in the dimly lit interior of the car.

Dornan sat on the seat above me, his knees wide, his face clean. He held an ice pack against the bridge of his nose, but the damn thing was swelling anyway. There were dark circles under his eyes, and cuts on his skin from the fight with John. He looked terrible.

'It's lucky I brought an extra shirt,' he said, taking the ice pack away from his nose. 'Though we're gonna have to retouch the photos.'

I sat up on my elbows, noticing the white dress now on me. The air-conditioning was cold between my thighs. I felt with one hand – no panties. *Figured.*

'How kind of you to dress me,' I said, dragging myself to my knees and sliding up onto the seat opposite. I was four feet away from Dornan, but if I'd been able to jump out of the limousine, I would have. We weren't moving. I looked out of the window to see a large, garish sign in the shape of an arrow, pointing down at a chapel that was adorned with Elvis.

Could life get any worse? I looked around the car for something sharp that I could use to kill myself. There was nothing sharp, unless you counted Dornan's eyes. I had the sudden urge to crawl over to him and rip those eyes out of their sockets.

Dornan tossed my purse at me. It hit my arm and fell onto the seat beside me.

'Put some fucking make-up on,' he said. 'You look like shit.'

He tossed something else at me. Panties. Black lacy ones. I rolled my eyes, hooking them over my shoes and sliding them up my thighs and over my ass. *Better.* That felt better.

'Why do I need make-up?' I asked, rummaging through my bag. I still had my gun. I pulled it out and pointed it at Dornan's head. I smiled, amused.

'I thought you would have taken this out,' I said, marvelling at the way it felt in my hand. It felt like power.

He grinned, holding out his open hand. Nestled in his palm, six shiny bullets.

I stuffed the useless gun back into my purse and yanked out my make-up bag. I took my sweet time applying foundation and blush.

***

'Why'd you want me to wear make-up, anyway?' I asked Dornan as we approached the counter inside the chapel. 'It's not like anyone's going to see this.'

He smiled a plastic smile, one hand pressed into the small of my back as he drove me towards the tired-looking woman behind the counter that screamed CHEAP WEDDING CEREMONIES.

'Our children will ask to see the photos one day,' he said, his voice steeled, his expression a mask of self-preservation. 'You should look beautiful for them.'

My knees actually buckled when he said that. They just plain stopped working, and the ground rushed up at me. Dornan's big hands were there to keep me steady, of course. He leaned me into him, tucked me into his side so I was pressed against him.

'I'm going to throw up,' I said, scanning the foyer for a bathroom.

'Oh, good,' Dornan replied, half-dragging me towards the sign marked BATHROOMS. 'Maybe you're knocked up again already.'

Fucking bastard. His casual indifference stung. He pushed me into the women's toilets and into the first stall, gathering my long hair up off my face as I dry-retched over the bowl.

'I'm more used to holding your hair when my dick's in your mouth,' he said, and I would have cringed had there not

172

been a steady stream of vomit coming out of my mouth. My stomach roiled again, once, twice. False alarms. I flushed, jerking back from Dornan's grip as I pushed past him and out of the cubicle.

A woman was washing her hands, wearing a wedding dress so enormous it took up most of the square footage in the small area. She looked at Dornan in the mirror, and he stared back until she cast her gaze to the ground.

'You feeling better, honey?' he asked, rubbing my back in mock concern.

I could tell he was mocking me because of the pissy look on his face. I looked at his nose and wanted to punch it again. He glared at the woman and she scurried out of the bathroom, her dress bunching up as she got stuck in the door before she popped out onto the other side like a champagne cork being let free. The door swung shut again and we were alone.

'I'm not marrying you,' I said.

Dornan didn't say anything, just looked at the ceiling. I glanced at his fists. Yeah. He was about to fucking rage.

'Give me one of those bullets,' I said, gesturing to his pants pocket. 'I'll put it right in my head. You won't have to worry about me causing problems anymore.'

I'd put the bullet in him first, but he didn't need to know that, did he?

'That sweet act back at the apartment, what was that?' I was hurting. I felt like he'd stabbed me right in the chest. He'd been soft and tender and I had fallen for it, so desperate to believe that there was still some good in him. I'd been betraying him for months. I was in love with another man. But the way

173

he had been with me – tender – it tore my soul to shreds. He had tricked me. I had fallen for it.

'Do you know where Murphy is?' he asked me, his tone deathly calm. Too calm.

Oh, God. My stomach lurched again as I remembered the taste of Murphy's blood in my mouth, the way he'd bled everywhere. All over me, all over my bed, all over the floor.

Dominoes. We'd piled them up, he and I, and they were starting to fall. One by one, the lies would set us free, even if that freedom meant certain death.

'No,' I replied. 'No, I don't.'

And the truth was, I didn't know. John had handled the burning of his body. And, I assumed, the disposal of whatever had been left over. Gravel and ash. Hell, maybe he was still at the same crematorium where Guillermo and I had taken the baby only yesterday. As far as I was concerned, the whereabouts of Christopher Murphy – what was left of him – was a mystery to me.

I would have to ask John what he did with Murphy's remains, assuming I made it out of Vegas alive.

'The FBI are looking for him,' Dornan said, taking my hand again and squeezing my wrist.

I didn't bother pulling away, the image of Agent Lindsay Price clear in my mind – the FBI agent who'd cornered me in the locker room at the gym Guillermo and I frequented, stolen my towel, and asked me where Murphy was. I'd never told Dornan. I couldn't. I no longer trusted the man who, once upon a time, would have laid down his life to protect me.

'The FBI are looking for him,' Dornan repeated, 'and they're getting closer.'

'Great,' I replied. 'Maybe when they find him, they can ask him where he stashed hundreds of thousands of dollars of your father's money.'

Dornan turned and smashed his fist into the mirror. Shards exploded in a rain of cold glass, sharp and tacky.

'They're going to call you as a witness, you stupid bitch,' he said, ignoring his bleeding knuckles as they dripped all over the floor.

Something reached into my chest and squeezed violently, the part of me that screamed MURDERER. *I* killed Murphy. The blood was on *my* hands, in *my* apartment, in the grout between *my* bathroom tiles. And even though John had it swept clean by a specialist crew, I'd watched enough TV to know that it'd only take a single missed speck of blood to put me away for the rest of my natural life.

And I couldn't be in prison. I could plot and thieve and run from the Gypsy Brothers and Il Sangue, but I couldn't break out of a federal penitentiary. That was beyond my particular set of skills. I couldn't ever, *ever* be caught for the terrible things I had done in the name of survival. Two police officers – Murphy, and his squeeze and DEA partner, Allie Baxter – were both dead by my hand.

Dornan must have seen something on my face. 'You know where he is, don't you?'

I shook my head vehemently. 'No.'

'Then why do you look like you're about to pee all over the fucking floor?' he growled.

'They'll arrest me for money laundering,' I said quietly, my eyes wide, my breathing laboured. I wasn't putting on an act. They really would arrest me for that. And ironically,

the sentences for white-collar crimes like funnelling money –
profits of drug supply and human trafficking at that – to every
known tax haven in the world were probably harsher than if
I'd just stepped out onto the strip with a machete and started
hacking gamble-happy tourists to pieces.

America, the land of the free, really fucking liked collecting
taxes. It didn't like it when you tried to hide money. Especially
when you got that money for doing very bad things.

'Why do you think we're here?' Dornan asked, his anger
subsiding for the moment. I glanced at the broken mirror, the
remaining shards casting a haunting image of us, shattered and
warped a thousand times over as our reflections existed in tiny
slices of glass.

'Because you don't have to testify against your spouse in
court,' I said vacantly, rubbing my wrist as faint bruises began
to appear. I mean, I'd been a little slow to catch on, but I wasn't
an idiot.

'Bingo,' Dornan said. He wrapped his hand in paper towels
to stem the bleeding. Then, as I continued to stand there like a
waste of space, he put his hands on my hips and guided me over
to the unbroken mirror that hung over the neighbouring basin.
He started to fuss with my hair, moving strands to where they
belonged and smoothing down the knots he'd created when he
fisted clumps of my hair and pulled. There were flowers woven
into my hair, my messy topknot.

'Did you put these in my hair?' I asked slowly, horrified
at the way he'd dressed me and arranged me as if I were his
doll.

'I did,' Dornan replied, tucking a small pink rose back into
my hair. 'You can thank me later.'

Somehow the act of decorating my hair was more disturbing than almost anything he'd ever done. It was his way of communicating that he could do whatever he wanted with me – and if I didn't like it, he'd force it anyway, just to get things the way he wanted.

I watched him silently in the mirror's reflection, weighing my options.

They were feather-light. *They didn't exist.*

'You good?' he asked. It was like the fight had bled out of him. Maybe it had. I nodded.

'Then let's go get fucking married,' he said, pulling the bloody napkin from his knuckles. 'Don't worry. If you still hate me this much in a year, we'll just get fucking divorced.'

His casual words belied the intent in his eyes. I knew that look. We would be married, but we would not ever be getting divorced. The only way I would ever be undoing what was about to happen would be if one of us died and the other was widowed.

John was going to want to murder Dornan when he found out about this.

'Does your father know about this?' I asked again, my heart hollow as the answer knocked around it like a frenzied moth in the dark. Because I already knew the answer.

'Of course,' Dornan replied, ushering me out of the bathroom. I glanced back at the shattered glass one last time, a sense of doom crushing down on me.

'Esteban and I were going to get married,' I said softly, letting him lead me to the altar, his reluctant bride. 'But your father had him killed before we could do it.'

'Lucky me,' Dornan said, as Elvis started singing 'Suspicious Minds' at top volume over the speaker system. *Oh, the irony.*

'Now I get the honour of calling you wife while he's napping in the dirt.'

I made a choking sound in the back of my throat as his words slammed into me.

'You motherfucker,' I shot, anger blossoming in my chest like noxious fumes.

He took something from his pocket and held it out to me, seemingly unaffected by my reaction. 'Have some gum. You need it.'

If looks were knives, he'd have been sliced clean in half. 'How thoughtful,' I said, snatching the packet from him.

I unwrapped a stick of gum and stuck it between my teeth. Mint flooded my mouth, sharp and tangy, and from that moment on I'd always associate white dresses and Elvis with sticky-sweet mint and broken bones.

CHAPTER EIGHTEEN

DORNAN

The ceremony was short. It wasn't, however, remotely sweet. When it was time for them to kiss, Dornan could have sworn Mariana flinched.

He'd have to punish her for that.

And he had just the punishment to fit her crime. The crime of not loving him anymore. The crime of checking out. She was physically here with him, but her mind was just gone.

But her body would be his. He would mark her so that any man who touched her knew she belonged to him. He would dig into her flesh until her eyes burned from the pain.

He'd seen the threads of them unravelling, but by the time he understood how serious it was, she was already somewhere else.

And he couldn't figure out where.

The phone, the incriminating evidence against her, was like a ticking time bomb in Dornan's existence. He'd almost asked her about it so many times, but he had never actually spoken the words aloud, because he didn't want to know the answer.

She was all he had, the only person who loved him that wasn't required to by virtue of sharing his DNA, and he couldn't bear the thought that she might have betrayed him.

That fucking phone, though. It was prepaid, a flimsy piece of shit that led nowhere. No details, no call history that he could find when he scrolled through the phone's basic functions – nothing. Murphy was the one who could get things like call logs easily and discreetly, and that motherfucker was either ghosting all of them, or dead. Dornan had packed the phone for this trip specifically, taking the opportunity to steal it from its hiding spot while Mariana was packing. Because he was tired of waiting around for answers, and it was time to get them himself.

The phone was in Dornan's suitcase now, locked inside his gun case with his Beretta – his other piece, the one he wasn't currently hiding in the waistband of his jeans. He had a smaller handgun for everyday concealed carry. A Beretta was too fucking heavy to carry around all day, and it made him itch.

The phone. The phone. The *phone*.

Now, if fucking Murphy hadn't disappeared, he could have checked the official call records for it, subpoenaed information, gotten answers. But Murphy was nowhere to be found, and perhaps that was because he was the one she was calling from this goddamn phone in the first place. Dornan's other investigative contacts didn't have FBI clearance, so they had to do some shady shit to get answers. Shady shit took time.

Fucking Murphy.

If he was still alive when they found him, Dornan was going to murder him.

If she was going to double-cross the cartel, it made sense that Ana would work with Murphy. He was a DEA agent. He was shady as fuck. And Dornan hated him.

But Ana hated Murphy, too. So if the phone had come from him, then he was either blackmailing her somehow, or giving her something she wanted.

But what?

Her family? The people who thought she was long dead?

What was he missing?

Was it somehow tied to Guillermo, the man Dornan had entrusted with Mariana's security detail? He'd been loyal to Dornan always, but everybody had a weakness. He'd put the hot-headed Mexican in Mariana's apartment for protection, but was he sticking his dick in Dornan's girlfriend – wait, his *wife* – behind his back? If that was the case, he'd chop the fucking thing off and barbecue it, and force Guillermo to eat it.

'Nice ring,' Mariana said, peering at the rock on her hand. 'Who'd you steal it from?'

Dornan grinned, but inside he felt cold. This wasn't the future he'd imagined for them. This wasn't how he'd pictured their wedding.

He hadn't even asked her to marry him, he'd forced her.

If she's betrayed us, I will fucking kill her. I will rip her fucking head off, and Murphy's too.

'It was my grandmother's,' he said, a hollow ache inside his chest. He'd had that ring since his mother's mother died and he was a young man, unwed and sowing his wild oats. He'd intended to give it to Stephanie, but then she left him. He'd never felt Celia was worthy of it. And somewhere in the depths of his black soul, he imagined Mariana would be buried in the ground wearing it, very soon.

'Oh,' Mariana said quietly.

Dornan got the driver to take a detour on the way back to the hotel: Franco's ink shop, right on Freemont. He knew Franco well. He'd been tattooing Gypsies for years, until he moved out to Nevada and started making bank by tattooing tramp stamps on drunken brides instead.

Mariana glanced at the store's sign warily as Dornan pressed his hand into the small of her back, directing her into the front of Franco's studio. Needles whirred noisily, the air-conditioning so cold it was like being in the fucking Arctic.

Better than sweating, Dornan thought. He pulled Mariana right up to the counter and knocked his fist against the glass display case once, twice, three times. A young punk girl wandered out, and Dornan couldn't help but stare at the stretcher earrings that had turned her earlobes into giant holes.

'Can I help you?' she asked, clearly unimpressed by him. That's right, he wasn't in LA. Nobody knew him here, at least not by sight, and definitely not when he was in civilian clothing, nary a Gypsy Brothers patch to be seen.

He looked the punk bitch up and down. 'Tell Franco that Dornan Ross is here,' he said, the smile he flashed her more like a wolf baring teeth. The girl's eyes went wide and she nodded, scurrying away.

'Wow,' Mariana said, leaning back against the glass counter. 'The place where everybody knows your name.'

He raised his eyebrows. 'They got *Cheers* on TV in Colombia, wife?' He liked the sound of that word when he said it. She was his wife. And she'd come around to embrace her new position. Eventually. Probably.

She didn't really have a choice.

She frowned. 'I haven't been in Colombia in ten years, *husband.*'

She said the word like she was talking about stepping in dog shit. It brought that rage out of him, that cloying, violent need for blood.

'Where'd you watch *Cheers*?' he asked, not really caring, but needing to fill the silence until Franco got his ass out here.

'In the apartment,' she replied. 'Guillermo and I watch reruns.'

'He rub your back and fix you tea, too?' Dornan asked. That fucker better not have laid a hand on her.

'Sometimes,' she said, catching his eye. She was fucking with him, and he hated it, but it didn't matter, because he was about to fuck with her.

Franco, a short, rotund man with a white beard and a shiny bald head, barged out of the back of the shop, making a beeline for Dornan. They exchanged pleasantries, Dornan slapping the man on the back hard enough that he thought he might break him, and then the three of them went into a back booth.

'Alrighty,' Franco said, peering up at them from his five foot nothing stance. 'What's the big bad biker getting today?'

Dornan smiled. Gotcha. He gestured to Mariana, draping an arm over her bare shoulders. 'My wife would like a more lasting reminder of our union. Apparently a ring isn't good enough these days.'

Mariana's head snapped around like the kid in the fucking *Exorcist* movie. She tried to pull away, but Dornan was strong. He held her to his side, squeezing her shoulders under his broad arm.

'What the fuck?' she hissed. Franco looked between the two of them, apparently not in a hurry at all. 'Do you want a moment to talk amongst yourselves while I get the needles?' he offered.

Dornan nodded. 'Sounds like a plan, Franco.'

Franco wandered out back and Dornan released Mariana. She backed up, away from him, but it didn't matter. He had her cornered, and she knew it.

'What are you doing?' she snapped. 'Are you out of your fucking mind? You want to brand me like I'm an animal?'

He grabbed her wrist, not bothering to be gentle, thinking she fucking deserved it rough after the performance she'd put on. He'd done everything for her, and she was freezing him out at every turn.

'It's tradition,' Dornan said. 'All the wives of Gypsies get a tattoo. It's part of your role. Or would you prefer to be marked with cum and lines of coke like all the club whores? Like I said, we can get a fucking divorce. But I need me a wife, babe. If it's not you, I'll have to donate you to the fine members of my club.'

'Fuck you,' Mariana said, shoving him in the chest. Of course he didn't move. 'As if you'd share me.'

Dornan chuckled. 'I might not like it, but, darlin', I'd do just about anything to prove a point.'

Mariana's smirk dropped, replaced by unadulterated horror.

'No,' she said. 'Don't do this. You don't have to do this.'

Dornan guided her to the chair and sat her down, marvelling at how beautiful his trapped little bird was, now.

'Yes, I do,' he said, nodding to the ring on her finger. 'Take that off and put it on the other hand. It'll be a few days until the swelling goes down.'

CHAPTER NINETEEN

MARIANA

I slammed the door in Dornan's face, closed the lid of the toilet seat, and sat. I looked at my ring finger, swollen, hurting so fucking brutally I wanted to rip the whole finger off. I wondered if the needle and the tattooing equipment had even been sterile.

I didn't want this fucking abomination on my finger. A skull. He'd had them tattoo a skull on my finger, and a matching faux band so that it represented a ring. Because a piece of paper legally binding us together and a diamond the size of my pinkie fingernail wasn't enough to seal the deal. I was surprised he hadn't just tattooed PROPERTY OF DORNAN ROSS over my face for everyone to see.

I didn't want this marriage.

I didn't want to be holed up in a fucking bathroom in Las Vegas while Dornan raged outside the door, ravenous for the release that only my body could give him. He had wed me, and now it was pretty clear that he wanted to fuck me. Consummation of a commitment ten years in the making.

Fuck that.

I didn't want him on me. In me. Near me.

I wanted John.

But John wasn't here. He was somewhere else, and I was here, and nothing else mattered.

'What the fuck are you doing in there?' Dornan asked. 'You can't stay in there forever.'

'Fuck you!' I yelled back, wrapping my arms around myself and resting my forehead on my knees. I knocked my finger against my leg and cried out. Goddamn it. It hurt.

I caught sight of myself in the mirror across from me. Pale. Not the actual colour of my skin – I was Colombian, after all – but the pallor. It screamed misery. So did my eyes. Red and bloodshot. My hair was messed up. My stomach was screaming for food and my hands shook from stress and lack of sugar.

I'm married to the man who is going to kill me if I don't get away from him.

I was a mess.

More than that – I was fucking doomed.

I rested my face in my hands and cried.

CHAPTER TWENTY

Mariana hadn't said a word while Franco was tattooing the ring onto her finger. It was tradition, but neither of his other wives had gotten them, and Dornan hadn't pressed the issue. But his Mariana … she was something to be coveted. She was something to be marked.

And marking her was exactly what he wanted to do right now. He wanted to rip the fucking bathroom door off its hinges, pick her up, throw her onto the bathroom vanity and fuck her until she screamed and he had to gag her. He wanted to kiss those soft, dewy lips, get them wet and swollen, and then push her onto her knees so that he could slide his dick right into her wet mouth. He wanted to come all over her face, her beautiful tits, her ass. He'd been waiting for the day when he could have her freely, when his father would finally allow their union to be official … But there was one problem.

She was locked in the bathroom.

Had been for the better part of an hour.

She wasn't coming out.

He smashed his fist against the bathroom door.

Inside, he waged a war. Against her. Against himself. Against every shitty thing he had ever done.

He lifted his fist to smash the door again, even though his knuckles were already a bloody mess, even though he didn't deserve her forgiveness. He craved it. He'd stood in the sunshine of her love once, and now on the other side, it was midnight, and he was cold.

Fist in the air, he almost hit her in the goddamn face when she yanked the door open abruptly and stood there, wearing her pretty strapless white dress, her tattoo angry and red-black around her ring finger.

'What?' she snapped.

He felt the angry wall inside of him collapse, if only for a moment. He was just *tired*.

'I want to go back to that first time in your apartment,' Dornan said gruffly, flexing the fist he'd just about driven into her face by accident. He reached out a hand, cupped her face tenderly with his rough skin.

'Why?' she asked tightly.

He sighed. 'I want to do better. You deserve better.'

Her eyelashes fluttered as she looked at him briefly, and then back at the ground. She was fucking beautiful. She was his wife, and he couldn't quite believe it. She smiled wryly, and for a moment he thought she might have been going to drop this shit.

The words that came out of her mouth, though, were like a cold pickaxe she was jamming into his heart.

'I want to go back to that night your father came for me,' she muttered, 'so that I could shoot him in the fucking face, and never have to meet you.'

Mariana smacked his hand away from her face like it was fire, and he was burning her skin. He saw red. He saw Mariana on the floor of her apartment, as he laid his fists into her for daring to defy him, and he saw the puddle of blood that had greeted him afterward, when she was already in the hospital, their baby long dead. The sting of her rejection was acute; it was utterly unbearable.

'When are you going to stop punishing me?' Dornan roared, slamming his palm against the wall beside her head.

CHAPTER TWENTY-ONE

MARIANA

I saw red.

'You think I'm punishing you?' I screamed, pushing him. 'I can't even fucking look at you without feeling like you're beating me against a wall!'

And maybe I was goading him. Maybe I wanted him to force me, so then at least I could say it wasn't my fault. That he wouldn't take no for an answer. Because I could already tell, from that psychotic glimmer in his dark brown eyes, that he wasn't taking no for an answer tonight. He'd claimed me on paper, and now he wanted to claim my body with his.

'I'm sorry, I'm SORRY!' he raged. He started to pace in front of me.

I watched, not daring to leave the safety of the bathroom doorway. If he came at me, if he tried to grab me, at least I had a chance at shutting him out and going back to my safe room.

But he didn't grab me, or try to kiss me, and that surprised me. If anything, the pacing seemed to calm him.

At least, I thought he was calming down, until he spoke.

'You've been avoiding me for months,' he said coldly, levelling his black gaze at me.

'What?' I tried not to squirm under the spotlight of his words.

He just raised his eyebrows. 'I know you, Mariana Rodriguez. Mariana *Ross*. You are a woman who demands to be fucked. You used to be addicted to my cock. So if you haven't been fucking *me*, who *have* you been fucking?'

My stomach dropped. 'What?'

'Who. Huh? Guillermo? I'll slit his dirty throat and screw you beside him, in a puddle of his blood.'

I grimaced at the visual. I didn't doubt him for a second. 'No, I haven't been fucking *Guillermo*,' I replied. *As if.* 'I'd rather sew my vagina shut than fuck him.'

'Who, then? Someone from the club?'

Getting warmer. He was pacing and pacing and this was so very bad. He'd never been suspicious before. Ever.

He stopped dead in his tracks, lifting his eyes from the shitty red and yellow checkered carpet. 'Did my father touch you?'

I thought of all the times Emilio had *touched* me – pinched nipples, pulled hair, slapped cheeks. He'd been rough. Threatening. But in all these years, Emilio Ross had never once tried to have sex with me.

'No,' I snapped. 'There's nobody. You're being paranoid, Dornan.'

He chuckled, the gesture devoid of any joy. He was in pain, I realised. He was crying out for me to love him in the way I showed him love – with pain, and sex, and blood.

'I know what you want,' I whispered through gritted teeth. 'And you're not going to get it from me. You don't deserve it.'

'WHO ARE YOU FUCKING?' he roared, raising his hand as if he were about to hit me.

'Nobody,' I replied calmly, refusing to cower under his physical threat. I would show no weakness, even though inside my alarm bells were screaming, *Get out! Get out!*

There was nowhere to go. *There was never anywhere to go.*

I stood my ground against my dark lover, glaring at him as emotion rose thick in my throat. And then, in an act of entirely false bravado, I slipped underneath his arm, still braced against the doorframe, and headed for the minibar.

The hotel we were staying in wasn't amazing, but the minibar was. They'd laid out a selection of spirits that made my mouth water, and I ran my fingers along the lids, selecting a small bottle of vodka. Opening it, I poured half the bottle over my tattooed finger, squeezing my eyes shut as they teared up. I gasped, blinking away the hot moisture that had gathered at the corners of my eyelashes, as I slammed a mouthful of vodka and felt it burn all the way down inside of me. All the while, I felt Dornan's eyes drilling into me, his questions, his suspicion.

He came to stand beside me at the minibar, running a hand through my long hair. I still had the damned flower wreath in it, and as soon as I'd finished the vodka, I was going to rip it out and throw it into the trash. I didn't want to look pretty. I wanted to be left alone to scream into my pillow and sob until the sun came up again.

The fingers in my hair turned into a fist, the gentle caress turning into a tight tug as he wound strands around his fingers and pulled, hard. I didn't resist, letting my head go with the swift motion. I didn't fancy losing any hair today.

'You're telling me you've been fucking yourself? Getting yourself off?' he asked, his breath hot on my cheek.

I nodded as much as I could with the way he was holding my head back. What else could I say without placing John under suspicion?

'I don't fucking believe you,' he growled.

I turned my gaze to him, an open challenge in my eyes. 'I'll show you.'

He appeared to think about it for a moment, his eyes lighting up with what looked like lust. He let go of my hair, dropped his hand to his side. 'You'd better,' he replied, reaching for the vodka bottle in my hand and pointing to the couch. 'Now.'

We stared off for a moment. *Oh, this is actually going to happen*, I realised. Well. Whatever. I'd give him a show he wouldn't soon forget. I'd make his cock ache until it was painful instead of pleasant.

I snatched the vodka back, took a long slug, and slammed the bottle down on the counter, wiping my mouth with the back of my hand. I stalked over to the couch, standing in front of it, facing away from Dornan as I hitched my dress up to my hips. I hooked my fingers into my white panties and tugged them down, bending at the waist until they reached my ankles. Then, without kicking off my patent heels, I turned, sat my ass down on the couch, and spread my legs, bracing my feet against the edge of the cushions.

Surprisingly, Dornan hadn't moved from the minibar. I'd half expected him to grab me while I was bent and removing my panties, but it seemed my *husband* possessed restraint I wasn't aware of. He'd left the vodka where it was, and selected a bottle of bourbon instead.

'You have a very pretty cunt,' he growled, squeezing his dick through his pants. His jaw was so tight, it looked like it might shatter if he clenched it any harder.

'I know,' I said, reaching down and spreading myself open for him to see. He let out a small growl in the back of his throat, his erection bulging through his pants, the black material stretched thin.

Something inside me broke mournfully apart as I realised the only way I'd be able to keep up this pretence would be to keep fucking Dornan until the very last minute. I didn't know how I'd be able to do that, not after what he'd done and what he'd put me through, but I knew it was the only way to evade suspicion. To avoid being caught out.

I slipped one finger inside myself, sliding it back and forth in my wet heat.

'You fuck yourself like that?'

I nodded, never breaking our gaze. In my peripheral vision, I saw him squeeze his cock, moving closer to me, the neck of the bourbon bottle still clutched tightly in his hand. I sank two fingers inside myself, letting out a small moan, surprised at how wet I was. How fucking aroused I was.

It wasn't about sex, I realised. This was about power. Being the one in power was getting me off. Having Dornan in front of me, knowing all he wanted to do was throw himself on top of me and push into me until I broke in half, that was power. The fact that he hadn't touched me yet, but continued to watch my bizarre little show, *that* was power.

'You want a front row seat?' I offered boldly. Kicking the edge of the coffee table in front of me to make room for his bulky frame, I pointed with my free hand. Dornan smirked, dropping the bottle onto the carpet with a heavy thud.

Taking three steps, he didn't stop until he was standing above me. He sank to his knees in front of me, his eyes greedily taking in my wet pussy, my swollen clit, my nipples that peeked out of my plunging dress.

Grinning, Dornan stuck two fingers into his mouth, wetting them as he watched me fuck myself. He took hold of my wrist with one hand, pulling my own fingers away from myself, his own fingers braced to enter me.

'Hey.'

He stopped, his fingers millimetres from my entrance. He looked dazed, as if the lust inside him was consuming him like a virus in his blood.

I took his wrists and guided his hands to my ankles. He wrapped his fingers around my flesh and squeezed.

'Keep them there,' I said, gazing into his dark eyes, shocked at how complicit he was being. 'Don't interrupt me, or I'll never do this again.'

He squeezed my ankles in response, breathing heavily.

'You're so wet,' he murmured. 'I want to be inside you.'

He licked his lips as he stared at my slick pussy, and I could tell this was killing him. He was dying to press me into the couch and fuck me into oblivion.

Wasn't going to happen.

I continued to massage my swollen bud with my fingers, using my free hand to reach down and tilt his chin, forcing him to meet my gaze.

'Look at me,' I breathed. 'I have some things I want to say to you.'

He didn't look away. I was impressed by his restraint. I took a deep breath, preparing to relive the horrors of the recent past.

'You put life inside me,' I whispered, continuing to rub myself. I squirmed under my own touch, so close to coming. He nodded, slow-blinking.

'You made me feel the worst pain imaginable,' I breathed. I felt my words leak out of me, a confession of sorts, and settle upon him. They entered him, soaking into his soul. He wasn't trying to make me stop talking. He was hanging on my every word, my every hitched gasp, my every touch as I brought myself to the brink of orgasm in front of him.

'You put life inside me,' I said, lifting my hips slightly as I slowed my fingers. If I didn't settle down, I was going to come before he'd paid his penance at all. 'You put life inside of me, and you turned it into death.'

'I'm so sorry,' he whispered, his expression so fucking anguished, so fucking bereft, that it took everything inside myself not to stop and pull him onto me, into me, to sate his sadness and his regret with my body, the same dance we had danced for a decade.

'What do you want?' I breathed, writhing as I continued to slowly finger-fuck myself. 'You want to fuck me? You want to come inside me?'

He nodded, his eyes hooded with lust as he stared, mesmerised, at what I was doing to myself. He took one hand away from my ankle and used it to pull his dick out of his pants, squeezing it until his knuckles turned red.

'Too bad,' I whispered, withdrawing my fingers from my pussy and pressing them into his mouth. He sucked them until it hurt, getting every single drop of me from my skin. 'You want to fuck me? You *earn* it.'

He was panting, hard, on his knees in front of me, and I saw the way he kept glancing at my bare pussy as he stroked his cock in his fist.

'You taste so fucking good,' he murmured around my fingers. 'So fucking good.'

I stopped abruptly, and Dornan's eyes widened, as if I'd broken the spell. *Bullshit*, I thought. I slid my hand into his short hair and pulled, bringing his face right up to mine.

But I didn't kiss him.

'Make me come with your tongue,' I demanded. '*Only* your tongue. You want me to forgive you? You'd better start by making me feel good.'

My voice was suddenly thick with emotion. Why? Why now?

Maybe because, after ten years, I was finally starting to take some goddamn responsibility for my own fate. In the beginning I'd needed Dornan's brutality, I'd needed his domination, but now I needed his submission, his reparation. I needed his desire to soothe me, to beg my forgiveness.

With my hand in his hair, I pushed his head down between my thighs.

His eyes gleamed up at me, full of lust, inexplicably calm. It was as if, by taking charge of the dynamic we shared, he was momentarily relieved.

'I might be yours on paper, but this pussy belongs to me now, you understand?'

CHAPTER TWENTY-TWO

DORNAN

Her dark blue eyes gleamed with conviction, simmered with anger as she stared down at him. In her rage, she was absolutely *stunning*.

'This body is mine,' she whispered to him. 'It was yours, Dornan, and you did what you did, and it's not yours anymore. If you want it back? You earn it. You earn my love. You earn your place inside my cunt. *You earn my fucking mouth around your cock.*'

He nodded, breaking their stare, his eyes sliding down her beautiful tits, her stomach, before coming to rest upon her sweet cunt. He stilled for a moment, breathing in the scent of her.

He licked his lips, pressing the flat of his tongue against her swollen bundle of nerves.

'Fuck!' she exclaimed, her fingers pulling his hair to the point of pain. He didn't care. He liked pain, especially with sex. The two belonged together. Pain and fucking. But, as he licked her he was gentle. She'd suffered too much because of him, felt too much pain, and it was time for him to reel it the fuck in and crawl his way back to her side. She was his now, legally, but she was broken. His bird was broken. And it was up to him to fix her.

'You worship me,' she moaned, as he sucked her clit into his mouth. 'You make me believe in you again. You– Oh!' She ground herself against his mouth desperately. 'You make me remember why I fucking *love* you so much, Dornan. You're the fucking kingpin in of all this– *oh, fuck!* And you just made me your ... *queen.* You just tattooed my status on my skin. It's time to start treating me like a fucking queen.'

And this time, when she came against his tongue, he didn't try to cover her mouth or muffle her noises. There was no reason to silence his queen. No, as she cried out and writhed under his tongue, he revelled in the sweet noise of her unsuppressed joy, her exhilaration, as he sucked in a final breath and squeezed his cock, coming violently against his thigh.

***

The next morning, Viper called him. His LAPD contact had done some digging and found the call logs for Mariana's secret cellphone. The contents of which were very interesting indeed.

She was still sleeping peacefully, out cold, when Dornan took the call in the hallway and then came back into the room. Seemed he and his new wife had some talking to do.

That was, if he didn't kill her first.

CHAPTER TWENTY-THREE

MARIANA

My hand hurt.

The pain had extended beyond my ring finger and my entire hand was just throbbing now. It pounded with the rhythm of my heart, relentless, nauseating. It wasn't physically that painful, per se, but it was knowing it was there, wanting to rip it off with my fingernails but knowing I couldn't. Laser removal was in my future, assuming I survived being the wife of California's most notorious biker and the daughter-in-law of the most lethal drug kingpin of the entire Gulf.

I saw a dirt grave in my future, too.

I'd fallen asleep in my dress, my make-up still caked on. My eyes itched from the clumped mascara, and concealer streaked my pillow. I was beyond caring. Try washing blood out of a pillowcase and then come talk to me about a few smears of liquid make-up.

I sat up in the bed – the large, downy, luxurious bed – and immediately lay down again as the room began to circle me viciously. The vodka. The lack of food. The reminder that Dornan and I were married.

If I'd had anything left in my stomach I would have surely thrown it up. Instead, I curled back into the foetal position and pulled the sheets over my face.

The other side of the bed was empty; I wondered where Dornan was. Reluctantly, I sat up again, scanning the room for him.

He was sitting on the end of the bed, staring at me intently, something in his hand.

'Hello, Mrs Ross,' he said, his voice sticky-sweet with fake enthusiasm, his teeth bared in a large grin that didn't reach his dark eyes. Oh God, what had I done now?

'Morning,' I said, crossing my legs in a yoga pose and arranging the blankets around me like a protective shroud. It had to be a hundred degrees out, the sun blazing a path straight to my eyeballs, but the room was as cold as ice. I rubbed my hands down my arms as goosebumps sprang up on my skin.

'You okay?' I asked Dornan. Something was up. Better to get it over and done with. Rip the bandaid. It was always about making the pain as quick as possible. No point extending our misery.

Dornan dropped the grin, his eyes on mine. He ran his tongue over his teeth and looked at whatever he was holding. I let my eyes follow his, but his big hands were mostly obscuring the object.

'Can I trust you?' he asked me.

I raised my eyebrows. 'What kind of question is that? Can you trust *me*? Can I trust *you*?'

I didn't even see the blow that hit me. Something in his hand, hard and blunt, smashed into the side of my head, just above my left ear, and I went down faster than an old Vegas casino with a wrecking ball and some explosives. That is to say, I flew off the bed and onto the floor, the the carpet cushioning my fall.

'Wrong answer,' Dornan said coldly, standing above me. I rolled onto my back, taking in his expression: serious, distant.

Shit.

I opened my mouth to speak as he held up a cellphone. My cellphone.

The burner cellphone John had given to me.

'You hit me with a fucking cellphone?' I asked, getting up on my elbows as the side of my head throbbed painfully. 'What if I was pregnant, you fucking idiot?'

He kicked me in the stomach for that. I made an oomph sound as he crouched beside me, his hand stroking my hair. 'If you were pregnant,' he mused, 'you drank enough last night to destroy any baby's brain cells. Besides, you just finished your period three days ago. You couldn't be pregnant, unless we made a baby in the apartment before we left yesterday.'

My mouth hung open in shock as he rubbed circles on my stomach with the tip of his finger. 'It could be happening right now,' he said, tracing a path from my pelvis right up to my belly button and jabbing his finger in hard enough to make me wince. 'What do you think?' he asked. 'Would it be my baby, Mariana? Or would it be someone else's? Because if there's even the slightest chance it isn't mine ... I'll stick my hand inside you and rip your fucking womb out.' He made his free hand into the shape of a claw and made a pulling motion in the air.

If I thought I'd known fear before, I didn't. Not until that moment.

I swallowed, incredulous, that image in my mind completely fucking disturbing. 'What is wrong with you?' I exclaimed. 'Seriously, what the fuck is wrong with you? You bring me here and marry me and then *this*?'

I was stunned, but he had the phone. *He had the phone!* He was going to kill me. I would die here, now, in a hotel room in the middle of the fucking desert, and it would be a fitting end to our union.

'I'm going to ask you one more time,' he said, standing and holding a hand out to me.

With great reluctance, outweighed only by self-preservation and the desire not to be kicked again, I accepted. He hauled me to my feet and took me by my arms, backing me into the kitchenette. Brazenly, I reached for a bottle of anything to hit him with, but he was faster. He grabbed my wrist and bent it so hard I thought it would snap.

'Fuck!' I yelled.

He responded by hitting me again with the phone, the plastic smacking into my cheekbone. I gasped for air, my head flying back, my body pinned by his hips.

'Fuck you,' he said. 'You see this?'

He held the phone in front of my eyes and I squinted, trying to focus.

'What?' I half-asked, half-begged. '*What?*'

'Blood,' Dornan said. I saw the dried red blood on the phone and my entire body stilled. A tiny speck of red. It looked innocent enough. Innocuous. Dazed, I felt my cheek for broken skin. My scalp. None. I wasn't bleeding.

I knew it wasn't my blood.

'Whose blood?' I asked. 'Yours?'

He cocked his head to the side, eyes raging like a wildfire burned inside his skull. And it probably did – my psychotic husband. I stumbled over the word. *Husband.* Seven letters, my death sentence.

'How stupid do you think I am?' he said.

I held his gaze. 'Stop. Stop! Just ask me. Just tell me what's going on, because I don't understand!' My voice got louder as I spoke, rising to a feverish pitch by the end of my sentence. I didn't know if I was yelling or begging at that point. All I knew was, he had that hand on me, the one he'd just threatened to disembowel me with, and I couldn't stop shaking, *and he had the phone.*

'Is. This. Your. Phone?'

'Yes!' I screamed.

His eyes lit up like wildfire. Oh God. *OhGodOhGodOhGod.*

His face gave away nothing. I wondered if it would be the last thing I would ever see.

I tried not to struggle as Dornan traced a finger underneath each of my eyes, in the hollow part, the socket, and it took every ounce of self-restraint not to flinch. I was half-convinced he was going to poke my eyes out, but his finger travelled down to my mouth. He pushed it between my lips and I let him, because more than anything, I really did not want him to hit me with that fucking phone again.

Had he found phone records? I deleted John's number every time I called him. Still, a lot had changed in ten years. It was 2008, and you could find almost anything you wanted information-wise if you looked in the right places.

'It's not what you think,' I said around his finger, needing to break the unbearable silence that stretched between us.

'I don't believe you,' Dornan whispered. I couldn't respond, because his finger was halfway down my throat, but I shook my head anyway.

He dropped the phone onto the counter that he had me pinned against and brought his free hand to my throat, squeezing.

Idiot. He had a finger in my mouth. I bit down as hard as I could, and suddenly I was flying through the air again.

'You fucking cunt!' Dornan yelled, as I crashed into the bathroom door.

Dazed, and with blood in my mouth – his, not mine – I scrambled to my knees, crawling away from him.

I wasn't fast enough, and the only escape in this room was the goddamn door anyway. He was between me and that precious exit, so I had nowhere to go.

There was never anywhere to go.

How many times had I repeated that thought to myself lately?

Too many.

Hands found my hair and yanked me up. I decided I was going to shave my head so he couldn't use my hair as a weapon against me anymore. For now, wanting to keep my scalp, I followed his momentum as he tossed me onto the bed.

'This finger is very fucking important,' he said, holding up his bloodied index finger. 'I use it to shoot people. I use it when I ride. I use it when I fuck you.' He leaned down so that his nose was touching mine, his breath hot on my mouth. 'If you've damaged it, I'll cut yours off. I'll cut all of them off.'

'*Don'tbesuchababy,*' I said, my words slurring together. He slapped me across the face, but I barely felt it. Something had dulled in my head when it hit the bathroom door. My thoughts were slow. My pain receptors slower.

A hand wrapped around my throat and squeezed, Dornan's expression resigned as he stared down at me. 'Whose fucking blood is it?'

Tears were streaming out of my eyes of their own accord, an entirely reflexive response. I felt like I was about to die.

'Mine,' I said. 'The blood is mine.'

He shook me. 'You're LYING!'

Jesus, fuck, he was going to kill me.

'I cut myself!' I gasped, fighting for breath, for the ability to speak. 'You know I cut myself. It's my blood. I swear.'

Dornan appeared torn. 'You promised me you didn't do that anymore.'

'I started doing it again,' I lied.

He loosened his fingers a little and I tried to get up, but he wasn't having that. Staring twin bullet holes into my head, he straddled me, one knee on either side of my chest. I tried to push him off, but he was too heavy. Too strong. His knees squeezed my ribcage until I thought my lungs would burst.

'Keep talking,' he ground out. 'Why? Why should I believe you? Why would you start hurting yourself again?'

'I found out my whole family was dead.'

Shock registered on Dornan's face. 'What?'

The truth, now. My eyes filled with tears and spilled over.

'Your father had them killed,' I whispered.

I could barely make out the expression on Dornan's face anymore. My eyes weren't focusing, and I wanted to pass out.

His fingers tightened. *This is it. This is where I die.* Tears leaked from the corners of my eyes as I ached for my son. For John. They'd never even know what had become of me. They'd never know that I didn't want to be married to Dornan, or that I'd fought to get back to them. They'd just never know, and I'd be gone. I wondered, in those moments, my fingernails scratching against Dornan's hands, if he'd burn me or bury me. Would I sink into the earth? Would he bury me in the desert? Would he just leave me here, in this room, for the maid to find when she came to make the beds and restock the minibar?

Please, I mouthed. Dornan was killing me, and he wasn't even watching as I died. I could feel the life ebbing from me as I starved for oxygen, my brain screaming for a single breath of air, my chest locked and shuddering. He seemed momentarily distracted, his fingers loosening a little, and I took the opportunity to twist my head to the side and bite his hand.

He pulled his hands away, giving me an annoyed glance and a smack on the cheek, but nothing compared to what he'd been doing earlier.

I choked and gasped for air, prompting Dornan to reach for a bottle of Evian that sat on the bedside table, courtesy of the hotel. A five-dollar bottle of water, but I would have paid a million dollars for it. He unscrewed it and handed it to me, watching silently as I chugged it down. I drank it too fast and I coughed, getting water down the front of my dress in the process.

'You done trying to kill me?' I asked.

Dornan got off me.

I couldn't stop coughing. My throat was on fire.

'What do you need?' Dornan asked, as if some water or some fucking food could fix the fact that he'd beaten me ten shades of black and blue and then almost strangled me to death.

'Who did you think I'd be calling?' I asked him. I put on my best wounded face, which wasn't a stretch. 'Because I know you wouldn't react like that if you thought I was calling my family in Colombia.'

He stared at the wall. 'I don't know,' he said. 'I just … you get further away from me, every day. Every single day. You used to melt when I touched you. Now you recoil like I'm a monster.'

Apt words from the man himself. He understood what he was, even then.

'You know why I recoil,' I said, my voice throaty and rough. I coughed, drank some more water. 'I don't trust you.'

Dornan growled. 'I've done everything for you! Everything, you understand?'

I nodded. 'Yeah. Still doesn't change what you did to me. To our baby. To Stephanie. To your *son*.'

'That's it?' he said. 'That's why you're acting like this?'

'*That's it?*' I repeated, dumbfounded. 'Yeah. How many more innocent lives do you snuff out because what they do is inconvenient to you?'

He didn't respond.

'Don't you want to know how he killed them?' I whispered. 'How your father wiped out my entire family?'

He levelled his glassy eyes at me, and I took that as an invitation to continue.

'Your father had his men go to Villanueva and burn their house to the ground. But first they tied them up, so they burned too.'

'Who told you that?' Dornan asked. He seemed shocked. Like his father had never told him.

'It doesn't matter who told me,' I said. 'All that matters is that it's true. Your father nullified his bargain with me when he killed my family. Me in exchange for their lives, that was the deal. And he killed them anyway.'

'I'm sorry,' he said.

He opened his mouth to say something else but I cut him off with a sharp flick of my hand. 'I can't, okay? I just ... can't.'

Dornan didn't argue. He went to my suitcase at the end of the bed and unzipped it, my skin crawling as I remembered the baby suitcase. I shook my head to try and get rid of the memory, my neck screaming in protest. I watched as Dornan lifted a grey knee-length dress and a blue scarf from the bag, bringing them over to me.

Dornan basically dressed me in the new dress, as if I were a child. He sat beside me and watched silently as I applied heavy foundation to my bruised neck before working on my face. I was red and blue from my wrists to my head, and although I tried my best, when I was done I still looked like shit. I needed a shower and about three weeks at home, where nobody could see me.

John. What was he going to say when he saw this?

'You should have told me about your family,' Dornan said, shame burning in his eyes.

I shook my head, resisting the overwhelming urge to roll my eyes. 'How long are we staying in Vegas?' I asked him.

He shrugged, standing up so that he was in front of me. 'How long do you *want* to stay?'

Oh, yeah, almost get killed, and now I get to decide how long we were staying.

Suddenly I felt like a little girl. Not a happy one. I felt powerless. Scared. Exhausted. 'I want a shower and some food and I want to go home,' I whispered. 'Can we please just go home?'

Dornan stared down at me for a long moment before nodding. 'Yeah,' he said, and I wondered what was going through his head at that moment. The phone was seemingly forgotten, the urge to murder me on hiatus for the time being. He looked remorseful. I didn't care.

He picked up the room service menu and handed it to me. 'Whatever you want,' he said.

How generous of you, I wanted to snap, but I bit my tongue, taking the menu silently. 'I think I'll shower first,' I said, putting the menu to the side and sliding off the bed, the room spinning as I straightened on my feet. Dornan put his hands out to steady me, and I looked at them like they were cockroaches on me. I pushed him off, making my way into the bathroom with him hot on my heels. Guess he didn't want me to lock myself in here again.

Without speaking – I was still coughing – I turned around, motioning to the zipper in the back of my dress. The room spun around me like a vortex of patterned tile and dark green wallpaper. And him.

Dornan unzipped me and I let the stupid dress fall to the floor, vowing to burn the fucking thing as soon as we were back home. I didn't want any lasting reminders of this trip. I'd have to find a way to lose the ring, too. Maybe I'd cut my finger off in a 'freak' accident in the kitchen. I could live just fine with nine fingers, right?

I wrapped my arms around myself and waited, staring at the wall, as Dornan turned on the shower and adjusted the temperature. He held out a hand to help me in, but I side-stepped it, practically hugging the tiled wall as I inched under the hot water. Avoiding any eye contact, I shuffled to the far corner of the shower, as far away from him as I could get, and slid down the wall, sitting underneath the high-pressure shower head with my knees drawn up to my chest. I covered my face with my hands, parting my fingers slowly so I knew where Dornan was. Because, more than the fact that I couldn't trust him, I could also no longer even try to predict what he was about to do next.

I peered at him through a river of mascara and my webbed fingers and saw his erection clearly bulging from his jeans. I wondered how it could be that a man could find such erotic thoughts while looking at the woman he'd almost just killed, as she sat naked in the bottom of a shower and wept.

CHAPTER TWENTY-FOUR

MARIANA

I didn't even know what time it was. I'd showered, wrapped myself in a fluffy robe, and come back out to the bed, where I now sat. My stomach was empty and growling for food.

'I'll order us some food,' Dornan said. To go from such violence to total normality in such a short span of time was frightening, but a relief all the same. I'd almost died just now by Dornan's hand – literally, his hand around my throat, cutting off my oxygen – and it was time to form some kind of escape plan.

An immediate one.

First, though, I had to survive the here and now. My stomach grumbled insistently, so loud that Dornan heard it. 'You want eggs?' he asked. What a fucking gentleman, this guy. A whirlwind (forced) wedding in Vegas, almost murdering me, and now he was offering to get me eggs.

'I'll be fine,' I said, waving my hand dismissively. 'You go shower. I'll order for us. What do you want?'

'Surprise me,' he said, and I cringed. Surprises were bad. I didn't ever want another surprise in my life again.

I waited until the shower was running and grabbed the room service menu. I did briefly contemplate the idea of running while Dornan showered, but it would've been for nothing. I had no money, no ID, I was an illegal immigrant, and I didn't know Vegas. I could call John, sure, once I found a pay phone somewhere, but he'd get caught. We both would. The grip of the cartel was just too powerful.

I decided to stay in the room and avoid having to think about any of this for at least another twenty-four hours. I settled on what I wanted to order – eggs and bacon for me, eggs and steak for Dornan – and was about to pick up the phone when the fucking thing rang so loudly, I almost fell on the floor. I answered the phone as Dornan poked his head out of the bathroom door, a towel around his waist and dripping water everywhere.

'Who is it?' he asked.

'It's room service,' a familiar male voice on the other end said.

'It's room service,' I parroted back to Dornan. Oh, shit. I knew that voice. Velvet-smooth and cunning. Somebody who was looking for Murphy.

'Act normally,' said FBI Agent Lindsay Price. 'You're going to meet me downstairs in one hour, do you understand? Say yes so Dornan hears.'

'Yes,' I replied, well aware that Dornan was still watching intently.

'You're going to come unarmed. Say "scrambled eggs".'

This was ridiculous. I didn't want to meet Lindsay downstairs. He was probably here to fucking arrest me. I couldn't leave Los Angeles with John and the kids if I was being arrested. *I couldn't get back to my son if I was being arrested.*

'No, that's wrong,' I said. 'That's not what I said.'

I rolled my eyes at Dornan and said something into the phone in Spanish. 'This guy's English is terrible,' I whispered, my hand over the receiver. 'Go finish your shower.'

'Don't forget coffee,' Dornan called, closing the bathroom door. I heard the shower start up again and returned my attention to the phone. 'What the hell are you doing?' I hissed. 'Are you trying to get me killed?'

'I was about three seconds from busting into your room this morning. How's your neck?'

I felt like someone had knocked the wind out of me. Again.

'You're listening to us?' I whispered.

'Mostly watching,' Lindsay replied.

Oh, for the love of all that is holy. Cameras!? A scarlet blush crept up my body and settled in my cheeks as I thought about what I'd been doing the night before. Putting on a porn show for an audience of one.

I hadn't realised there was an audience of more than one. I felt like I'd been punched in the face. I mean, I had basically been punched in the face by Dornan – but this felt even worse than that.

'Your boyfriend's pretty violent. Seems like even he thinks you've got something to do with Agent Murphy disappearing into thin air.'

Boyfriend. He hadn't said husband. So obviously they hadn't been watching everything. He hadn't picked up on the fact that Ms Rodriguez was now a reluctant Mrs, complete

215

with a black and red wedding band tattoo that had started to scab over. How disgustingly delightful.

'Watching *how*?' I exclaimed, looking around the room.

'The FBI is blessed with a generous technology budget. Trust me. We got plenty of angles.' He seemed to hesitate for a moment. 'Are you okay?'

'I'm not okay,' I seethed, watching the bathroom door intently. 'Isn't that against the law? Filming someone without their permission?'

'It's called a warrant,' Lindsay said.

A warrant? *Fuck me.* I was ready to hang up, but something about his tone, and the mention of a motherfucking warrant, kept the phone glued to my ear.

'He almost killed you, you know that, right?'

I wanted to throw the phone out of the window. 'I guess I'm just lucky the FBI were watching out for me,' I replied, my words dripping with sarcasm. 'Thank you.'

Lindsay sighed. 'We were in the hallway. Another few seconds and we would have been busting your door down.'

I didn't respond. I could barely hear above the screaming in my head.

'I'm on your side,' he added. I snorted. 'Mariana, I know how violent Dornan is. I understand the danger you're in. I can help you. I might be the only one who can help you at this point. Let me help you.'

The words I'd uttered to John came back to haunt me: *I don't need a man to save me.* Maybe I was wrong. Maybe I did.

'Here's what's going to happen,' Lindsay said, shifting gears. 'I'm going to send two cups of coffee up with your food.

One will be drugged for your dear boyfriend. He needs to take a nap so we can talk. The drugs will last at least an hour, but I only need five minutes.'

'What if I don't want to talk?' I asked. 'What if I'd rather you just went away?'

I heard him shuffling papers. 'You don't have to talk,' he said. 'But I'd strongly suggest that you at least give me five minutes of your time, Ms Rodriguez. Do you really think you'll be able to make it back to your son and protect him without the FBI's help?'

'Okay,' I said, cutting him off before he could make any more mention of my *son*. 'But,' I added, switching the receiver from my left ear to my right, 'Dornan's a big guy – he needs a horse tranquilliser to knock him down. A Percocet isn't going to cut it.'

'I'll keep that in mind,' he replied. 'The black coffee's for him. Don't drink it. We want him asleep, not you dead.'

'Whatever,' I snapped, my ears buzzing, the line already dead.

Somehow the FBI had tracked us to Vegas. Shit. Shit. SHIT!

***

I thought I'd throw up waiting for the knock on the door and for 'room service' to appear. When a guy in his mid-thirties appeared at the door, wearing an ill-fitting hotel uniform and wheeling a tray bursting with breakfast foods, I glared at him so intently I'm surprised he didn't catch on fire from my death rays. Sure enough, two cups of coffee sat in the middle of the tray, steam billowing from them. That right there was the biggest giveaway. I'd never had room service coffee delivered at any temperature but lukewarm. They were obviously camped out in a room nearby, watching us and preparing poisoned coffee to send to our room.

Fuckers.

I debated telling Dornan about Lindsay's call and the spiked coffee, but I decided against it, sipping at my latte as I watched Dornan down his black coffee in about three gulps.

The coffee worked quickly. I'd already anticipated Dornan's suspicion at suddenly feeling woozy and drugged, so I figured I'd lessen it a little if possible. While he drank his coffee I gave him the quickest blowjob in the history of blowjobs, hating myself the entire time, and now armed with the knowledge that Lindsay could see everything I was doing. *Great.* As I swallowed, Dornan's hand on my head, I made a mental note to thank Lindsay for saving my life when I was being choked out.

Seriously. They couldn't have knocked and pretended to be cleaners or something?

Instead, they'd watched as I fought for my life. More embarrassingly, they'd watched while I had, quote, 'fucked myself', and given Dornan a peep show to rival all others. I'd made myself come in front of him, and probably half of Lindsay's unit.

I started to panic as I contemplated where else they might've had cameras. In my apartment, the place where I'd killed Murphy? That didn't make sense, though. If they'd had cameras hidden in my apartment, I'd already be sitting in a cell, serving my life sentence without parole.

That was the punishment for killing a federal officer of the law, last time I checked.

Add money laundering, drug running and (unknowingly) balancing the books for an entire human trafficking operation for the better part of ten years, and it was easy to watch the consecutive life sentences stack on top of one another like Tetris bricks.

Dornan was snoring soon after he finished his coffee and I'd finished him. He didn't even make it to the bed, sprawled out on the couch in the sitting area. I prodded him a couple of times, then, relatively comfortable with the fact that he was deep asleep, I got dressed, brushed my teeth, grabbed my purse and headed downstairs.

A black Escalade was parked at the front entrance to the Wynn, the door already open for me. I picked the guy holding the door straight away – black suit, short hair, one of those little earpieces in his ear with a cord that ran down under his suit jacket. He held out a hand to help me step up into the SUV, but I ignored it, preferring to use the handle inside the doorframe to pull myself up and onto the black leather seat that flanked the rear of the interior. I winced as the door closed and the central locking clicked with a sound of permanence.

FBI Agent Lindsay Price sat beside me in the dim cabin, the dark tint on the windows saving us from the worst of the unrelenting Nevada sun. He was still the same as I remembered – green eyes and dark hair cut close to his skull, military style – but he looked a little rougher around the edges than the first time we'd met. He looked like he'd missed a day of the impeccable shaving routine he obviously adhered to. His chin bore a five o'clock shadow and his eyes were lined with fatigue, despite it being only nine in the morning.

'Your bag, please?' Lindsay asked.

'Well hello to you, too.' I clutched my bag tightly, glaring at him.

Lindsay raised his eyebrows. 'Look,' he sighed. 'We can do this the hard way. I can take out my gun,' he patted his hip holster, 'and I can threaten you, maybe throw some cuffs on you. But I don't want to. I'm not going to.'

I didn't say anything.

'Just give me the bag,' he said, holding out his hand. 'Please.'

I don't know what it was. Maybe it was the fact that I was so tired. Worn out, frayed. It seemed I'd momentarily lost the ability to resist. Without breaking eye contact, I placed the bag on the seat between us and he scooped it up, rummaging around until he found my gun and pulled it out.

'That's mine,' I said, reaching for it.

Lindsay opened the chamber, presumably to check for bullets. 'A woman carrying an unloaded gun, and there are no bullets in her bag. Did your boyfriend take them?'

I didn't bother correcting the term boyfriend to husband. He'd find out soon enough, no doubt.

'What, were you filming us on the car trip, too?' I asked.

'Educated guess,' Lindsay shrugged.

'How'd you know I'd bring a gun?' I asked.

He smiled. Not in an arrogant, cocky way. Just a smile. 'Because I told you not to.'

'You think you know everything about me?' I asked.

'Twelve years in the FBI profiling unit, there's a good chance I know more about you than you know about yourself.'

'Oh yeah?'

'Yeah. I know you're planning something. I know the only thing stopping you from running is one John Portland.'

I sat back, stunned. I don't know why I was stunned. I mean, if they'd been watching me, then they'd probably know about John.

'I know you're still hoping you can get out of this without anyone getting hurt,' Lindsay added, his voice softening.

'And let me guess,' I said evenly. 'You're here to tell me I can't. Right?'

'I'm here to implore you to do the right thing.' He patted the gun on his lap – *my* fucking gun, the one I'd used to kill Murphy and Allie.

Panic began to rise in my throat. 'Why do you need my gun?' I asked.

'Insurance.' He paused for effect. *Insurance for what?* 'That's all. Go see your little boyfriend. Stay out of trouble.'

With great irritation, I flashed him the skull tattoo on my ring finger. 'You mean my husband.'

Lindsay snatched up my hand and studied the tattoo. 'What is this? You guys got matching promise rings?'

I rolled my eyes, holding up my right hand, where my actual wedding band sat. 'I can't wear it until the tattoo heals. Apparently gold just doesn't seal the deal like ink these days.'

Lindsay's mouth practically hit the floor of the SUV. 'You're legally married?'

'Yeah,' I replied. 'Dornan finally decided that he wanted to marry me. I found out when I got to the altar. Aren't I lucky?'

His expression was grave. 'You don't understand what this means for you and me.'

'Oh come on, Agent Price,' I said, pursing my lips mockingly. 'You can't be jealous, surely.'

His green eyes were ablaze. 'You do know why he did this, don't you?'

I shrugged. 'Entrapment. Control. Paranoia. Or maybe he just really, really loves me.'

Lindsay wet his lips with his tongue, at the same time shaking his head. 'He married you so you wouldn't have to testify against him. The FBI is building a case against his father's cartel. A case that very much hinges on your testimony against these men, Ms Rodriguez. Sorry, Mrs *Ross*.'

I felt my stomach sinking. 'Who says I was going to testify?'

'Your kid,' Lindsay said pointedly.

He had me, and we both knew it. I'd do anything to protect Luis. I already had, indirectly, when I'd killed Murphy and Allie.

Speaking of.

'I need to deliver Agent Murphy's subpoena,' Lindsay said quietly. 'Any idea where he might be?'

I narrowed my eyes. 'No.' *Not unless you count the fact that little pieces of him were probably left over in that crematorium I'd visited again the other day.*

Nobody spoke for a long, uncomfortable moment. I watched as cars pulled up to the front entrance of the Wynn and people got out. Regular people, excited to gamble and take in a show and eat way too much at the seafood buffet. People who were oblivious to the seedy underbelly of the world, their masks still firmly over their eyes as reality painted a very different picture.

'I haven't had a lot of sleep lately,' Lindsay said, changing tack. 'Do you know why?'

I feigned boredom. 'No, but I bet you're going to tell me anyway.'

222

'I've been investigating a murder.' *Great.* 'A young woman.' *Awesome.* 'A fellow federal officer, actually.'

Fuck.

My heart skipped inside my chest. The dominos. They kept falling.

No, the fucking sky was falling.

'She was a DEA agent,' Lindsay said, his eyes drilling into me so intensely I itched. 'Somebody shot her.'

No shit. I wanted to look away, but to look away would be admitting guilt.

'And?' I challenged. I tried to recall whether looking up or looking down signalled a lie. In the end, I couldn't remember at all, so I kept my gaze glued to Lindsay's eyes.

'I think you killed her,' Lindsay said softly.

There it was. The real reason he wanted to see me so desperately. My head swam – drowned – in what might happen next. I saw walls and prison bars, and a cell door slamming shut in my face.

'Fuck you.'

Lindsay didn't answer.

'What do you need from me?' I asked slowly, a crushing feeling of defeat pressing down on me.

'I need to know what they did to you,' Lindsay said. 'And what they made you do for them.'

'How? When?'

'Soon. Very soon.'

I swallowed thickly. 'How am I supposed to trust you?' I asked. 'What if you're just like everybody else?' And suddenly I wanted to cry. Because he didn't seem like everybody else. Lindsay Price seemed like a real stand-up guy. Maybe he

wasn't. He could have been an axe murderer, for all I knew.
Could have been working for Emilio.

'I'm not like the men you're used to,' Lindsay said. He put
his hand on my arm in a comforting gesture, and surprisingly,
I didn't shrug it off. It was warm.

'What are you like, then?' I whispered. My eyes burned
with unshed tears as a lump grew in my throat.

'I believe in justice,' he said, handing me the gun back. 'But I
also believe in survival. I believe that sometimes, the law doesn't
understand what a person can endure before they break.'

I stared at the gun in my hands in disbelief. 'I thought–'

'A gesture of goodwill,' he interrupted. 'That gun is my only
piece of evidence linking you to Alexandra Baxter's murder. I
know you killed her, Mariana. I don't need to take your gun to
know that. I only need to take your gun to *prove* that.'

'If Emilio finds out I've spoken to you, he'll kill me,' I said,
my hands shaking as they cupped the gun.

Lindsay nodded. 'Don't tell anyone. Don't write it down,
don't even think about our conversation until the next time we
meet. Understood?'

I nodded.

'I know what they did to your family,' he added. 'For what
it's worth ... I'm sorry.'

In the edges of my mind, I saw them screaming as they
burned. I didn't want to see that. I looked out of my window.
'How long does that sedative last?' I asked him, changing the
subject as I stared at the gold-tinted stack of glass that made up
the Wynn.

Lindsay tapped a button in his armrest and a screen unfolded
from the ceiling. He aimed a small remote and it flashed to life,

a black and white image of a hotel room becoming visible. He pointed to the middle of the screen. 'Long enough.'

I peered closer, picking Dornan's still frame on the couch in the centre of the suite. I glanced at Lindsay as something unsettling occurred to me. 'What happens next?' I asked quietly.

'That depends,' Lindsay replied. 'The situation isn't as clear-cut as it was. You're now not compelled to testify. You'll have to choose. We can't force you to give evidence against your husband.' He said the word 'husband' like he was talking about having to wipe dog shit off his shoe. I got the feeling he really didn't like Dornan.

Neither did I, anymore, so we had that in common.

'No shit,' I replied. 'Could've gotten here a day earlier, saved me the pain.' I flashed my tattooed finger at him.

'I think you like the pain,' Lindsay murmured, his tone almost sad. 'I think you don't remember how to survive without pain. You're always either running at it, or away from it, but what you can't see is that you're going to drown in it. Either that, or your husband will kill you. At this rate, I'd put my money on him.'

Ouch.

Neither of us said anything for a moment. I glanced at the screen in front of us again. Dornan hadn't moved. Maybe he was dead. That would solve some of my problems.

'I'm tired of the pain,' I answered finally. 'I don't want it anymore.'

I was only too aware that Dornan would stir if I was gone much longer.

'You testify against Emilio, against Dornan, and the rest of his club, and you get immunity. You get your son back.'

Fuck him for using my son as blackmail material. 'I'm not saying one word for you unless you can guarantee John's safety. We both get immunity.'

Lindsay lifted his eyebrows. 'No can do. He goes down with his club.'

'I love him,' I said quietly. 'I can't let him go down with them.'

'You loved Dornan once, too. And see how that turned out?'

I closed my eyes and tried not to have a total meltdown. I had to agree to whatever Lindsay was saying or he'd never let me out of his sight again. I couldn't very well slip away into the night if I was being tracked by the FBI.

'You say you're tired of the pain,' Lindsay added. 'Let me help you. Let me take it away. All you have to do is say yes.'

I rested my forehead on the back of the seat in front of me. Everything, it seemed, hinged on the next thing that came out of my mouth. Three letters or two.

'Yes,' I lied. Without Lindsay agreeing to give John immunity, I wasn't testifying. I was running. We were running. I just had to get back to John and formulate a get the fuck out of town plan. I sucked in a breath as a wave of dizziness slammed into me. I had to get out of the car before I passed out. I stuffed the gun back into my bag, searching for the door handle. I heard a click as the doors unlocked and I opened the door, gulping in the hot Nevada air as the same dude on the outside of the car held out a hand to help me down.

I slid out of the SUV, turning back to face him as my feet hit the ground. The last image I had of Lindsay Price was his serious expression as he watched me silently. He almost seemed … relieved.

I slammed the door so hard, I swear the car moved. My wrist throbbed from the sudden exertion, and I rushed back into the hotel lobby, parting a sea of tourists with the force of my heels against the polished floor.

Soon. Something was going to happen soon.

How was I going to tell John?

We had to leave Vegas *now*.

I rode the lift back to the hotel suite with one hand against the mirrored wall. I was tired.

I was so fucking tired of this life.

CHAPTER TWENTY-FIVE

JOHN

Two days.

Two whole days and he hadn't been able to contact Mariana. Something was amiss, but he had no fucking idea what it was or how to find out.

Oh, and they were driving to San fucking Diego, on Emilio's orders. Caroline, who for once was straight and sober, was driving down with Juliette, for some event Emilio had insisted the entire club attend. And John was riding his motorcycle with the rest of the Gypsy Brothers, because presidential duties demanded he lead the pack. For the moment, at least. After the shit that went down at the strip club with Dornan, he was fairly sure he wouldn't be presiding over his club much longer. An invested man would have cared. A man who wanted to pull the trigger and run had no time to care about such things.

John had been at home when he'd received a call about an urgent club meet. 'Stay away from that boy, you hear me?' he had said to his daughter, as he grabbed his leather jacket and the keys to his motorcycle.

Juliette rolled her eyes at him, barely looking away from the television. 'Daddy, I don't even like him. I just feel sorry for him.' Stretching her long legs out on the sofa, she finally turned her gaze to John. Her expression grew troubled. 'His brothers are so horrible. They're always hurting him.'

John shrugged. 'Boys can be rough, baby. Especially those boys.' He thought of Dornan's sons, pack of wildlings that they were. They'd never had a sister to soften them, to teach them that sometimes you had to be gentle. They were loud and brash and they communicated with their fists. Dornan's oldest sons were in their twenties now, patch-wearing Gypsy Brothers with little kids of their own, and they were still animals.

'Why did Uncle Dornan do that to Jase's mom?' Juliette asked quietly. 'He's part of our family. He's always been good, Dad.'

John rubbed his hand across his stubbled chin, contemplating how to answer that question. His daughter was his only child, his world, and how was he supposed to explain to her what his best friend had done to his own son? How was he supposed to explain to his teenage daughter that dear Uncle Dornan had murdered his son's mother in cold blood and left her in a bathtub full of blood for him to find?

He couldn't. He refused to put that mental image inside Juliette's precious mind. He prayed that the young boy had been vague on the details of the visceral horror he had endured upon seeing his slain mother.

John sat on the arm of the sofa, wondering what the fuck he could say. He bit the inside of his cheek, the memory of Stephanie's bloody corpse at the forefront of his mind.

'It's not for you to worry about,' he said. 'I can't talk about it anymore.'

Juliette's face fell. 'Okay,' she said, looking back to the TV. It was clear she was hurt, but she didn't say anything. She was a good girl. Always had been. Sometimes too good.

'Sweetie,' John said, cursing the Gypsy Brothers' existence as he reached out a hand to his daughter. She looked at it like it was a piece of shit and pulled away, out of his reach.

'Did you help him kill her?' Juliette asked suddenly. There it was. Her attitude. He was almost relieved to hear it. It was better than her fear.

'No,' he replied. 'I didn't help him kill her. I would never hurt a woman. A mother.'

'But you do hurt people. Don't you?' She looked at his messed-up knuckles, and John found himself shoving his hands in his pockets, ashamed.

'Your Uncle Dornan was out of line,' John said tightly.

She blinked her big green eyes up at him. 'It was because Dornan found them, wasn't it? Jason said he knew–'

John's expression must have changed, because she stopped mid-sentence. 'Never mind,' Juliette said, looking at the floor.

'You can tell me, Julie,' John said. He felt sweat gather on the back of his neck. Too many secrets. Too many lies. *Don't shut down on me now, Julie.*

'Jason said he knew you before,' she said. 'That you sent them money. Is that why we never have any money?'

John looked around the cramped living room, acutely aware of how well Caroline could hear things, even when she was high. 'Where's your mother?'

Juliette shrugged. John looked around again, feeling deeply unsettled. 'We can talk about this later,' he said, taking a twenty out of his beat-up wallet and passing it to Juliette. 'Order pizza if you get hungry. And don't tell anyone about what you and Jason discussed, okay?' He lowered his voice to a barely audible level. 'If your mother hears talk about sending money off, she will lose her goddamn mind. Understand?'

She nodded.

'Don't go to his house,' John added. They both knew who he was referring to.

Juliette frowned. 'Don't tell me I can't see him, Dad,' she said. 'If I don't go see him, he's all alone.'

He could hardly argue with that. Instead, he kissed the top of her head before shrugging into his leather jacket. The thing seemed to get heavier with time, and it was true, the burden of who he was and who he had to be was a weight he bore alone, a weight he couldn't bear to hold for another moment but which stayed with him, unrelenting, pressing down on his shoulders with every step he took. He glimpsed himself in the hallway mirror on his way out. He looked worn out, used up. He looked like somebody who should've gotten out of this game a long time ago.

Before he could go anywhere, though, he got the phone call from Viper. Club business in San Diego. Dornan had demanded John's presence immediately. And Caroline's. And *Juliette's*.

Not just club business, though. A celebration. Seemed the woman he would have laid down his life for, the woman he loved more than anything, had been unreachable for two days because she was busy marrying Dornan.

CHAPTER TWENTY-SIX

MARIANA

Dornan's father lived on a compound that belonged in a Hollywood movie. It was ridiculous: a massive parcel of land, the main part of which was surrounded by a six-foot solid brick fence. A fence topped with razor wire and broken glass. Basically, unless Emilio wanted you to enter or leave, you were fucked.

Which was why it seemed such an odd place to hold a party. Yeah, you could jazz the place up, get out some tables and break out the crystal wine glasses, but at the end of the day the place resembled a prison more than the palatial homestead it was obviously trying to convey. Perhaps I was just biased; I'd started my days as a captive in this very place, locked underground in a tiny cell, stripped and humiliated and prepared for an auction where Emilio had planned to sell me as a slave.

Dornan had been the only reason I hadn't ended up living in a dog cage at the end of some psychopath's bed, naked and wearing a chain around my neck. Maybe. Probably.

But now I was one of the *familia*, welcomed with open arms. It was surreal, like a nightmare that you can't quite wake up from but that you know is about to give you a heart attack if you stay in it for a moment longer.

After Dornan had finally woken from his drugged slumber around noon, we left Vegas. We'd stopped off in LA briefly on our way back, for showers, extra clothes and Dornan's motorcycle. I'd voted to stay in the limo, but Dornan rejected that. He hadn't told me anything about where we'd be going on the motorcycle, other than that we were celebrating our quickie nuptials with his family. Something I was just thrilled about. He also hadn't seemed suspicious about the way he'd passed out for several hours after drinking the drugged coffee Lindsay had sent up to our hotel room, which was a small mercy.

At Emilio's compound, four hours later, I had to fight to keep my jaw off the pavement as I surveyed no less than fifty Harley-Davidson motorcycles parked up inside the compound, flanking the long driveway that culminated in a large circle in front of the main house. There were dozens of cars too. I spied John's, and wondered where he was. How he'd been told about what had happened in Vegas, and by who.

If he thought I'd betrayed him.

A deep sorrow spread through me. My finger was still throbbing. How had it come to this? Marrying a man by force, letting him flaunt our union in front of everyone he knew? In front of the man I actually loved? Lying to everyone, conducting secret meetings with the FBI after allowing them to drug said husband ... Things were spiralling completely out of control.

And in the middle of the raging storm was the image of my son. He was waiting for me. He was safe, but for how long?

I pushed him out of my mind as Dornan pulled me from his motorcycle, placed his hand into the small of my back and propelled me along the path that led to the front door of Emilio's mansion. It wouldn't do me any good, thinking about Luis when I was about to enter the lion's den. I needed strength, not weakness.

I needed cunning, not despair.

'Are you ready?' Dornan asked me, and I plastered on my fake smile. I let the mask fall into place and steeled myself for the biggest act of my life. The lie. *I love you.* When really, I wanted to burn this place to the ground with Dornan and his father inside. Lindsay's words played on repeat in my head, a soothing chant, a reassurance that this was all going to be blown up *soon*.

'I'm ready,' I murmured, leaning into him.

He liked that. It seemed to make him proud as he looked me up and down, from my throbbing finger marked with his brand, to my eyes, covered expertly with layers of heavy make-up to hide the marks. The scarf around my neck, to conceal the bruises he'd raged upon my skin. I was beaten and broken, but in that moment, all I felt was impatience. I wasn't afraid. I was just waiting. The FBI was coming for us. Lindsay Price was going to make sure Emilio and Dornan were punished for their sins.

I just had to get to John and let him know what had transpired before he was punished, too.

***

It was a lavish party, to say the least. Every Gypsy Brother seemed to be in attendance, as well as at least half of the children fathered by the club members. I caught John's eye as Dornan and I walked into the room to applause and cheers, but he looked away. It didn't matter; what could I communicate to him in a crowd of Gypsy Brothers and cartel members who would murder us if they knew the truth? I had to find a way to get to him. But I had to be patient. Get Dornan hammered, break away and hope John came looking for me. I knew he'd be dying to get me alone, if only to demand an explanation as to why the fuck Dornan and I were now married.

The minutes dragged on. It was almost like an out-of-body experience – I was there, but I wasn't. Somebody had made a wedding cake, but instead of a bride and groom on top, there were two tacky motorcycle helmets. I tried not to throw up in my mouth when I saw that. I spoke to so many people I'd never even met, and it was strange, going from being the girl hidden away and not talked about, to the girl Dornan suddenly wanted to parade around like a prized head of cattle. He kept worrying, too. Kept taking me aside and touching my neck and asking if I was all right, until I snapped at him and told him to relax and quit reminding me of what he'd done. He largely ignored me after that, which was a blessed relief.

John, I screamed inside my head. *I need you. Where are you?* I had to warn him before Lindsay and the FBI moved in, and closed off our only hope of getting out of this alive.

CHAPTER TWENTY-SEVEN

DORNAN

Dornan left Mariana with Jase and Juliette and approached John. He'd been planning this moment since John's fist had connected with his face a few nights earlier. When he'd dared to question Dornan in front of their club. You didn't question a brother. Ever.

John needed to be displaced.

'Congratulations,' John said, looking anything but congratulatory.

Dornan could empathise. He'd just gotten rid of his own ball-and-chain in the form of divorcing Celia, and John was still stuck with that whore Caroline, who was currently harassing a poor young waitress for more champagne.

'Thanks, Johnny Boy,' Dornan said, slapping John on the arm. He hadn't used that name for his best friend in a long time. He didn't pause before he delivered his next line.

'Boys are waiting in the garage,' he said. 'We're voting. Now.'

John's eyes seemed to cloud over momentarily when he heard the words. *We're voting.* John didn't ask what they were voting on. Something told Dornan he already knew.

John quickly regained his composure, passing Dornan as he made his way to the large garage at the other end of the house. Dornan followed, watching the large, red and black Gypsy Brothers patch that sat in the middle of John's back. Everyone else had black and white patches. Only the president got red.

They'd have to get someone to unravel all that thread. Dornan might be taking the patch, but he'd never take the jacket off a brother's back.

CHAPTER TWENTY-EIGHT

JOHN

The vote for prez went in Dornan's favour. Overwhelmingly.

John understood. It was like a chain reaction. He stared at the faces of his brothers in arms as they sat around a makeshift table and cast their votes for the Gypsy Brothers presidency, men he would have laid down his life for – many that he actually had risked his life to protect. Yet, one by one, they voted against him. They were afraid, John realised, about halfway through the proceedings. Not Dornan's sons, of course – the board was half made up of people somehow related to Dornan by marriage or blood, so it wasn't surprising that his coup was so successful.

What was surprising was that John didn't care. He just couldn't muster a single fuck about what was happening. No, instead a nervous buzz began in the pit of his stomach and spread through his body. At first he didn't understand what it was, and then he could have laughed when he figured it out.

He was excited. He was thrilled. He was getting out.

Then he remembered that Dornan and Mariana were married, and his brief elation was tempered by rage.

John sat back and watched as Dornan was sworn in as president. That buzz became an angry scream in his ears, as he imagined Mariana having to say the words 'I do' to this motherfucker. That was the sole reason for his violent need to kill Dornan in that moment. If it were just a matter of being usurped by the Gypsy Brothers, he would have gotten up on the table and done the fucking moonwalk.

After they voted Dornan in, it was time to decide on a new VP. Not surprisingly, almost half the men voted for John. Perhaps that was their way of trying to make amends for essentially betraying their president by overthrowing him and installing a madman as leader. But despite the votes, one person got more – Dornan's oldest son Chad, who was possibly the least intelligent person John had ever encountered. Jacked up on a daily cocktail of roids and speed, Chad was a surprising choice.

It just showed how far things had gone.

It was only when Dornan was passing his VP patch to Chad that John realised he needed to give his patches to Dornan. He'd lived in this jacket for years, ever since the last one had been shredded by knife slashes when he'd been in a fight with a rival cartel member. The patches were originals, having survived the past several decades unmarred. Stained with engine oil and probably blood, but always with him.

John slid off his jacket, realising for the first time how heavy the thick leather was. The thing weighed a ton. No wonder his shoulders always felt like they bore the weight of the world on them. Was this how it felt to be free? To be a normal person?

Just a thin shirt on your back, no traces of a club patch that acted as a homing beacon for violence?

John turned the jacket over, but before he started to tug at the thread holding the club insignia to the beat-up leather, he stopped. He held the jacket out to Dornan, who didn't move.

'I'm not taking your jacket, John,' he said, and for a moment John could have sworn he saw shame flicker in Dornan's eyes.

Undeterred, John dropped the jacket onto the table in front of Dornan. 'I want you to have it,' he said, stepping back. 'I'll get a new one.' *I'll trade you my fucking jacket for your wife.*

Dornan regarded him gravely. 'We gonna have trouble, brother?'

John smiled, reaching out and slapping Dornan on the shoulder. 'No trouble, brother. My loyalty is to the club, whether I'm president or not.'

An awkward silence fell over the room. John let his eyes roam around once more, and then he turned and left the only friends he'd ever known.

CHAPTER TWENTY-NINE

MARIANA

'Are you okay?' I asked Jason.

He nodded, looking jumpy as always. His eyes travelled around the large sitting room that had been dressed up and filled with party guests. I opened my mouth to ask him why he had a black eye and a cut on his lip when I felt a cold hand on the back of my neck. I jumped, expecting to see Dornan. Instead, when I turned around Emilio stared back at me with his beady black eyes, bringing one hand to my cheek.

'You look so pretty, Mariana,' he said, using a single finger to pull my scarf down enough to expose the bruises on my throat. The sight of them made him smile, a grotesque expression that made him look like he was about to eat me.

'Thank you,' I replied, swallowing my discomfort as best I could.

'It looks like my son got a little excited,' he said, dropping his eyes to my throat again. 'He gets that from me, you know.'

'I can only imagine,' I said.

'You ever pull a stunt like that again,' he said quietly, tucking a stray hair behind my ear, 'and I'll take you down to Budget Funerals and put you in the oven myself. Alive. Do you understand?'

Budget Funerals. He'd mentioned the place by name. Had it been on the box of ashes that I'd dumped on his desk? I couldn't remember. The hairs on the back of my neck started to prickle uncomfortably as my heart raced to a gallop.

Out of the corner of my eye, I could see that Jason and Juliette were taking this entire conversation in, their eyes like saucers, their mouths slack with shock. I moved ever so slightly, making sure they weren't in Emilio's line of sight, and nodded. 'I understand.'

'Nobody is irreplaceable, darling,' he said with a grin. He still had his hand on the side of my head, just above my ear. I wanted him to stop touching me, but what was I going to do? I was in a room full of his family and his people. He could literally have murdered me where I stood and nobody would have dared to stop him. Well, except John, but he was MIA, along with Dornan and half the Gypsy Brothers.

'You might think you've got power now that you're married to my son, but he's been married before. You replaced Celia. I won't have a problem finding somebody to replace you.'

I nodded, trying to stay outwardly calm. I wanted to lean over and throw up all over Emilio's expensive Italian loafers, but he'd probably make me lick them clean as punishment. Instead I stood there, frozen, until a warm hand snaked around my waist and squeezed. Jase flinched as he made eye contact with whoever it was hugging me to their side.

I smelled John, but that couldn't be right. I whipped my

head to the left, confused. Dornan was beside me, but he was wearing John's jacket. My heart rate rose to fever pitch as I stepped back, almost ending up in Juliette's lap as I tried to understand what was going on.

'What are you wearing?' I asked Dornan, frowning in confusion as I re-read the patch above his heart that clearly said PRESIDENT. 'Why are you wearing John's jacket?' *Did you kill John?* I mean, why else would he have his jacket?

Dornan grinned. 'We just voted. You're looking at the new president of the Gypsy Brothers.'

I opened my mouth to ask where John was, but then I saw him in the corner, talking to Viper but casting glances our way. He was okay. He was not the president anymore, but he was okay. Thank God.

I looked back to Jason, and my heart broke. He'd flinched when he saw his father, I realised. He was that terrified of Dornan that he couldn't even be near him. I heard Lindsay's words replay in my mind. Soon. I'd get away sooner. Me and John and Juliette and Jason. I would insist, and John would do it because he loved me. Because it was the right thing to do.

I heard the sound of cutlery clinking on glass. Emilio had disappeared, making his way to the centre of the large room.

'A toast to the lovely bride and groom,' he called out, a hush settling over the crowd as Dornan took hold of my arm and dragged me towards his father. His fingers hurt as they dug into my arm. There'd be more bruises tomorrow to add to my collection.

'My dear friends and family,' Emilio said, 'let's give a warm welcome to my son's new wife, and my new daughter. I give you Mariana Ross.'

There were claps and cheers, and hugs from Emilio. First he embraced his son, something I'd never seen him do in ten years, and then he hugged me, almost crushing me in his arms. He might've been old, but the man was strong. Just as I thought he was letting go, he leaned in and gave me a wet kiss, right on my mouth. I almost jerked my head back, stopping myself just in time. If I made him angry he'd kill me, and then there wouldn't be any escaping for a new life and a chance to finally be reunited with Luis.

'We're a very affectionate family,' Emilio whispered in my ear. 'We share ... *everything*.'

I gritted my teeth and kept my fake smile plastered on. Beside me, Dornan was oblivious, his friends and fellow club members congratulating him in a steady procession. Me, I was just there to look good. None of them gave me so much as a sideways glance. Then again, maybe they were too scared of Dornan yanking their eyeballs out for daring to look at his property.

As Emilio was finally disentangling himself from me, there was a scuffle and yelling from the edge of the room. A female voice. *Juliette*. I batted Emilio's hands out of my path, rushing to where I'd been standing in front of Jason and Juliette only moments earlier. Jason was on the ground, curled into the foetal position, his older brothers standing around him but nobody paying him any regard. Only Juliette was helping him, on her knees beside Jason, her hands pulling his shirt up to look at the damage.

John appeared by my right side, and Dornan soon joined him on my left. Oh, the irony of being flanked by your husband and your lover as you look at the son one of them hid away from the other.

'What happened?' I asked, acutely aware that the entire room seemed to have eyeballs on us. Juliette looked up, her eyes wet with tears, and that's when I noticed the blood on her hands.

I fell to my knees next to Juliette, searching for the source of the blood. Juliette lifted Jase's shirt, and I saw a long red line across his stomach, one that was seeping blood at an alarming rate.

'What happened?' Dornan asked, his voice deathly calm.

The boys started to fidget. I mean, they were hardly boys. All six of Dornan's older sons were patch-wearing Gypsy Brothers, ranging in age from Chad, the oldest at twenty-four, to Ant, the youngest at seventeen. Ant was only a few months older than Jase, but the difference in the two boys was stark. Ant was already a tattooed, drinking, drug-taking little smart ass, whereas Jason – apart from the tattoos he'd been forced to have inked upon his flesh – was relatively unmarked by the life.

Except now he had a dirty big slice in his belly, and his blood was all over the floor.

'It's just a flesh wound,' Jase muttered, his ghostly pale face telling me otherwise.

John yanked Juliette to her feet and tucked her under his arm, apparently not worried about the blood on her hands making a mess of his clothes. He'd likely seen a lot more blood in his time, and while it was true that Jason didn't exactly seem to be bleeding to death before everyone's eyes, he'd still been gouged deep enough to make him hurt.

'Dornan,' I snapped. 'Do something.'

He looked vaguely irritated by my directness. Well, fuck him. His son was bleeding on the floor at the hand of one of his other sons and he was standing there looking almost bored.

'Which one of you shitheads did this?' Dornan asked. There was much snickering and pushing between the brothers before Ant cleared his throat. Little fuck. I should've known it would be him. He followed Juliette around like a sick puppy, even though she told him constantly that he was like a brother to her, and no she would not date him. The kid was a date rape waiting to happen.

'It was an accident,' Ant shrugged, mirroring the way his father often acted when confronted with the truth. Deny, deny, deny.

'How do you accidentally stab somebody?' I interjected. 'No, really, I want to know.'

Ant sneered at me. I wanted to punch his head in, but I was well aware that we had a rather large audience.

'Ant, take your shirt off,' Dornan ordered, snapping his fingers. 'Now.'

With seemingly great reluctance, Ant took his shirt off and slapped it into his father's open palm. Dornan fixed him with a hard stare before turning to me. 'Here,' he said, handing me the shirt. 'For the blood.'

I took the shirt and pressed it to Jase's wound. The blood had already slowed to a trickle, but that wasn't the point. Who would do that? Hurt their own brother so brutally, so casually?

Little fucking savages.

'Get the fuck out of here,' Dornan said, and his older sons dispersed like rats in torchlight. 'You'll toughen up soon enough,' he said to Jason, and then he walked away. I stared at him as he left, incredulous.

'Let's get you to one of the bedrooms,' John said to Jason, kneeling beside me. 'Clean you up.'

Jason nodded, and together we managed to help him into a guest room on the ground floor without making his wound bleed too much. By the time Jason was lying on the bed, Juliette sitting by his side, I was ready to find a knife of my own and slit Ant's throat.

John located a first aid kit and I made quick work of the long cut. It looked like Ant had simply walked past Jason and dragged the tip of a knife along his stomach until it split open. I wanted to kill that kid.

Once Jason was bandaged, I left him to find some painkillers. I was barely two steps down the hall when an arm shot out of a doorway and yanked me inside. John. Before I could even open my mouth, he had the door locked and my hand held up to the light, examining the skull tattoo on my ring finger.

Our eyes met and I fought back tears. 'I didn't know where you were,' he breathed, dropping my hand and putting his fingers up to my mouth. He leaned in and kissed me, so softly that I could hardly believe it was the same man who'd picked me up and fucked me against a bathroom basin less than a week ago.

'I'm sorry,' I said, swallowing the rock in my throat. 'I didn't want to – I had to go along with it or I don't know what he would've done.'

John shook his head. 'Doesn't matter. We're getting out. We're taking those kids with us.'

I breathed a sigh of relief. Those kids. I nodded. 'Yeah, we are,' I agreed. 'And we have to do it now. This week. The FBI thinks I'm going to testify against Dornan and Emilio in exchange for immunity.'

'What?' John said.

I told him about how Lindsay had drugged Dornan and insisted I meet with him in Vegas. How they were planning to move on the cartel and the Gypsy Brothers very soon. John listened intently, his forehead lined deep with worry.

'We need cash,' he said.

I nodded excitedly. My insurance policy was about to pay off. 'I've got cash,' I replied. 'Lots and lots of cash. Think you can gather it up for us?'

John smiled, shaking his head. 'I knew it,' he said. 'I'm impressed.'

I rested my head on his shoulder for a brief moment, terrified at the prospect of having to go back out there and interact with Dornan and Emilio.

'I play the long game,' I said quietly.

John chuckled. 'That's good,' he said. 'Because I've got twenty-seven dollars to my name. Shit, I don't even own a leather jacket anymore.'

I looked up sharply as the puzzle pieces slammed together in my brain. 'That's your jacket Dornan's wearing? In front of you? Parading around like you're not even here?'

John nodded, cupping my chin with his hand and pulling my face to his. 'That would be the one,' he murmured against my lips, kissing me again. 'So we'll have to go somewhere warm, okay?'

'Okay,' I agreed, grabbing onto his wrists for dear life as he held my face in his palms.

'Now,' he said, grinning, 'tell me where I need to find this money.'

I couldn't help but grin back. I'd always been a planner. A saver of options for rainy days and escape plans. Thank Christ. Life on the run was going to be so much easier when we were millionaires.

CHAPTER THIRTY

MARIANA

We rode back to LA, a motley procession of motorcycles and the occasional car. I wasn't lucky enough to be a passenger in air-conditioned comfort, unless you counted the air blasting past my skull at a hundred miles an hour. No, I got the same four-hour ride on the back of Dornan's motorcycle that I'd endured on the way to San Diego, my entire body numb from the waist down by the time we rattled into Santa Monica.

Dornan deposited me at the gate to my apartment complex. 'Pack your shit,' he said, his sunglasses showing me my own reflection. I didn't look good. I looked sick with stress and anxiety.

'Pack my shit?' I echoed. 'What do you mean?'

He looked at me like I was an idiot. 'Pack your shit because I'm coming back tonight with my pickup and we're taking your stuff to my house.'

I snorted. 'I'm not living with those fucking savages.'

'Yes, you are,' Dornan snapped. 'They're not savages.'

'Honey,' I said, placing my hand on Dornan's shoulder

as I spoke in the sweetest, most sickly sarcastic voice I could muster, 'your sons told me last night that they'd like to feed you sleeping tablets and then, quote, take me "for a spin". I don't think they were talking about taking me for a motorcycle ride.'

Dornan didn't say anything.

'That's what I thought,' I said, turning on my heel and walking towards my apartment.

'We got a meeting tomorrow,' Dornan called to me. I stopped in my tracks and turned back to face him. 'Tomorrow? What for?'

Dornan shrugged. 'Something about Sunday being a holiday in Italy,' he shrugged. 'My father's going away on business, so we're meeting tomorrow.'

Shit.

'And the club's meeting as well?'

Dornan peered at me with what seemed like suspicion. 'Yeah. Why?'

I rolled my eyes. 'So I can mentally prepare myself to see those boys of yours again. You should teach them how to treat a lady with respect.'

Dornan revved his engine loudly. 'If I have spare time, I'm going to use it disrespecting you in that bedroom up there, not teaching them shit.'

What a stand-up father. I fought the urge to respond with something sharp and condescending. Instead, I stood and watched as Dornan took off down Santa Monica Boulevard, not taking my eyes off him until he'd disappeared.

As I was turning to head upstairs to my apartment, something made me look back to the road.

A black Escalade was parked on the corner. No big deal, right? Common car, especially in LA. Except the window was down, and the guy at the wheel was staring right at me. He was wearing dark tinted sunglasses, and had one of those earpieces attached to a cord that disappeared under his shirt collar. He was FBI, plain as day, and he wasn't even trying to hide it. *They're watching me*, I realised, sickened. *Lindsay's making sure I don't slip away.* Maybe he did know me better than I thought. I turned and took the stairs two at a time, bursting into my apartment and slamming the door behind me.

Guillermo was at the breakfast bar, shovelling Cheerios into his mouth. I ignored the drips of milk all over the counter and walked right up to him, my hand outstretched.

'I need your phone,' I said, breathless and insistent as my eyes bored into his.

He lowered his spoon slowly, licking milk from his lips. 'Why do you need my phone?' he asked slowly, pushing the cereal bowl away as he held my gaze. I didn't respond. I just looked at him, and sure enough, he reached into his pocket and withdrew his cellphone, placing it in the centre of my palm.

'You've got five minutes,' he said, his face unreadable. I watched as he walked past me to the front door, opened it, and then closed it silently behind him.

I dialled John's number. He answered after two rings. 'Yeah?'

'It's Ana,' I said. 'There's FBI sitting outside my apartment.'

'Shit,' John muttered. 'Watching you?'

'I don't think they're watching Mrs Mayflower downstairs,' I said, referring to my geriatric neighbour who was both legally blind and almost deaf.

'What's your feeling?' John asked.

'My feeling is bad,' I said, looking around the apartment nervously. Was this place bugged like the hotel room had been? Shit, I hadn't even considered that possibility. 'Wait a minute.' I switched on the small radio that sat on my kitchen windowsill. Placebo blasted out of the tiny speakers, and I turned that fucker up as loud as it would go without drawing suspicion. Then, I stepped out onto the balcony and closed the glass door behind me. If the balcony was bugged, I was shit out of luck, but I felt like it was the safest option.

'Okay,' I continued. 'Dornan says the Sunday meeting's been moved to tomorrow at noon. I say we leave right after. Any longer and the FBI will make it impossible. Any sooner and they'll notice we're gone before we even make it through downtown LA traffic.'

'Yeah. My thoughts exactly.'

Something else occurred to me. It was useless to leave if we didn't have a means to fund our escape.

'Did you find it?' I asked.

He knew what I meant by *it*. 'All of it,' he said, and it sounded like he was smiling.

'Good,' I said, sagging back against the balcony wall as relief flooded my limbs. 'That's really good.'

CHAPTER THIRTY-ONE

LINDSAY

'Morgan,' Lindsay barked across the packed briefing room.

Lindsay's colleague and fellow FBI officer, Peter Morgan, stood up at the desk he was occupying and made his way to the front of the room. Standing next to Lindsay, he addressed the twenty-odd federal agents who were assembled, ready to jump into action as soon as they were given the command.

Another officer handed out clipboards with photos and vital information while Morgan elaborated. 'There's a shipment of young girls coming from Mexico,' he said, his expression grave. 'There are babies, people. We have to take these bastards down before we end up with a shipping container full of dead Mexican children.'

The room was deathly quiet. Mentioning children and trafficking tended to have that effect.

Their raid had been scheduled for Sunday, but intel suggested that the Gypsy Brothers members and their overlord, Emilio Ross, had brought the meeting forward to Friday – and today was Friday. Lindsay had scrambled to grab as many bodies as he could to help pull off such a raid, and so long as the LAPD sent over a couple of officers for manpower if things got ugly, they'd be fine. He could have waited until the following Sunday, but something in his gut told Lindsay not to give Mariana Rodriguez a week to rethink her agreement to testify, or for Emilio Ross to be tipped off by someone inside the Bureau and hightail it to Colombia.

Morgan finished his briefing and Lindsay took charge once again, detailing floor plans of the Gypsy Brothers clubhouse and the surrounding areas. No exit left uncovered. No stone left unturned. No member of the Ross family left uncuffed.

And then, after he'd finished talking, it was just a matter of waiting the morning out. This was always the hardest part. Sitting on your hands and waiting for the bad guys to be in the right place at the right time, when all you wanted to do was go in, guns blazing, and drag them out of whatever hole they were currently hiding in.

'This'll be good,' Morgan remarked after the briefing had ended.

Lindsay smiled. 'Like shooting fish in a barrel.'

CHAPTER THIRTY-TWO

It was 11:43. Church was due to start in seventeen minutes, and Viper wanted to talk?

'It'd better be fucking urgent,' Dornan muttered, showing Viper into the office where his father was already sitting, flicking through the newspaper. He didn't even look up to acknowledge Viper's presence.

'It can't wait,' Viper said, and something about his expression made Dornan baulk.

'Shit, did somebody die?'

'Yeah,' Viper said. 'Somebody did die. We'll get to that.'

Emilio looked mildly interested.

Viper pulled several folded pieces of paper from inside his leather jacket and placed them on the desk. Dornan went to reach for them, but Emilio was faster. 'The fuck am I looking at here?' he asked impatiently.

'If I'm right,' Viper said, 'you're looking at sixteen years' worth of money being wired from John to Stephanie.'

Dornan felt like he'd been punched in the heart. 'Come again?'

Viper looked deeply troubled. He was implicating the man who, until this week, had been his club president, the man he'd sworn loyalty to.

'John knew where Stephanie was the whole time. He sent her money every single month. Plus extras. Doctors' bills from her pregnancy. From Jason's birth. School fees.'

Dornan snatched the papers from his father, who scowled but didn't say anything. Heart racing, fire in his veins, Dornan swept his eyes down the columns that didn't really mean anything – until he started to focus on the titles of each column. There were dates and times and ... Holy shit, John had really kept Stephanie from him for the better part of two decades. John had kept his son's existence from him.

Dornan made a growling sound in the back of his throat, charging for the door. Viper cut him off. 'Move or I will rip your head off,' he strained.

'There's more,' Viper said, blocking Dornan's path. 'It's about your wife.'

CHAPTER THIRTY-THREE

MARIANA

It was weird going to our weekly meeting on a Friday instead of a Sunday. Sunday was 'church', after all, even if the Gypsy Brothers' church had nothing to do with God or religion. It was a tradition, one they never broke. I was betting that the new president was keen to get his hands dirty, and he sure as shit didn't want to wait until Sunday to start throwing his weight around.

John and I had a plan: as soon as the meeting finished we were going to head back to the strip club, grab the money he'd hidden there, collect Juliette and Jason from John's house, and get the hell out of town. John assured me he'd organised a car for us, a Chevy Tahoe. He'd arranged for it to be parked outside the clubhouse, down the block a few hundred metres, the key to be taped behind the licence plate.

Once we got out of town, there was a car switch, several states to pass through, and then a private jet that would take us the last part of our journey. Colombia beckoned with open arms and the promise of my Luis. And once we had my son safely in our custody ... we could literally go anywhere in the world.

All we had to do was get through our respective meetings – John with his fellow club members, and me with Emilio and Dornan. We did this every week. We could do it one more time. Right?

I was on edge. Jittery. My stomach was tied in knots and I kept feeling like I might throw up. But I could act. I could poker-face my way through anything. I'd been acting my way through the last ten years of my life without ever getting caught.

We were going to make it.

Only we were screwed before we even got a chance to head into our meetings.

We arrived at the clubhouse early, as was custom. I arrived with Dornan, as usual, and John strolled in at 11:47 a.m. Thirteen excruciating minutes until we could get this over and done with and then disappear into the wind. Our new life taunted me relentlessly. I wanted it more than I'd ever wanted anything in my life.

Dornan had already peeled off somewhere, and Emilio was nowhere to be seen. John was talking to another Gypsy Brother, and I leaned against the wall and tried not to attract any attention – easier said than done when you were the only woman in a club full of men. It didn't matter at any rate, because while I was trying to remain inconspicuous, the doors to the club burst open, and FBI officers started streaming in. I saw Lindsay across the room, before he could see me. I acted on autopilot. I locked eyes with John, gestured to the fire escape at the back of the club, and we ran.

CHAPTER THIRTY-FOUR

DORNAN

Dornan backed up and let Viper speak.

'After I found these transactions, I decided to take a look at John's house ...' he trailed off.

'Don't get shy now,' Emilio said. He seemed intrigued, but it wasn't his money. It was John taking pity on some girl and sending her some of his cash. Dornan could tell that his father thought this was no big deal.

Viper placed a cellphone on the desk. He looked like he was about to have a damned heart attack.

'Whose is it?' Dornan asked. His head was throbbing. He almost didn't want to know. He definitely didn't want to be blindsided while his father was standing beside him.

'I found this phone in John's garden shed,' Viper said. 'It was hidden thoroughly. When I unearthed it and turned it on, guess which number was first on the call list?'

Dornan closed his eyes briefly, pinching the bridge of his nose. He already knew the answer. The phone in front of him was a cheap burner phone. He'd seen one exactly the same.

'He's been calling your wife,' Viper said, his eyes darting around as if he didn't know where to look. 'Or rather, they've been calling each other.'

Dornan's resolve shattered. It made perfect sense. Of course! He knew she'd been seeing somebody else, even when she tried to deny it. Of course it would be John – the man who was everything Dornan had never quite been able to emulate. The good one. The kind one. The one who didn't beat you until you miscarried. Or, for that matter, the one who didn't beat you at all, because he was just a fucking stand-up guy.

'There's more,' Viper said.

Emilio was openly entertained now, apparently having forgotten the time and their impending meeting. Seemed this juicy news was reason enough to be late.

'Please, by all means, go on,' Emilio said, steepling his fingers and leaning his chin on them. 'You're really very good at setting the scene. Very thorough.'

Viper glanced at Dornan. 'Once I figured out they'd been talking, I decided it was worth looking into something that's been bothering me ever since you told me about it, Mr Ross. The ashes you mentioned to me. You asked me to track down where she had the kid cremated at such short notice and I found it – Budget Funerals. We've already talked about this, but after I told you I decided to do some more digging. I asked the guy if I could look at his security tapes from the week Agent Murphy went missing.'

Emilio drew a sharp breath. There was nothing playful about his attention now.

'John took a body to be disposed of the same day Murphy disappeared,' Viper said. 'I asked the guy about it, convinced him that John had sent me to make sure any personal effects had been destroyed along with the body.'

He dug into his pocket and pulled out an ID badge, with Murphy's face staring out next to the letters DEA.

He slid it across the table for Emilio to see. 'I rechecked the tapes. Mariana was waiting in the car while John loaded Murphy's body for burning.'

Emilio stood, pounding his fist on the desk. 'That fucking cunt!' he roared, his eyes so big Dornan thought they might explode out of his head and roll along the floor. Dornan didn't know what to do. His wife was a traitor. His wife wasn't loyal to him. She was loyal to John. She was in love with John.

And they were both standing five feet away, separated only by the soundproof walls this office boasted; thank God for small miracles in a sea of shitty news.

'I'll kill them both,' Dornan decided out loud, reaching for his gun.

'Stop,' Viper said. 'There's more. I checked the accounts after I found all of this. She's been skimming your money. I didn't have time to put it all together, but the amount so far is over seven figures.'

Emilio looked like he was about to cut Viper's skull open and rip out his brain, just to see if he could get the answers faster than Viper was relaying them.

'But seven figures is–'

'Millions,' Viper confirmed.

Dornan and Emilio both moved for the door at the same time.

But they never reached it. It exploded open, a stream of FBI agents yelling commands at the three of them, and then

Dornan was on the floor, hands behind his back and his face pressed into the rough carpet as the bony knee of an FBI agent dug into the small of his back.

Emilio was cursing in Italian, the same sentence, over and over again. '*I will cut her fucking head off. I will saw their fucking heads off!*'

No, he wouldn't. Dornan would beat him to it. And he wouldn't need a blade. No. Dornan would rip his pretty wife's head from her body simply with the force of his rage, and then he would do the same to his best friend, the man he'd trusted more than anyone else in his entire life.

CHAPTER THIRTY-FIVE

MARIANA

I'd like to say we escaped, that our plan was brilliant, but our plan was hasty and panicked. John went first, sliding down the fire escape to the back alley below, hidden from street view. This was even better, I surmised, as I felt John's hand on my ankle, guiding me down so I didn't fall and break my neck in these ridiculous high heels Dornan insisted I wear to meetings. We could make a clean break while the others languished in police cells. We'd be in Colombia before some of them even made bail.

But that's where the illusion shattered. Because I looked down, and the man holding my ankle wasn't John. It was Lindsay.

'Mariana.' He smiled, pulling me down to the ground and then pushing me up against the wall, cold handcuffs wrapping around my wrists and clicking shut. 'How nice of you to join us.'

In my peripheral vision I saw John, handcuffed and gagged, as he was dragged away. He hadn't even been able to yell out to warn me of the danger below. Lindsay wrenched me away from the wall and pushed me forward. I moved awkwardly in my heels as he propelled me around to the front of the clubhouse, following in John's footsteps, where at least fifteen police cars sat waiting to be filled. I looked on in horror as I saw John being wrestled into one car, Dornan into another, and Emilio into a third. Cuffs firmly in place, Lindsay spun me around to face him. He smiled again, and Christ almighty if he didn't look like some Hollywood movie star who'd been plucked off the street and handed a gun and a badge. His bright white teeth were dazzling, and he looked clean. Too clean. Even his navy blue suit jacket looked freshly pressed.

We, on the other hand, we were all dirty, even if we didn't look it on the surface. Emilio's dirt was the poison that ran through his veins, the beady look in his dark eyes, the bit of phlegm that always seemed to be trapped in his chest, that rumbled when he spoke and made me want to scream at him to clear his damn throat every time he opened his mouth.

Dornan and John were dirty anyway, with their beard scruff, the tattoos that covered their skin in various stages of bright and dull colouring, the leather vests they never, ever washed, their palms stained with engine oil and probably blood.

We were all dirty, dishevelled, less than.

Lindsay, though, was resplendent. He had us now, and he knew it.

And he beamed.

CHAPTER THIRTY-SIX

LINDSAY

Divide and conquer – that was the key to getting people to turn on each other. Lindsay was well versed in this technique, and it was perfect for today's situation: a group of highly paranoid criminals with shady moral codes who would just as soon rat on someone as take a bullet for them. It was the law of averages. Eventually, one of them would turn on the rest.

Speaking of. In front of him sat Mariana Rodrig– no, it was Ross now, wasn't it? Mariana Ross. Didn't roll off the tongue as nicely as Rodriguez, but Lindsay suspected that she'd roll off his tongue nicely no matter what her name was. He tried not to think about how beautiful she was, though. It had already made him go softer on her than he should have, when he gave her the gun back in Vegas. It was a dumb move. He knew the second she got out of that car that she wasn't going to testify for him.

He'd been questioning her for at least thirty minutes but the woman was like a vault. She wasn't saying anything, and she looked bereft. Lindsay suspected he'd interrupted her escape plans. Well, he had literally interrupted her shimmying down the fire escape in heels and a pencil skirt, but he suspected she'd planned to be on her way to some exotic locale by now, instead of sitting chained to an interrogation table inside the LAPD's downtown station. As much as Lindsay loathed this place, the FBI headquarters simply couldn't handle this volume of arrests at one time.

'This is your last chance at getting immunity,' he reminded her. 'I mean it. Just because I feel sorry for you doesn't mean I can make the murder charge go away.' He slid a piece of paper over to her side of the table. 'We know you killed Allie Baxter. You're going away, for twenty-five to life. Not that you'll survive that long. The cartels run the prisons. You'll be dead before you get to dinner on your first day.'

It was only then that she started to communicate.

'You'll never get immunity approved for a cop killer,' Mariana said to him. 'Why would you offer such a thing?'

Lindsay smiled. 'Killing a dirty cop isn't quite the same as killing, say, a cop like me.'

Mariana raised one eyebrow. 'A cop like you?'

'Exemplary. Unblemished record. Solid cases. You definitely don't want to get caught for killing a cop like me.'

She didn't look convinced.

'Your testimony could bring an entire cartel to its knees,' Lindsay said. 'It could dismantle their drug operations. Their arms deals. Their human trafficking.' He saw her flinch. 'You want to help the women and children Emilio is selling, don't you? The babies? The babies he sells while they're still in their mothers' wombs? Mariana, don't you want to stop those children from being sold to porn rings and paedophiles?'

'Stop,' she said, covering her ears. 'Please stop.'

'Do you think anyone stops when those children beg them to stop?'

Mariana glared at him. 'John and I are a package deal,' she said. 'We both get immunity, then I testify.'

Lindsay laughed. 'What? You're kidding, right? Immunity for the president of the club who was running the trafficking in the first place? I don't think so.'

'He didn't have anything to do with it,' she said forcefully.

'Guess you can tell that to your buddies in your prison cell.'

'Do you really think I'm afraid of prison,' she shot back, 'after the life I've lived? Prison would be a walk in the park compared to that. You can either give us both immunity, or you can process me, because I'm not saying another word without John.'

Lindsay realised that she didn't care what happened to her. She was in love with this guy, and she was never going to cooperate unless he was part of the deal.

Mariana sat back in her metal chair and smiled at Lindsay smugly. 'You should see the things I could get for you,' she teased. 'I think the word "damning" ought to cover it.'

Lindsay was finding it harder to smile at her. She was asking him to do the impossible.

'Wait here,' he said.

***

Fifteen minutes later, Lindsay marched John Portland into Mariana's interrogation room. Her eyes practically popped out of her skull, she looked so surprised. She covered her reaction

268

quickly, though, with a smile. 'See, that wasn't so hard,' she said to Lindsay.

He just made a noise at the back of his throat. He could technically lose his job for this, but if an entire cartel was taken down through his efforts, then all would be forgiven. Probably.

Lindsay left them alone for a moment under the pretence of getting John a chair, but when he peered at them through the one-way glass window, they remained silent. They were smart. They'd almost been smart enough to get out before Lindsay had scooped them up. Almost.

After a few moments of watching them exchange silent glances, he headed back in, a chair in one hand, coffee in the other. The coffee was for him. Criminals didn't get coffee until they gave him something. If these two delivered, he'd buy them a lifetime supply of Starbucks to go with their immunity.

John sat in the chair. Lindsay leaned against the table and sipped coffee. They all looked at each other silently. And then Mariana Rodriguez began to talk.

***

Mariana had insisted on going to the clubhouse to collect the financial evidence herself. She'd also insisted on taking John with her. Said she wouldn't do a thing if he was out of her sight for a single second. John hadn't said a damn thing.

After much toing and froing, Lindsay sent them both with Agent Morgan to recover the evidence Mariana was so adamant about – the financial records that could prove a link between Emilio Ross, the Il Sangue Cartel, and the human trafficking ring. He watched them leave, relieved that he was able to cut a deal that would see Mariana kept safe. He'd only met the woman twice, but he'd watched her for hours upon hours over the last few months. There was something about her that endeared her to him, even if he couldn't quite articulate what it was.

His coffee long since cold, Lindsay gathered his files and dumped them on his desk, and then headed down to the lock-up to see who he could rattle next. Yeah, he had Mariana's testimony, but it didn't mean he couldn't make his case even more bulletproof with additional testimony. He was looking forward to interrogating Emilio and Dornan Ross. He was practically giddy about the prospect of waving their life sentences in their faces, because that's what they'd get for the things they'd done. He intended to impress upon them that his case against them would bury them so deep, they'd never see the light of day again.

He was feeling pretty chipper as he approached the police officer on duty and held out his badge for verification. 'I'm ready for Dornan and Emilio Ross to be brought upstairs for questioning,' he said, scanning the lock-up for the father and son.

The officer shrugged. 'They're gone.'

Lindsay just about died on the spot. 'I'm sorry, what?'

A senior officer who was sitting at a nearby desk chimed in. 'Yeah. Apparently they had some hotshot lawyer down here, demanding to know what they were under arrest for. He got them out, like, three hours ago.'

'We'll have all the evidence we need to convict those two sorry sons of bitches. It's being collected right now.'

'Well, you needed it three hours ago,' the senior officer replied. 'We had no choice but to let them go.'

Lindsay was incredulous. 'It's an FBI case. It's called a twenty-four hour hold, for Christ's sake.'

The duty officer opened his mouth to speak but Lindsay cut him off as a fresh wave of panic slammed him. 'Wait, did you say they've been gone for three hours? *Fuck!*'

CHAPTER THIRTY-SEVEN

MARIANA

We were completely and utterly screwed. Emilio had somehow skipped his holding cell and beaten us to the strip club, pouncing the moment we'd entered the place with Agent Morgan.

The same Agent Morgan who was now bleeding to death at my feet, courtesy of a bullet to his chest. Two of Dornan's sons held my arms behind my back. Viper and two other Gypsy Brothers were holding John. It had taken three men to restrain him.

Behind the desk John usually sat at, in the office we shared, Emilio paced.

He'd already filled us in on the information Viper had pieced together. We were fucked. Emilio knew everything. He knew I'd killed Murphy. He knew John and I were together. He knew I'd been skimming cartel money for years. And he knew John had been responsible for Stephanie's disappearance.

This was it. Our final moments. I'd always wondered what would happen if the house of cards came crashing down, and now I knew. This.

Death.

Turns out, I didn't much like waiting to die.

'You're going to kill us,' I spat at Emilio. 'What are you waiting for?'

He didn't stop pacing as he locked those cold, dead eyes on me. 'A call. I'm waiting for a call from my son. He went to your house, John, assuming that's the first place you'd hit. Such a family man, we all thought you'd go back for your daughter before stopping here. Who knew?'

John growled, straining against the stronghold his three club brothers had on him.

'I wonder what they'll do with your precious daughter,' Emilio mused.

'I'll fucking kill you if you touch her!' John roared, lunging over the desk.

Emilio smiled. 'I won't touch her,' he said, smirking. 'But I will watch.'

***

They locked me in a room by myself and left me there. It was more of a broom closet really, full of cleaning supplies and towels. There was nothing sharp. No windows. The best hope I had was to try to set something on fire. I'd probably die very quickly, though. So I refrained.

I paced the tiny room, once my eyes had adjusted to the darkness. At least I paced until I heard the screams coming from downstairs. Once I heard those screams I started screaming. It didn't matter, though. Nobody came to let me out.

CHAPTER THIRTY-EIGHT

DORNAN

Dornan didn't quite know what he was doing. It was as if his need for vengeance had overtaken his mind. He'd gone to John's house in search of John, with a bag of smack as a bribe to get Caroline to tell him where John had gone if he wasn't there.

Caroline didn't tell Dornan anything. But it didn't matter. He'd handed over the heroin willingly. He'd taken her child as payment.

Juliette. The baby he'd taken in after Caroline abandoned her in the hospital in search of her next fix. The baby who John hadn't been able to meet until she was already months old and staring into Dornan's eyes like he was her daddy. The only parent she'd known from birth. They'd always had a special bond, he and Julie.

And now he had taken her from her home, and he was going to hurt her. The darkness inside him clamoured for her blood, even though part of him was distraught at the prospect of what he was about to do. He was about to take that girl he'd

274

once thought of as his own, the girl who meant more to John Portland than breathing, more than air, more than living ... and Dornan was going to destroy her.

An eye for an eye, a tooth for a tooth. A life for a life. John had taken everything from Dornan. He'd taken Stephanie. He'd taken Jason. He'd taken Mariana.

And so Dornan would take Juliette from John. Break her into little pieces so that she could never be put back together again. It was a fitting revenge for such a systematic betrayal.

'Please,' Juliette begged, tied to a chair on the empty stage of the strip club. Before her stood a video camera on a tripod, a flashing red light indicating that it was recording. He would hurt her. He would break her, and then he would force John to watch the highlights reel.

'Dornan!' she implored. 'You don't have to do this!'

But he did have to do this. Because in that moment, he didn't even see Juliette, the girl he'd treated like one of his own. He didn't see his father, watching silently from the floor below.

He only saw Stephanie, crying as he beat her half to death. The woman who'd taken his heart, and his son, and his hope that he could ever be something better than what he was.

He saw John. The man who he'd trusted above all else, the man who'd now taken not one, but two women he loved, and made them despise him. Yes, in the girl's green eyes he saw treachery and betrayal, but most of all, he saw her fear, and *he liked it*.

John had taken Stephanie. Sent her away. John had taken his son in the process, and now Jase hated him. His own father. John had taken his youngest son once, and now he was planning to take him again? Yes, as if the betrayal was not cutting enough, John and Mariana had been planning to take Jason when they fled town.

John had stolen Mariana from Dornan. And she had gone to him, like a moth to a flame, like none of the shit they'd been through in the past ten years had ever happened. Dornan had risked his life for her, taken a bullet for her, left his wife and married her! He would have fucking died for her, and none of it mattered, because she wanted John.

He'd always vowed to protect this girl, Juliette. But he didn't protect her. He took a knife and cut her clothes from her body, and when she was naked and sobbing he told his sons to destroy her.

And they had tried. All of them. All except Jason, who'd been found and brought to the strip club, kicking and screaming blue murder, who was now unconscious at Dornan's feet because he'd been so distraught at the sight of Chad laying his body upon Juliette's and violating her. All six of his older sons had done as Dornan had told them to. Some more willingly than others. They'd all walked away after committing different variations of the same heinous act upon the defenceless girl, and she was still here. She was still breathing.

She was a fighter, like her daddy. It was going to take more to break her.

It was going to take Dornan to break her.

It was just the two of them now, on the stage; them, and a camera and a small table where Dornan was laying his clothes in a neat pile as he pulled them from his body.

As she continued to protest.

'You're supposed to be my family!' Juliette screamed, bleeding all over the fucking place.

He stared at the girl in front of him, and something inside him said *stop*. It was a whimper, not a scream, that voice of dissent that said *It's not too late to let her go*. But something else, something much louder and more powerful drowned that protest out. The beast inside him demanded vengeance, demanded destruction. And the beast needed to be fed.

Dornan swallowed. Took a deep breath, took a step towards her, his belt in his hands.

And he became the monster he was born to be.

CHAPTER THIRTY-NINE

DORNAN

'Get up.'

Jason was at his feet, his face bloody and swollen from being beaten unconscious.

'Where is she?' he begged. 'Please, where is she?'

Dornan reached down and grabbed the back of his son's neck. His anger gave him brute strength, and it was the easiest thing in the world to drag the insolent little fucker away from the stage where a naked Juliette lay, unconscious and bleeding from what Dornan had done to her. In one hand he gripped his son. In the other, the remnants of Juliette's clothing – a macabre souvenir of the dignity he'd stolen from her.

He entered the small office where John was being held, still dragging Jase. As soon as they were both safely in the room and the door locked, he shoved Jase away. He fell to the floor and scrambled into the corner, getting as far away from his father as he could.

'Where's Ana?' Dornan asked, scanning the faces around

him. Viper and Jimmy and … oh yes. John. Tied to a chair, his face much like Jase's – bloody and swollen and bruised.

'She's down the hall,' Jimmy replied. 'Want me to get her?'

Dornan shook his head. 'Not yet.'

He circled John's chair once before stopping in front of him.

'Johnny Boy,' he said.

John refused to look at his oldest friend. Dornan thought that was odd. Shouldn't he be begging Dornan to let Juliette go?

But then he remembered, John didn't know about Juliette.

Dornan steeled himself, the sticky bunch of fabric in his hand. He dropped the bloodied clothing on John's lap, piece by piece. John looked at the material, either disinterested or confused, Dornan couldn't tell which.

And then he dropped the last piece. The piece of T-shirt with the little rainbow icon that, just two hours ago, had sat above Juliette's heart as she wore her regular clothes and lived her regular life.

John's eyes widened when he saw the rainbow, his head whipping up so that he could look at Dornan.

'No,' he said hoarsely.

Dornan smirked.

'No!' John screamed, bucking against his ropes. 'No! No! No!'

Dornan, who'd started pacing in front of his bound, traitorous friend, stopped on his heel and turned in front of John. He stood so close, their legs touching, that had John been able to pry his hands free from their bindings, he'd have been able to swing at him.

'Sixteen years you kept Stephanie from me.'

John looked down at the bloody ribbons of clothing in his lap, horrified. Transfixed. 'What did you do?' he breathed.

'Sixteen years, I could have had my son.'

'WHAT DID YOU DO?' John roared, his face bright red, his knuckles white as he tried to twist them away from the chair.

'How long were you fucking my wife?' Dornan asked. It suddenly occurred to him that it was the last time he'd likely refer to Mariana as his wife.

'If you hurt Julie–'

Dornan tutted. 'I already hurt Julie. Jesus, John, didn't you hear her screaming? That was your daughter and my sons, but she was the only one who screamed.'

John made a guttural noise in the back of his throat, pulling against the ropes that bound him to the chair. He was going to either make himself bleed or snap the rope soon enough.

Dornan drew his gun and pressed it against John's lips, against his teeth. 'We're talking about my wife first, John. She suck your cock, *John*? Did my wife suck good cock?'

John's eyes flashed with anger. Dornan drew the gun away and used it to pistol-whip him across the face. Blood flew from John's mouth and through the air, landing on the ground with a sickening splat.

'What else, huh? You steal my wife, you steal my money, you steal my FUCKING SON?'

'Why is there blood on her clothes?' John panted. 'Why are her clothes cut up?'

Dornan grabbed a second chair and planted it right in front of John's, straddling it. He rested his elbows on the top of the backrest, watching John as an eerie calm descended upon him. Little by little, the angry buzz was starting to recede. *This is what it feels like*, he realised. To switch it all off and walk away from ever caring about anything else again. *This is what it feels like to be my father.*

It felt ... oddly freeing. No more worry. No more pain. Just the self-assured conviction that the man in front of him – the man he'd trusted with his own life, his own *wife*, his own fucking kids – that this man would suffer for his betrayal.

John levelled his gaze at Dornan. 'Why are her clothes cut up?' he repeated. 'ANSWER ME!'

Dornan responded by taking his gun, pressing it down into John's groin, and pulling the trigger. The blast was deafening; John's howl of pain even more so. His pain rocked him to the side and he crashed to the ground, still tied to the chair at an awkward angle. Dornan could only imagine the pain John must have been feeling. A bullet in the cock. There were major arteries down there. The steady stream of blood pouring from John's lap made sense then. His skin went pasty-white and he started to hyperventilate, gasping for air.

'Now bring her in,' Dornan said to Jimmy, who obliged, scuttling away and coming back not thirty seconds later with Mariana in tow.

'Oh God,' she cried, running towards John.

Dornan stopped her, a hand around her throat as he drove her against the wall. 'Nuh-uh,' he said, grinning at her. 'No touching.' He pressed his hips against Mariana, effectively pinning her to the wall. 'Jimmy!' he barked. 'Get out your gun. Take all the bullets out. Leave one in the chamber and give it to Jason.'

Everyone looked at Dornan as if he were mad. 'What if the little fuck shoots you?' Jimmy asked. 'Or me?'

Dornan glared at him. 'He won't shoot you. Just fucking do it.'

With great reluctance, Jimmy handed the gun to Jason. He immediately pointed it at Dornan.

'If you want to redeem yourself,' he said to his youngest son, 'you'll put John here out of his misery. He's in pain. You don't want him to be in pain, do you, son?'

Dornan motioned for everyone to leave the room. Soon it was just Jase and John, Dornan and Mariana. She was saying John's name, over and over. Dornan didn't like that. 'Stop, bitch,' he ground out. She didn't stop.

'I said STOP, BITCH!' He pulled her head forward and then slammed it back into the wall, watching in fascination as her eyes rolled back in her head. He dragged her out of the room and closed the door, and waited for the gunshot. Either Jason would kill John to ease his pain, or he'd turn the gun on himself and blow his brains out. There really was no telling which way it would go. But one thing he did know, he couldn't stay and watch.

In the hallway, Mariana continued to struggle, and Dornan continued to brace her against the wall. She was fading fast; pretty soon she'd be still. Jimmy and Viper leaned against the opposite wall and said nothing. Dornan wondered where Guillermo was. Whose side he was on. He made a mental note to find out. But first, he had to wait for that blast.

What he didn't expect was that Chad would wander up the hallway, looking almost rueful, his hands covered in blood.

'Pop,' Chad said, holding out his blood-soaked hands.

'Whatever you did to Julz – I can't wake her. I think she's dying.'

Mariana found a second wind and started struggling again. 'What did you do?' she wailed. 'Oh God. Oh *God*. What did you do to her?'

Dornan opened his mouth to speak as a deafening gunshot rang out. He felt his breath hitch for a moment as he wondered who was dead in the office just a few feet away – his best friend, or his son.

'Hold her,' Dornan snapped, throwing Mariana at Viper. He opened the office door, and saw his son on the floor, the gun to his temple, desperately pulling the trigger over and over again to a series of empty clicks.

Dornan watched him do this for a few moments, unable to look down at John. And then he forced himself to look.

John was dead. Gone.

A moment of horrified shame lurked at the back of Dornan's pitch-black mind. He pushed it down, though, with the rest of the terrible things that he'd done. He didn't have time to ruminate now. His best friend was dead at his feet, and his son was now smashing the barrel of his gun into his face.

'Chad!' Dornan snapped. 'Get him out of here.'

Chad obliged, hooking his bloodied wet hands under Jason's arms and dragging him from the room. As they passed, Dornan snatched his gun from Jase and jammed it into the back of his jeans again.

Emilio entered the small office, coming to a standstill beside Dornan. He put his hand on his son's shoulder, and it sat there, like a dead roach that Dornan desperately wanted to throw off.

'We always hurt the ones we love,' Emilio said, squeezing his shoulder. 'Remember when you begged me to keep her? I told you, son, this day would come.'

He let his hand drop.

Dornan continued to stare down at the body in front of him as Emilio cleared his throat.

'We have to go,' Emilio said, his tone becoming urgent. His tone was never urgent, which meant the situation was dire. 'We have to get out. The Feds are going to find one of their own dead here, and we need to be gone before then. Clean up crew will sort this, but only if we move. Kill her and let's get the fuck out of here. Unless you want me to do it?'

Dornan started to pace. He tugged at his hair.

'I'll do it,' Emilio snapped, drawing his gun.

'Don't fucking touch her!' Dornan yelled at his father. 'I'm about to shoot my fucking wife,' he choked out. 'Give me a goddamn minute, will you?'

Emilio fixed his son with a hard glare. 'You've got five minutes,' he said through gritted teeth. 'Then you're on your own.'

CHAPTER FORTY

DORNAN

Emilio was gone. John was dead. The boys had all cleared out, taking an unconscious Juliette and a crazed Jason with them. It was just Dornan and Mariana, locked in a room together. They were ending exactly as they'd begun, only this time there was a dead man lying on the floor between them, a man they'd both loved dearly at one time in their lives. A man who Mariana had just spent the past few moments trying to save.

But there were some things that were beyond repair. A bullet in the brain, for example. John was dead. He'd been dead since the moment Jason planted a bullet in his skull. Now Mariana was standing again, only this time she was covered in John's blood.

'Hurry up,' Mariana said, her eyes full of tears, her entire body shaking violently. 'Just do it. Just kill me!'

Dornan was crying now, too. The shock was starting to dissipate, and the rage along with it. Now he just felt a hollow ache inside, that familiar emptiness that defined his existence. He'd killed John. Juliette was almost dead. And his wife stood in front of him, begging him to kill her, and he couldn't bear to end her life like this.

He still loved her. Despite the treachery, the betrayal, the lies, he loved her. He would always love her.

'I don't want to kill you,' he rasped. 'I want to save you. I want you to run.'

'No,' she protested. 'No, Dornan.'

'You have five minutes,' he said to her, his hand coming to rest on her cheek. His fingers burned where their skin met.

She was sobbing. Hysterical. 'What if I don't run?'

He shrugged, his own eyes burning with regret. 'Then I take you back to Emilio, and he can do whatever he wants to you.'

Her sobs stilled. She looked up at him, her eyes wide, hands thick with John's blood. The sight made him bitterly jealous, for no good reason. John was dead; he was gone. But blood had been their thing, the thing that bound Dornan and Mariana together, from the very first time he'd bandaged her wounds all those years ago.

'Did you ever really love me?'

She slapped him across the face, hard. Enough so that he tasted blood. How did somebody as small as his Mariana slap him so he bled? The taste of his own blood set off something primal, and he growled, grabbing her wrist and twisting it until she cried out.

She ripped her hand away and stepped back. 'Of course I fucking loved you. I loved you so much I thought I would die. Don't you know the things I did for you? For us?'

All he saw was her with John. It consumed him until he thought he might go totally insane.

He narrowed his eyes. 'Enlighten me.'

She shook her head, laughing mirthlessly. 'You stupid bastard,' she said. 'I loved you until the end. I loved you even after I saw what you did to Stephanie. What you did to your own son. I still loved you.'

He nodded, his throat tight. 'So what was it, then? The thing that destroyed us?'

She straightened, took a step back. 'You *know*.'

And it was true, he did know. He'd killed their child. Hurt her so much, it had died and bled away.

This was his fault.

'It was always going to end like this,' she whispered, tears dripping onto her dirty cheeks. Her words stunned him, physically, to the point that he had to step back to keep his balance.

'Like what?' he asked.

'With blood. We started with blood, and that's how we ended.'

'Is this what this is?' he asked sadly. 'The end?' He'd been so fucking happy when he married her. It was the first day he'd truly been able to say that she was his and not his father's. But now, looking at the weeping mess in front of him, the traitor, the seductress who'd been lying to him all this time, Dornan Ross had to wonder – had she ever been his at all?

'Yes,' she said, looking down at John. His eyes were still frozen open, unseeing. It wasn't fair.

Mariana knelt beside John, reaching her hand out. With love. She reached for him with so much tenderness, so much despair, that it took everything inside Dornan to stop himself from putting the gun in his own mouth and pulling the trigger. Had she ever looked at him like that?

287

'Don't fucking touch him,' Dornan said, jealousy surging through him as he aimed the gun at the woman he'd loved.

She swallowed thickly, guiding the gun up to her forehead. 'Do it,' she urged, tears streaming down her face. 'DO IT!'

He grabbed her, pulled her back to her feet. He wanted to kill her. He wanted to save her. He wanted to take it all back.

'I'm sorry,' he said hoarsely. 'For everything.'

She was sobbing, staring at John.

'Ana. He's not waking up.' Dornan just needed to ask her one question. 'Ana?'

She waited for his next words, searching his face.

'The way you … looked at him. Did you ever feel like that about me? Or was it love because you needed me? Because the alternative was too much to bear?'

Her eyes flashed with emotion as she stepped back to him, taking his face in her bloody hands. He heard her chest rattle when she breathed and sobbed all at once.

'I looked at you like that,' she implored, her gaze the truest thing he'd ever seen. 'I looked at you all the time.'

'I didn't see it,' he said, his resolve faltering, his gun dropping to his side.

She shook him, and he let her. 'You were too busy looking at everyone else!' she cried. 'All I ever wanted was you, don't you understand, Dornan? All I ever wanted was the man who saved me. He was my everything.'

He wanted to hold her to his chest and never let her go. He wanted to give her fat babies and a house she could feel safe in, and most of all, her freedom. Her own name. He'd always wanted those things for her, but right now, more than ever before, he saw the life they could have had, he saw the baby he'd killed as if it had survived and been born happy, he saw every single thing that would have happened if he'd played a different hand.

He wanted to make it right.

It would never be right.

He staggered back, pushing her away. 'Go,' he said hoarsely.

'Dornan,' she protested, reaching out.

'Go!' He gritted his teeth. 'If you touch me again, Ana, I will grab onto you, and I will never, ever let you leave me. We'll end in blood when I decide, and we'll end together. It won't be pretty. I'll take everything from you, whether you give it to me or not.'

She shrank away like he was fire and she'd burn if she touched him. 'If you loved me, you wouldn't.'

'I loved Juliette!' he roared, and for the first time he let the weight of what he'd done to John's daughter sink into his bones. Fifteen years ago, he'd watched her be born. He'd taken care of her. Today, he'd tortured and raped her and left her for dead. The girl who'd been like a daughter to him. The girl who'd been punished for her father's sins.

Why can't we ever turn back the fucking clock?

Still, Mariana didn't move.

'GO!' he repeated.

And then, just as he'd decided to reach out for her, she turned on bare feet and fled.

Don't chase her. Don't fucking chase her.

Dornan turned slowly away. Every bone in his body screamed to go after her, until he saw John. Fuck. He crumpled to his knees beside his friend, the floor slick with blood, and shook his friend.

'John,' he whispered. 'Johnny Boy.'

Dornan let out a guttural sound, the sound an animal makes when its child has been killed. With much difficulty, he shifted John's dead weight onto his lap, his tears falling down onto his friend's still face, a face now marred with a perfect round bullet hole, smack in the middle of his forehead.

'John,' he whispered. 'Brother. *I'm sorry.*'

He thought of Juliette, then. Of Mariana.

He looked at the gun and thought about blowing his brains out.

It was tempting.

CHAPTER FORTY-ONE

MARIANA

My chest screamed in agony as I tried to draw another ragged breath. Stones and old bits of glass bit into my bare feet as I ran blindly in the night, without any idea of where I was going, if anyone was following me, or what I would do if I ran into Emilio. In the distance, the busy streetlights beckoned through a fog of haze that blanketed my vision.

John. Juliette. He'd killed them. I sobbed as I ran away, every step a jolt that said *turn around*.

Every step reminding me that I was a terrible human being.

Jason was still alive. I'd told him that I would protect him. That I would take him away from all of this, to the safety of a life that would now only ever be an idle thought, a daydream, an ill-placed fantasy.

I was a terrible person, because he'd trusted me, and because I was never, ever going back. I was getting the fuck out of here. My brain had been reduced to the most basic of operations, and it said: RUN.

So I did. Achingly aware that I was out in the open, that if the wrong person cast a glance my way I'd be shot in the back and left to bleed out on the ground, I kept running.

Headlights loomed in the distance.

Fuck! They'd found me. Dornan had changed his mind. Emilio had put his men on the scent. Something. All I knew was, I'd been found, and my brief taste of freedom was coming to a close.

'Mariana,' a self-assured voice called out.

I froze.

'I know you can hear me.'

'Go away,' I said, wincing as the soles of my feet bled.

'Come on,' Lindsay said, holding out his hand as he drove alongside me.

I shook my head, sticking to the pavement. No. I wouldn't go with him. I couldn't trust anyone. All people ever did was lie and cheat and spill blood like it was nothing. But it wasn't nothing. How much more blood would be taken from me before I'd be empty? How many more wrong moves?

'I'm not going with you,' I said, his eyes and the headlights appearing in double as the world started to spin around me. I stumbled and fell to my knees, and suddenly there were warm hands on my shoulders.

'Come on,' Lindsay said, draping his suit jacket around me as he led me to his car. 'I'll keep you safe. I promise.'

'Where?' I argued, too weak to fight him. 'In prison?'

He opened the back door of his Escalade and bundled me in, laying me across the backseat. 'I'm not taking you in, Mariana,' he said softly. He closed the door, and a moment later he was jumping into the driver's seat.

It took me a moment to register the words. 'Then where *are* you taking me?'

He pulled away from the kerb, and I lay on my back across the leather seats, the car accelerating so fast it was like we were flying.

'To a safehouse,' Lindsay murmured as he navigated traffic. 'There's someone waiting for you there, and I promise you, you're going to want to meet him.'

CHAPTER FORTY-TWO

LUIS

I met my mother for the first time when I was born. Briefly, and then I waited another fourteen years to meet her a second time, inside the walls of an FBI safehouse.

She was younger than I'd imagined, but when she raised her eyes to mine, I saw all those lost years in her stricken expression. Her bare feet were cut and bleeding. Her dress was torn and she was covered in blood.

They say you can never remember the first moments of your life. That it's impossible for the brain to be able to store that kind of information. But there are some things that transcend the realm of possibility, some algorithms too complex for us to explain away with just science. The nights I had spent looking at my mother's faded photograph paled in comparison to this moment, this flesh and blood, and *blood-covered* woman who sat before me, as if she'd just fought a battle and barely made it out alive. Maybe she hadn't made it out entirely. Her eyes were sad. They said she'd lost something very dear to her. That she'd left something behind.

'Mariana,' the FBI agent said, grasping one of her hands and placing his other palm on my shoulder. 'This is Luis. He's been waiting a long time to meet you.'

My mother started to cry, and it hurt inside my chest that she was so upset. What had happened to her? Had she been trapped somewhere? Had she just escaped?

'Don't cry, Mama,' I said, my throat tight. I was fourteen years old, and I didn't cry. I wouldn't cry. But in front of my mother? I wanted to crawl into her lap and cling to her and never let her go.

Her eyebrows rose in disbelief when I said *Mama*.

'Luis?'

There are some things that cannot be explained. A child can't remember his mother's voice from the day he was born. And yet ... 'Your voice,' I said. 'I remember your voice.'

That made her cry harder. I chewed on the inside of my cheek. I didn't want her to cry. I wanted her to speak so that I could hear her voice again.

We sat in stunned silence, observing each other.

'You look exactly like your father,' my mother said to me.

I nodded. It was true, I did. I'd seen the photographs. I was his spitting image.

'But I have your eyes,' I said to her.

She blinked fat tears, tears that wound a line through the dried blood and the dirt on her cheeks. It was incredible. Like the warrior I'd always envisaged her to be, here she was, risen from ashes, this mythical person who, until this moment, had only existed in hope and a faded photograph I carried around with me like it was my saving grace.

Agent Price nudged me, pointing at the empty seat next to this woman he called Mariana. I stepped over and sat down so that I was next to her.

My mother dropped the agent's hand and turned to face me, stretching her fingers towards me ever so slowly, almost as if I might disappear if she moved too fast, like smoke on the wind.

'Can I?' she asked hesitantly, her eyes darting to my hands.

I nodded, offering them to her. She took them in her hands, drawing a deep, almost choking breath when our skin met. I hated to be touched, hated to be hugged by my aunt or my cousins, hated to have any affection. My whole life, I'd always felt like a weird kid, the outcast, because I'd just wanted people to leave me alone.

But when my mother studied the ridges on my palms, when she turned them over to look at each finger, at my wrists, when she let my hands gently go and pressed her fingertips against my cheeks, it was like someone had poured a balm onto my skin. I didn't want to shrink away.

'You're real,' she whispered, cupping my chin in her hand.

I nodded, squeezing her wrist with my hand.

'I'm so sorry,' she said, 'that I ever let you out of my sight.'

She wrapped her arms around me and squeezed, and we stayed that way for a very long time. It was nothing like I imagined it would be. It was so much better.

After a long time, the agent cleared his throat. 'I'm sorry,' he said. 'It's time for me to take you both, now.'

'Where are we going?' my mother whispered.

I saw him glance at me before his gaze settled on my mother.

'Home. You're going home.'

CHAPTER FORTY-THREE

DORNAN

There was a hollow feeling in Dornan Ross's chest that he just couldn't seem to shake. He'd tried to fill it with so many things over the years, with fucking and money, and little lines of flake that made his brain spark and bubble but left him with a hideous comedown afterward. He tried to fill it with children, and wives, and control.

He tried to fill it with everything he fucking could, but it was like a black hole, and it demanded to be fed, and it never, ever fucking closed up. It was never full. It was never sated. It just got bigger, and greedier, until one day, it swallowed him whole.

All these things occurred to him as he watched six Gypsy Brothers lower John Portland's coffin into the earth. The day was brilliant, the normally hazy Los Angeles sky clear and blue. Sweat gathered around Dornan's collar as he tugged at his tie. It seemed like far too nice a day to bury the best friend you'd murdered. He glanced across to the second slightly smaller coffin that contained John's daughter's remains. Yes, the sky was much too blue to be burying the girl he'd once thought of as his own.

MARIANA

'Lindsay,' I said, smiling broadly as two machine-gun toting guards flanked me – one male, one female. You could never be too careful when the world believed you were dead. Especially when you alone controlled an eighty-something per cent stake in the South and Central American cocaine trade. 'It's been a long time.'

Lindsay smirked back at me, raising his arms as Guillermo patted him down for weapons or wires. I might have been happy to see my old FBI handler, but that didn't mean I trusted him. Men – especially extremely attractive men – were not to be trusted.

After finding nothing, Guillermo slapped him hard on the back and Lindsay lowered his arms to his sides.

My two guards, a black-belt badass by the name of Maria, and a hulk-sized Colombian called Alejandro, followed Guillermo out of my sitting room, the door closing behind them.

Lindsay shoved his hands in his suit pockets and paced the length of the large room where I spent most of my time. It's not that I was afraid to go outdoors, but it was summer in Colombia, and as soon as I went outside my flesh turned an angry red. For a native Colombian, it was annoying that I could no longer tolerate the sun in my own country, but ten years spent largely indoors had made my skin and my eyes incredibly sensitive.

'You haven't been here in months,' I said.

Lindsay threw his hands up in mock frustration. 'You won't let me see you.'

'I let you today.'

He laughed.

'You look beautiful in that dress,' he said in Spanish. He spoke the language almost as well as I did, a girl who was born and raised speaking the mother tongue.

'Thank you,' I replied, in English, smoothing down the black dress I wore. I would only address him in English, which annoyed him greatly, since he'd learned the language purely to impress me. I didn't need his silver tongue or his sweet Spanish adorations turning me soft. I knew he wanted me; I wanted him, too, and it had been a very long time between lovers. The last man I had slept with was Dornan. But I couldn't trust anyone, and so I was alone.

It was easier that way. Men only broke your heart. Burrowed in and settled, and then shattered you from within.

My heart was mine alone. It belonged to my children. No man would ever breach its solid walls again.

'Uncle!' Adelita cried, her long, messy hair flying behind her as she ran into the room and barrelled straight into Lindsay.

His eyes lit up, a smile he only smiled for her. They were not related to each other in any way, and they didn't see each other for months or years at a time, but Adelita loved Lindsay as if he were her family.

My darling Adelita. Almost six years old now, and beautiful, a female version of her father.

The blue eyes. The wide cheeks and angular cheekbones. The dirty blonde hair, thick and impossible to untangle. They have the same toes, the same fingers. Until the day I gave birth to her, I did not know who her father was. Whether I'd carried a part of Dornan or a part of John for nine dangerous months, as I fled and hid and swelled with a baby I was terrified to bring into my chaotic existence, where we'd be forced to live in the shadows until fate caught up with us.

I loved her anyway, my baby girl. I didn't care who her father was. I didn't hope one way or the other, because despite everything, despite the blood and the lies and the betrayal, Dornan had let me run. *He had let me go.* Even as I hated him bitterly for everything he'd done – for murdering John, and Juliette, for beating me so badly that I'd miscarried the baby that was his – I still loved him, deep down, somewhere where the light could never quite get in, in the dark. I loved him because he let me go free.

But when I'd given birth in a makeshift hospital room inside an FBI safehouse, Lindsay by my side, Luis pacing anxiously in the hallway, I'd known. My Adelita had cried, and before they'd even placed her wet, howling little body on my bare chest, I saw a tuft of her blonde hair sticking up, and I knew she was John's daughter.

'Lindsay, are you staying for dinner?' Adelita asked.

He shrugged his shoulders, looking to me. I nodded. 'Of course I am!' he said, wrapping her up in another hug, her little face pressed up against his neck. For a moment I imagined Lindsay was John and my throat ached.

'Why don't you go play, *bebe*,' I said to Adelita. 'We need to talk for just a minute. Can you find Lindsay some of that cake you baked the other day?'

Adelita agreed, skipping off to the kitchen in search of cake. That would keep her busy for at least a few minutes, and I could figure out what Lindsay was here for. Once she was gone, I gestured to the couch. 'Sit. You want a drink?'

'Please,' he replied, sitting down.

I went to the large oak cabinet that ran along one wall, and selected a bottle of whiskey. I grabbed two tumblers and poured us each a double, because from the look on Lindsay's face, we were going to need it. I handed one to Lindsay and sat beside him, waiting for him to speak.

'You look pale, Ana,' Lindsay said finally, his smile shrinking. 'You look tired.'

I smiled, despite myself. 'Your eyes look heavy,' I said quietly. 'Like they're weighed down with a terrible secret.'

He looked at the floor, a self-deprecating smile reappearing on his lips. 'You always did know how to read me,' he said.

'What is it, Lindsay? What is so important that you had to come to Colombia to tell me?'

He lifted his head and met my eyes again. 'We raided the Gypsy Brothers' clubhouse. We found a fingerprint in Dornan's room. Juliette Portland's fingerprint.'

I stared at him in horror, disbelief settling into my chest like an old friend. There was a chance that John's daughter – Adelita's half-sister – was still alive?

'It's old. It has to be,' I breathed.

'It's a fresh fingerprint, Mariana. We have reason to believe that, *somehow*, Juliette is alive. And she is with the Gypsy Brothers.'

MARIANA

When I was a girl, I'd dream about marrying my king.

When I met Esteban, I knew. I knew he was the one for me. Something about the way he looked at me seeped into my bones and settled there. Warm. Familiar. I loved him so much, there was this constant ache in my chest.

I was nineteen when I felt him take his last breath, in my arms in a dirty alley. My life was over. I thought I'd die, too.

I didn't. That heart of mine kept beating and aching, missing my lover, missing our son.

When I was a girl, I'd dream about marrying my king.

I never thought Dornan Ross would end up my king. But he did. He made me his queen.

I didn't want it.

He didn't care.

Our wedding night was spent in a hotel room in Vegas, with me locked in the bathroom, staring at the wall as he threatened to smash the door down and then beat my head in.

He'd already killed our child. I wasn't going to let him get inside me again. Wasn't going to let him poison me.

I wasn't going to let him corrupt me ever again.

It didn't matter. He broke the door down eventually.

He got inside me again.

And that's where he stayed, until the bitter end.

Because of all the things in life, love is the most confusing. The most all-consuming. The reason we breathe, the light in our darkness.

At sixteen, love devastated me, his perfect button nose and sweet baby smell overwhelming as my father took him from my arms and into the night.

At nineteen, love saved me, a dangerous man with a heart that was determined to own mine.

At twenty-nine love almost freed me ... but in the end, love broke me.

I wish I could tell you that things ended differently – but I'd be lying. I don't know if he regrets what he did, or if he's happy, but it doesn't matter, really.

It doesn't change the fact that the man who loved me ended up being the same man who would destroy me.

CARTEL

Book 1 in the smash hit *Cartel* trilogy

LILI St. GERMAIN

author of the *USA Today* bestselling Gypsy Brothers series

CARTEL

The first searing novel in the
Cartel trilogy

When her father's drug run goes horribly wrong,
Mariana is the debt he repays to the Gypsy
Brothers motorcycle club. Doing everything she
can to survive, falling in love with the man who
owns her isn't part of Mariana's plan.

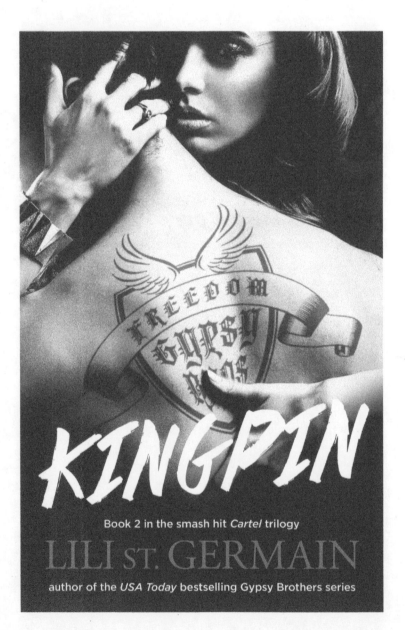

KINGPIN

Book 2 in the smash hit *Cartel* trilogy

LILI ST. GERMAIN

author of the *USA Today* bestselling Gypsy Brothers series

KINGPIN

The second scorching novel
in the Cartel trilogy

Mariana and Dornan struggle to define their
twisted relationship amid the wreckage of their
warring families. With their forbidden love built
on a foundation of lies, it's only a matter of time
before everything they've built comes crashing
down around them.